THE NAMELESS HEIGHT

J.D. NARRAMORE

This is a work of fiction. All of the characters, organizations and
events in this novel are either products of the author's imagination
or are used fictitiously.

www.jdnarramore.com

Citation:

"Remarks on Signing the Intermediate-Range Nuclear Forces
Treaty December 8, 1987." The Public Papers of President
Ronald W. Reagan. Ronald Reagan Presidential Library.
https://www.reaganlibrary.gov/archives/speech/remarks-signing-
intermediate-range-nuclear-forces-treaty (accessed 17 July 2022)

ISBN: 9798830118385

To my wife, Hallie.

ACKNOWLEDGMENTS

Mitchell Allen for his invaluable suggestions.

Rachel Wales-Latendresse for helping get the words just right.

Diane Narramore who provided honest and helpful feedback.

Clyde Wayne Allen, a role model and superb storyteller.

And Hallie, the love of my life, whose constant support made this book possible.

PART ONE

CHAPTER 1

October 1987

Libya

It had been Ahmed's idea to bring him here. The head of Libyan intelligence insisted, despite the tremendous risk of a leak, on having the fair-skinned man take refuge at the camp. A man on the run with a 'unique' skillset, Ahmed enthusiastically described him in that meeting three years ago.

"He'll never last," Akif Saeed argued. "You can't just take a man who knows only of snow and ice and make him into a desert rat. Besides, suppose they find out?"

Ahmed slowly removed a pair of large-rimmed glasses and bore his sunken amber eyes into Saeed's with a menacing glare. It was a look the subordinate had witnessed others receive that raised objections to various 'ideas'. He dared not utter another word. To this day, he'd refrained from speaking on the matter entirely.

The sun held court amongst a cloudless sky when the commandos resumed training on the sand-swept desert. Saeed had given strict orders for all to remain inside their huts from 1400 to 1430, lest the infidel's intelligence satellites catch sight of them. Twenty or so men lined up to take practice with their Soviet-made Kalashnikov rifles against targets a hundred yards away. Their training showed by the tight circle of bullets hitting each of their targets, making their instructor proud. Three hundred yards behind them, several other men were drenched in sweat as they hurried along an agility course. Libyan, Syrian, Lebanese, and the like crawled in the sand underneath barbed wire as their instructors yelled them onward before coming to and climbing over a thirty-foot wall.

Off in the distance, beyond the camp's outer perimeter, a black Land Rover was kicking up a cloud of dust as it soldiered on towards them. Saeed spotted it through his binoculars before the guard tower radioed word of its pending arrival. *What can he want now?*

Limited oversight. Plenty of latitude. Resources provided. Results guaranteed. It was the simple yet effective formula that the base commander ran his operation by. *How many years has it been? Eleven? Eleven years since the border wars with Chad. To think I survived all those raids. And now, in a position such as this.*

Both the Intelligence Director and his predecessor rarely meddled. When they did, it often backfired, resulting in a return in deference to Saeed's command. But the case of the fair-skinned man had upset everything.

Saeed met the SUV just as it pulled up outside the main hut. Several of the younger recruits stood off to the side gawking before an officer barked at them to move along. The camp commander was already saluting when the Director of Mukhabara el-Jamahiriya, Ahmed Raza, exited from the passenger's door in full uniform, medals reflecting the blinding light of the sun to all facing him. He noted the perspiration already on Raza's forehead. *Always indoors nowadays. The city-dweller wouldn't stand a week out here.*

2

"Director Raza, *ahlana bik*. It's always a pleasure to see you," Saeed exclaimed while standing at attention.

Ahmed nonchalantly returned the salute. "At ease. Come, let's get out of this heat," he answered as the two entered alone into the hut.

"Where's Boytsov?"

"Working the firing range at the moment," Saeed remarked while pouring two cups of Berber tea. "Would you like me to get him?"

Ahmed nodded as he took a seat. Saeed handed him a cup before stepping outside and ordering a guard to summon the instructor.

"How has he been since I last visited?" the Director asked.

"The usual. Acts sometimes like he's the Slavic Lawrence of Arabia," sneered Saeed. Ahmed laughed.

"Well, he does command the men's respect. The keffiyeh looks a bit ridiculous on him at times. But then again, isn't Gaddafi's as well?"

"What you have for him, a transfer, I hope?" The camp commander could hardly contain the resentment he felt towards the presence of his infidel consultant. How many times could he stand for this man to interfere with the way things were run here? Always talking about the ways of the Spetsnaz. One-upping him with Ahmed constantly. Saeed had half a mind to shoot Boytsov in his sleep.

"Now, Akif, do you really think we could deny these men his expertise and knowledge?"

Just then, a knock came at the door. "Come in," ordered Saeed in a resigned tone that didn't escape Ahmed's notice. Entering the room stood a man dressed in army fatigue pants, boots, sandstone t-shirt, and white turban. He was not quite tall, no more than 5'9, yet his adequately cut physique suggested he was more than able to hold his own in any fight. His skin was tan and rugged as leather. By all appearances, he did

3

seem to give T.E. Lawrence a run for his money.

"Ah! Come in, soldier," Ahmed exclaimed as he entered. "How do the new batch of recruits look?"

"*Bihalat jayida,*" Boytsov answered in an accent which, though subtle, stood out in the land of Bedouins. His face, meanwhile, gave but a cold, stoic expression. It constantly frustrated Saeed how the man was so unreadable. Rarely did he show emotion. Even rarer did he show his cards but on one subject.

"That's what I like to hear. Since you joined us, our Jamahiriya Guard and freedom fighter affiliates have nothing but praise for the effectiveness and discipline of the men you've trained. The Colonel thanks you. I thank you. All of Libya thanks you…"

What about me? Saeed was doing his best not to roll his eyes at the fawning. *Who does he think runs this camp?*

"Which leads me to why I'm here," Ahmed continued. "My friend, you are aware of the treachery inflicted on us by the Americans last year, are you not?"

"Bombing around Tripoli. Killing The Colonel's daughter, Hana. Yet we repulsed their attacks and achieved victory, shooting down their fighter-bomber."

"You remember well Konstantin Boytsov," Ahmed said with a smile. The instructor parroted the state media line quite well. Details, such as Libyan agents bombing a West Berlin nightclub frequented by U.S. servicemen (which caused America to retaliate), the mystery of whether The Colonel's daughter had ever existed or that the air strikes had in fact been a clear victory for the Americans, were unimportant here. "Colonel Gaddafi likewise has not forgotten. He demands action be taken and has instructed Mukhabara el-Jamahiriya to spearhead an operation that will long be remembered."

"How may I be of service then, Director Raza?" asked Boytsov.

"I've received word that our assets in America have uncovered the identity of a former CIA officer who caused us much trouble years ago. It happens he is the same one you first spoke of when we found you."

Boytsov's face immediately began to knot up. "*Ya poydu?*" he uttered in Russian this time.

Ahmed grinned like a jackal. Manipulation came easy to him. *All about finding the right kind of bait. Now, all that is left is to reel in the prize.* "What makes you think I want you to go? Maybe I came to ask who amongst your commandos might be ready for such a mission? A risky thing sending our finest instructor into harm's way."

"If you trust the training I give these men, then you should certainly trust I can complete the mission and return. With all due respect, Director, I've earned this."

"Perhaps. But even if you did manage to succeed in the hit, the risk we'd take in possibly losing you would require a great deal more in return."

The Russian already knew what he was getting at. "I've told you before, it's impossible. You cannot fathom the danger in acquiring what your Colonel wants."

He's fighting. Just like any real catch would. He need not get away though, Ahmed. Keep his focus on the bait. The second part of the plan will then fall into place.

"Danger to you. Not us, if done correctly. It's your decision: you can serve the Great Socialist People's Libyan Arab Jamahiriya in this manner while fulfilling your own personal vendetta, only if you then get from your old comrades what we've longed for."

Boytsov turned back towards the door without a word, opening it to stare out over the western vista. Memories of failure, loss, and desperate escape, long ago seared into his mind, were replayed once more. *If only I could make it stop.*

Revenge, it seemed, like so many before him, was the only way to make it end. Beyond the distant horizon, unfinished business awaited. Unfinished business that haunted his very being constantly.

Finally, the Russian turned back toward the Director. "When may we begin?"

CHAPTER 2

December 1987

Baltimore, Maryland

Audrey Davis's heart was pounding. As she made her way through the crowds at Harborplace Mall, the CIA instructor kept her eyes glued on the man carrying a backpack five yards ahead of her in a navy ball cap. For the last two hours, the man had been under constant surveillance working to break free, make a brush pass, and return to the designated checkpoint before time expired. All just part of a day's training in the Central Intelligence Agency's field officer program.

Without warning, the target spun around an upcoming corner past a clothing store disappearing from view. Davis quickened her pace. *He's figured out the best blind spots, that's for sure.* When she turned the corner, he was out of view. A hallway to her right led to the restrooms and a mall security office.

"He just exited down towards the security office," she spoke into a discrete microphone attached to her blouse. "Anyone near the emergency exit?"

"Negative, but we do have a car just outside," another instructor answered.

You're not going to pass this easily—not on my watch.

Davis scanned her surroundings as she moved through the hallway. "Any movement outside?"

"Negative."

She knew what to do. Moving towards a vending machine, she hid on the opposite side, out of sight from the restroom doors.

Three minutes later, two men emerged at nearly the same time. One was a slightly overweight man with a beard, wearing a suit and carrying a shopping bag. The other, a shaggy-haired janitor wearing headphones and carrying a broom. Both the same height. She'd no doubt her recruit had changed both his clothes and appearance in the stall. There's more to being a spy, however, than just wearing a disguise. Davis had learned that years ago. You had to not only look the part but act like one as well. Following behind, she watched as the two reached the entrance back out into the mall and went in opposite directions.

He's turning right.

She watched as the janitor bobbed his head up and down to whatever music he was listening to. A wire connected to his headphones went into his right pocket and to what most would assume was a Walkman of some sort. Passing a Santa meet-and-greet, the man boarded an escalator leading up to the second level into the bustling food court. Davis remained close behind, watching for anyone that could be making the brush pass.

A middle-aged woman dressed in a puffy amber coat was sitting alone at a table finishing up a slice of pizza. Though she was well away from the janitor's path, Davis noticed her eyes paying extra attention to the man approaching her on the right without even so much as turning her head. Casually, the woman stood up, pushed in her seat, picked up her trash, and began making her way toward him.

A sixth sense went off inside Davis. "All surveillance move in and get ready now!"

The janitor was now reaching inside the right pocket. Within seconds, in the midst of all the Christmas shoppers walking about the noisy food court, the two passed each other. Davis rushed in and grabbed the janitor's shoulder.

"Sorry, Mark, better luck next time."

Mark Jankowski let out a frustrated sigh. "Where did I mess up?"

"Training exercise over. Repeat, training exercise over," she relayed to the training team before answering him. "You did almost everything right but one thing: when you stepped out of the men's restroom, for the first few seconds, you acted like a spy. Your eyes shifted around too much. Sign of nervousness. That'll draw attention in the field. You want to act calm like no one's watching you."

The recruit nodded and resigned himself to the outcome. There would be another chance though. He'd just have to prepare himself better mentally next time.

Ten minutes later, all members of the training team had either left or were making their way to the parking lot. Davis glanced at her watch as she opened the door to her black Ford sedan. Five minutes past four. It would take her about an hour to return to her home in McLean, Virginia. *Should be plenty of time to make dinner.* Her mind tried to remember all that was in the fridge. She'd yet to go grocery shopping for the week. Taking 395 south to 95, she raced down the highway, hoping to beat out the 5 pm rush hour traffic. The radio was on as she drove. The INF Treaty was front and center on all the news talk programs. As they spoke about Reagan and Gorbachev, Davis found herself recalling how her path had once crossed with the General Secretary only four years ago.

The sedan pulled into the driveway of a white-washed two-story brick home in a mostly quiet neighborhood. The 'mostly quiet' was due to the ongoing renovations and construction of a house just across the street. *Looks like I beat them home.* Stepping inside, Davis set her keys on the kitchen counter and began pulling things out of the fridge. Her two sons, ages twelve and ten, would be home any minute.

"We're home!" A young voice soon came from the entryway as the front door opened. Her oldest Nikita entered the kitchen, followed by Sergei and a woman with dirty blond hair wearing a gray pantsuit.

"How was your day?" Davis inquired as she set a two-pound package of chicken breast on the counter. "Hockey practice go well?"

"Great!" beamed Nikita. "I made an eighty-eight on my math test and scored two goals in the scrimmage match."

"Mary got us chocolate chip cookies!" exclaimed Sergei, whose face could still could use a napkin.

"Made some last night. Only gave them two each. I didn't think you'd mind," FBI Agent Mary Holden said. Since the day Audrey and her two sons arrived from Moscow, Mary had been assigned to protect them. Over time, she'd become to them like a favorite aunt, who just happened to have a badge and carry a firearm.

"That's fine. Did you two say thank you to Ms. Holden?"

"Yes," Sergei replied as he set his backpack down. "Thanks again!"

"You want to stay for dinner?" Davis asked Holden. "I think I'm going to cook brown sugar chicken."

"Thought you'd never ask," the FBI Agent replied. "Any big plans this weekend?"

"We're going to go pick out a Christmas tree at a farm on the other side of the Potomac," Davis said as she began to preheat the oven. "Do you think I should make a salad too?"

"I can help with that. I'm off-duty now as it is," Mary said as she grabbed a bowl for the salad. "That sounds fun but I thought you had a date this weekend?"

Davis began to act busy pulling out everything for Holden to help with the salad. The Agent still caught her halfway blush. "Oh, well that's actually this Thursday," said Davis. "I've got a sitter and the Bureau is sending someone to keep watch outside."

"This the guy you met at the PTA meeting? What was his name, Landon?"

"No and no," Davis shook her head as she started seasoning the chicken. "It's nothing big. Just dinner, Mary. Only a second date with a guy at the Agency."

Holden grinned at the sheepish answer. She wasn't ready to let up.

"That's how you spooks like to keep it. Always tied to work. What's he like?"

"Tall. Kind of good-looking. Likes to go sailing on the weekend out in the Chesapeake."

"Seventh-floor guy who's got a boat. Way to go, Audrey!"

"You said seventh floor, not me. We'll see where it goes."

"Does he have a name?"

"Skylar. Jack Skylar."

Davis turned back to preparing dinner lost in thought. *There was never any time for romance. All those years in Moscow treating intimacy and affection as tools of manipulation. Maybe, just this once…*

CHAPTER 3

Davis, in fact, held two roles at the Central Intelligence Agency. When she wasn't training the next line of field officers for duty abroad, she would sit at a lone desk in a windowless room at Langley. The solitary workspace, rather than one in a more communal area, had been Deputy Director of Intelligence (DDI) Trent Ashcroft's idea when she'd first returned from Moscow four years ago. Best to avoid the unnecessary questions, he'd once told her. There in her Spartanesque office, she gave her latest analysis on key players inside the Kremlin. Who they really were, what their motives were, vices, passions, anything she'd learned while *married* to Boris Alexeev, then a personal assistant to rising star Mikhail Gorbachev.

Looking at the black and white photo paper-clipped inside the manila envelope, she tried her best to recall one Lavrentiy Gagarin. She'd provided a brief summary of their one encounter long ago in 1981. It happened at a party in Leningrad. Gagarin was then working in the Ministry of Foreign Affairs. Their meeting had been both brief and cordial. However, it was what Davis later learned about the man, now playing a pivotal role in the negotiations for the ongoing INF Treaty, that stood out.

"You remember him, Tatiana? The man from that birthday party for my friend who was dating the ballerina," Boris said to her once after a long day at work. "He came to the office this morning to meet with Gorbachev."

"By himself?" she asked. "He must be moving up the ranks."

"*Nyet*. A GRU officer from the Ministry of Defense was with him. Strange thing is, Gagarin appeared to be taking orders from the officer when they entered Gorbachev's office. He kept glancing his way every time he spoke, almost like he was looking for approval."

It was this observation reported back by Davis that led to the CIA uncovering the Russian's real job, unbeknownst to many. The intel had now become useful during the pending arms negotiations, giving the American negotiators a better idea of who they were dealing with.

But why is he staying in Washington? That was the question troubling the Director of Central Intelligence, William Webster, as well as Ashcroft. Word had already gotten out that he was taking up residence at the Soviet Embassy long-term. Without answers, there was no idea how seriously his presence should be taken. Their only immediate solution rested with the analysis of a woman who had gone out into the cold and lived to tell about it.

Davis took a sip of the cup of black coffee sitting next to her and rubbed her temples, seemingly in an effort to bring forth those long distant memories.

"Any luck?" Ashcroft asked as he opened the office door and peered in.

"Morning, sir. I was just thinking. Our source says he was coy about his intentions to stay in D.C.?"

"Correct," the DDI nodded. "We need to better understand what he's up to. The FBI already has the customary surveillance watching his every move outside the Soviet embassy off Virginia Avenue. If he's going to try and run agents, better to know now and apply a full-court press. But if he could be a potential ally..."

"You mean we turn him?"

"Not necessarily. We've had fewer eyes and ears inside the Kremlin since you served there. If he were someone we could have off-the-record conversations with at state dinners and get a true sense of what's going on, it would be huge. But, we have to know if he's a Gorbachev glasnost-type or sticks close to the ways of the old guard."

"My observation, sir, is that he's the type who keeps his cards close. The topic of a dissident came up, I recall, in conversation at the party. Some were quick to tow the party line, but a few gave a softer denunciation. When asked what he thought, Gagarin quickly changed the subject and smiled. It's that self-discipline that's allowed him to rise to the position he's in now."

"So you really couldn't say?"

Davis shook her head. "I'd just be assuming if I did. Honestly, the man's a wild card."

The straight-shooting persona and reluctance to embellish were just a few of the qualities the Deputy Director of Intelligence valued in Davis. She was more than just an ex-spy turned case officer instructor. She had the ability to apply her first-hand knowledge and analyze the other side's key players. All while keeping a good head on her shoulders. It seemed that a small but still too large number of analysts and case officers, eventually lost that ability to keep it straight—the stress of the job over time being the biggest culprit. Drug problems, broken marriages, and even double agents had at times been the result. It was something the Agency had begun taking steps to address. Davis, however, had managed to avoid those pitfalls. Ashcroft knew whom she had to thank for that.

"As fair an assessment as we can ask for," he noted before shifting gears. "Come on, got a meeting about to start in my office."

"The usual crew?"

"Yep, Soviet Select."

The stroll up to the DDI's office took less than two minutes, including an elevator ride upstairs. "Any big plans for the holidays?" Ashcroft asked as he pushed the seventh-floor button.

"We're having my aunt and uncle from Norfolk come to stay with us for Christmas. Speaking of which, the boys and I are getting a tree this Saturday."

"Your uncle, Commander Zachary Davis? Been a while since I last ran into the old submariner. Tell him I said hello."

Doesn't miss even the smallest of details on a personnel file. Always catches me off-guard.

"Will do," she replied as they stepped off the elevator. "Any plans yourself?"

"Grandkids coming to stay with us," he answered as they passed by his secretary's desk and entered his office.

The heads of the Soviet division, Toby Koufax and George Shelby, were already seated on the couch against the wall. The Deputy Director of Operations (DDO), Pat Clark, sat across from them on the other side of a coffee table. Jack Skylar perpendicular to both.

"Now, let's get started," Ashcroft bellowed as he grabbed a lone chair against the wall for Davis before sitting down.

Clark set down his cup of coffee and went first. "Counter-surveillance programs in Moscow over the last week have mostly confirmed our estimates. The Kremlin is eager to cross the finish line this week on the treaty. There's little appetite for any last-minute surprises." The Operations Director put on his glasses and picked up a folder. "With that said, we've already begun moving to reactivate assets that'll be key to monitoring the dismantling of their ICBMs. At least a dozen locations we'll need to stay on top of, as you can see by this map I'm passing around. Koufax?"

"Some new intel from THISTLE," the balding Soviet division director with a beard began. For more than thirty years, Koufax had worked on nearly everything Red. He'd cut his teeth as a Station assistant in Berlin right after college at Yale before returning stateside to rise up the ranks at Langley. Davis had always observed him to be rather an introvert. Koufax's wife had died only a year ago from a heart condition. They'd had no children together. It was assumed that, after her, his life revolved around his work at the CIA. "Moscow Station reports the Politburo was briefed on some new radar technology tests they're hoping could be effective at picking up stealth aircraft at the lowest of altitudes. Price tag could scare them away. Possibility of them activating it on a limited scope and/or selling the hardware to allies for a tidy profit."

Shelby followed—a near jack-of-all-trades liaison on the team but with a recent specialty for satellite observation. In many ways, he was the antithesis of Koufax. Young, brash, and always the life of every office Christmas party. After a brief period in counter-intelligence for the FBI, he joined the Agency and never looked back. "Troop and tank levels in East Germany are the same as they've been the last six months. We think we've made a positive ID on a Red Brigade training camp about thirty miles southeast of Lyon. Now just a matter of when we'd like to let the French know."

"Jack," Ashcroft motioned to his assistant, who had the distinction of being a consultant to the negotiating team for the treaty. Everything about Jack Skylar seemed polished, from his manner of speech right down to his Venetian hand-stitched leather shoes.

"Deal should get wrapped up this week," Skylar began. "I did speak to Gagarin yesterday morning. The man appeared pretty jovial. Made a comment about how he's already found his favorite spot to purchase Earl of Grey here in Washington."

"Which leads us to Audrey," Ashcroft spoke up.

"Gagarin keeps a good poker face," Davis began. "He's never come out strong for the old guard or Gorbachev's camp. He's shown neutrality to be a winning strategy in his rise to his current position."

"So you think we should watch him?" Skylar asked with an intrigued look.

"As in take normal precautions for a diplomat from the Soviet Union? Particularly one with ties to the intelligence division of their military? Yes, I'd recommend that."

A smile formed on Skylar's face. He appreciated the rarity of a colleague who wasn't afraid to both present the intel and also make a recommendation they were willing to put their chips on. That was Audrey Davis to a tee. It was this no-nonsense attitude, paired with charm and natural attraction few women could match, that led to him asking her out.

"Agreed," said Ashcroft. "I want you to continue keeping an eye on him, Skylar. You've already got the working relationship going with him, and I can point you in the right direction as needed with…" The intercom suddenly buzzed. "Yes?" Ashcroft growled.

"Skylar's secretary is outside with a folder he requested," replied Ashcroft's secretary.

"A detailed memorandum I wrote up," said Skylar. "More on Gagarin and a couple of his colleagues at the negotiating table. Copies have been made for everyone here."

"Send her on in, Julie," Ashcroft spoke into the intercom.

"Anything in there on Dubinin?" Clark asked.

Skylar shook his head. "Nothing new on the Ambassador. However, there's…"

The conversation halted as a young woman, no more than twenty-two and fresh out of college, entered the room.

"Here are those folders you asked for, Mr. Skylar. I'm sorry I'm late with them, but you see the copier was…

"No problem at all. Everyone around here has trouble with those machines, Brooke. Thanks for getting them to me."

Davis watched Skylar's gaze linger on his secretary as she handed out folders to each of the Soviet Select. A bit too long in her opinion, though she was never one to get jealous easily. *At least HR is still hiring them right out of school.*

A half an hour later the meeting was over. The two found themselves alone on the elevator headed down to the main level where the lunch crowd was already gathering.

"I get the sense Gagarin wants something from me," Skylar began. "Talking to me isn't part of his negotiating role. He's prodding with certain comments and questions."

"I only report the intel and try to recollect what I can remember," Davis smiled. "But for whatever it's worth, if he isn't too overly confident, he should realize we're already onto him and his GRU connections. My guess is that he's not looking to make an agent out of you. Yeah, he may be seeing if he can't trip you up a bit and say something on accident. Who wouldn't? A defector might also look to develop a relationship with a key official."

"But you don't think it likely?"

"Not really," she answered as they stepped off the elevator. "From when I met Gagarin years ago to now, he's been working his way up the ladder very carefully. He's not someone likely to make irrational decisions. Don't know if that helps any. As to what he really wants, I'd be just as curious. He's a tough Russian to read. By the way, want to get lunch?"

"Can't. I've got to drive up to State Department and go over some details for the treaty."

"Oh. Well, we're still on for this Thursday?"

"Ugh, afraid I'm going to have to cancel. Something's come up." He glanced down at his wristwatch before continuing. "You free Saturday though?"

"I think so." Davis was kicking herself deep down, wishing she'd instead concocted a story about already having plans earlier that day that may run into the evening and needing to double-check.

"Great. I got to run. I'll let you know the details later."

Watching him head out toward the lobby and out the building, there were but two things on Davis's mind. The true intentions of an aloof Russian and one Jack Skylar.

Holden first noticed it that afternoon while pulled into the driveway. Across the street was parked a grey service van. The FBI Agent quickly glanced and saw two men seated up front who appeared to be looking over a map. The one in the driver's seat was white, and the other possibly Latino, so she guessed. The boys ran to the door as she locked the car and followed them inside.

A half hour later, Holden got up from the kitchen table where she was reading and looked out the front living room window. Pulling back the curtain she saw the van, the driver visibly eyeing the Davis residence. Before she could react, the truck drove off.

Four years, Mary. Four years. Don't over-think a van probably with the utility company.

CHAPTER 4

Carson Cooper watched as the sedan made its way up the hill and along the winding dirt road. Standing on his porch with several boxes full of Christmas lights lying about, he reached for his thermos and took a last sip of coffee before glancing at his wristwatch. *9:30 am. Right on time.*

"Hi, Uncle Carson!" an excited Sergei yelled as he jumped out of the car before it had fully come to a stop in front of the old spymaster's house.

"You ready to cut down an evergreen today?" Cooper asked, shaking the young boy's hand.

"Hey, thanks again for letting us come over," said Davis as she and Nikita got out as well. "That one couldn't stop talking the whole drive over about picking out a tree."

"We've never had a real one, Uncle Carson," Nikita remarked with enthusiasm as well. "Only store-bought tinsel."

"You're in for a treat today then." Cooper gestured to the axes leaning against a chair. "I've got hot chocolate ready in the kitchen if you want some before we go out. How about it, boys?"

The two brothers raced up the porch stairs and into the house, slamming the screen door loudly. It was now just the former Chief of Station and his once top spy.

"How's work been for you lately? Still breaking in new recruits at The Farm?"

Davis gave a nod. "They've been keeping me busy."

Cooper nodded. Since retirement, he'd gone into the tree farm business. Evergreen conifers were just one of several types grown on his spread of land. So far, it had been a modest success. The itch to be out in the field for the CIA had long passed. Now he was ready to enjoy a more peaceful way of life.

"You keep up much with anyone from Langley still?" she asked while untangling a strand of red and white-colored lights.

"No, not really." He took the end of the strand Davis held and began to wrap it around one of the front porch columns. "Oh, Ashcroft did stop by once a year ago to get a tree and visit. Haven't had anything to do with the Agency since the day I drove out of the parking lot in the Bronco for the last time. The way I see it, my work is done. Served my country the best way I could. That book's finished. Now I'm onto a new one," he said as he surveyed the view of the farm. "Hey, whatever happened to that fellow you mentioned a while back? The dentist you're seeing?"

"7th-floor man now. Just a second date."

Cooper grunted, somewhat disapprovingly she guessed. "Well, as long as you like him, that's what counts," he answered.

Though she was trying not to giggle, Davis valued the old spy's opinion. Cooper had become almost a father figure to her. Since their return from Moscow, the two stayed in touch, eventually having each other over for cookouts and Thanksgiving dinners. The boys liked him a lot.

With no grandfather, he was the closest thing to it. The well-meaning advice could be a bit much at times, she felt. It was because he truly cared, however, and more often than not, he was right on the money.

"By the way, I've got a job for Nikita if he's up for it and you're okay with it. One of my guys left to take a job down south, and I'm going to be short on help until probably after Christmas. Nothing backbreaking. Mainly setting up some irrigation hoses.

"Fine by me. I'm sure he'll say yes."

The screen door swung open again. The two boys each had a mug in hand.

"You'll figure it out, Audrey," he said with a look of warmth in his eyes. "You always do. Just remember I'm pulling for you."

CHAPTER 5

The sound of champagne glasses clinking together echoed throughout the State Dining Room as yet another toast was being made. Only a few short hours before, Davis couldn't decide whether to kiss or kill Skylar for letting her know they'd be going to a black-tie event at the White House.

"You expect me to be ready for a state dinner at the home of the President of the United States in four hours?" she asked him in frustration over the phone earlier that day. "Really, Jack?"

"Hey, I told you we might be going out Saturday! No one said I needed to say where."

Just as Skylar was taking a sip, he felt an arm reach around his shoulder.

"Jack, my man. I propose another toast: to your health and successful work on that treaty."

"I'll drink to that one, Kyle. Cheers!"

"It's good to see you again," said Commander Kyle Billingsley, U.S. Navy, as he polished off his glass. "Been too long. Not since you boys came out on the *Nimitz*."

"It has. When did you arrive in D.C.?"

"Last Friday. Scheduled R&R for a couple more weeks. I don't think I've had the pleasure of meeting Mrs. Skylar yet?"

"Who? Oh, you saw Audrey. My date tonight. She's over there across the room with some of the women. I'd introduce you, but I know how you hotshot pilots are."

"Ha, ha," Billingsley replied as he rolled his eyes. "So, now that the Treaty is almost wrapped up, what's next?"

"A good intelligence official never tells."

"Worth a shot. Here she comes your way now. Wow, so are you going to introduce me to her?" he said with a mischievous grin.

It was then that Davis approached the two men. Why she'd kept the modern yet elegant black ball gown all this time, she wasn't sure. It paired well with the necklace she wore bearing a single three-carat sapphire.

"Kyle, this is my date, Audrey Davis. Audrey, meet my old roommate from Annapolis, Commander Kyle Billingsley, Squadron Leader of the Knights F-14 Squadron."

"Good to meet you, Commander. Knights, I figure that's Sixth Fleet?"

"Your figure is exact," he replied as his gaze drifted down but for a moment. Davis didn't miss it. "You work for Defense or the Navy?"

"Oh, no, I just make a point of knowing a little about everything."

"Well, you seem to be pretty good at that. If I were a betting man, I'd say you and Jack met through work."

"Perhaps," she answered before glancing over at Skylar. There was no use trying to gauge where this new dating relationship stood, for Skylar gave no expression but instead seemed distracted by something else across the room.

"Jack, how long have you guys been dating? Jack?"

"Uh, sorry. Just a couple weeks. I'm sorry. If you'll both excuse me, there's someone I need to see for a moment."

"Everything alright?" Davis asked.

"Yeah. Just work-related. You know how it is."

"Even at White House dinners, duty calls," Billingsley said as he shook his head. "Well, Jack, if I don't get to visit with you anymore tonight, it was good seeing you again."

The two shook hands before Skylar turned to Davis. "I won't be too long. I promise, Audrey."

"You're fine, Jack. Hurry back," she replied with a smile.

As Skylar turned and headed out the large doors of the State Dining Room, Davis and Billingsley found themselves alone. It was the Commander who spoke first.

"Care to dance?"

Davis looked somewhat taken aback.

"He won't mind at all. Long as you save the last one for him. Come on." Billingsley held his hand out.

With a bit of reluctance and one glance back at the entrance to the room, she took Billingsley's hand as he led her onto the dance floor where the Marine band was starting to play Cole Porter's *Begin the Beguine*.

"Tell me, Commander, are you always as fast as the Tomcats you fly?"

"You misunderstand me, Ms. Davis. I'd never move in on another man's date. Much less a friend's."

"Then what are you doing now then?" she asked right before he twirled her out. Davis found herself surprisingly impressed, not expecting the Naval Aviator to be this skilled on his feet.

Twirling her back in and holding her close, Billingsley answered. "I have a rule: never leave a woman with the right stuff standing alone. Even for just one dance."

When the song was finally over, the Commander escorted her off the floor.

"Think I'm going to try and find Jack now. Thank you for the dance, Commander Billingsley."

"My pleasure. You can call me Kyle, by the way, Ms. Davis."

Davis gave a slight nod. "Goodnight, Kyle."

The two parted company, and she was now looking around the room. *Well, how many times do you get to wander around the White House? Looking for your date. He's got to be around here somewhere.* Davis then headed out the door into the hallway known as Cross Hall. On her right, she peered into the Red Room. Guests had overflowed into here, glancing up at various paintings of past presidents and first ladies and enjoying what had once been Dolly Madison's famous salon. *No sign of him.* She continued down the hall and checked the Blue Room as well as the main entrance. At the far end was the closed-off East Room. Davis was about to give up and return back to the party when she noticed a door slightly ajar. Curiosity got the better of her as she grabbed hold of the doorknob and entered the Green Room.

"Jack!"

"Audrey, I ugh, fancy seeing you in here," Skylar stuttered as he disengaged from a woman who left more than her fair share of Yves Saint Laurent rouge on his mouth. Davis immediately recognized her as Skylar's secretary.

"Hey babe, I've some business I need to discuss. I'll find you in a bit," he said to the woman, who bobbed her head and turned to leave. It was all Davis could do not to give her the evil eye as she passed by on the way out.

"Having a good time?"

"I've gone out with my share of lowlifes," Davis fumed. "You, however, top the cake. Taking two women out to the same party. Really, Jack? Or should I say a woman and a girl?"

"Look, nobody is official here," Skylar replied with raised hands. "I originally asked out Brooke and thought she said no, so I asked you. Didn't expect her to show up at the White House gate and have a page track me down and ask if she was also my guest."

"You're playing a dangerous game. Think about that for a moment."

Skylar shook his head and took a seat beside a lit fireplace. Overhead, watching the entire spectacle, was a portrait of John Quincy Adams. He picked up a glass of champagne he'd brought into the room and finished it off.

"Nothing more dangerous than me going out with you. You're a co-worker as well, Audrey."

"Yes, a colleague. Not your fresh-out-of-school secretary!"

Skylar sighed. He knew, as just about everyone did, that the CIA practically encouraged employees to date. Better to keep secrets in-house and have someone who understands the stress and need for discretion. Ashcroft, though would have his head if he learned about any dalliances with a subordinate.

"Look. I'm sorry. The evening clearly hasn't gone as planned, and I never meant to hurt you in any way. Can we put this all behind us?"

"As in go out again? No," she said with a glare that made him look down at the floor in humiliation. "We're a closed case. You won't have any trouble from me on the 7th floor, however." Davis paused as she carefully chose the words she was about to say next. "As long as you end it with her. I mean it. That girl has the right to an honest day's work without the advances of her boss."

"Fine," he answered with a huff as he stood. "I'll see you at work tomorrow?"

"Like always." Waiting until he walked past her and out the room, she rolled her eyes and swore aloud.

It was on the drive back home in the back seat of a taxi when Davis first saw him.

She was lost in thought about how the evening had gone. *Too busy with work. Too much a player.* Well, she could definitely empathize with the former. *The arms negotiations work alone probably has him needing to blow off steam. Skylar just isn't up for anything serious. Not now anyway.*

Her eyes drifted off to the sidewalk. The taxi was only a few doors down from her house when a lone figure appeared to be on a walk. A man who seemed to be glancing around as if he were making some sort of mental notes. His face appeared rugged, with a scar on the side of his jaw and a weather-beaten complexion. The headlights revealed his eyes to be a harsh green color as they turned towards the light and faced Davis. A chill could be felt in her bones as his direct stare gave way to an unsettling feeling. It lasted but a moment before the car finally passed him by and pulled into her driveway.

That face. I've seen it before. But where?

CHAPTER 6

Camp Peary near Williamsburg, Virginia

It was the gun range that Davis most enjoyed at The Farm. There since the early 1950s, neither the CIA nor the federal government had formally acknowledged the clandestine training center nestled in the 9,000 acres which made up the highly restricted Camp Peary. A naval base, it had originally been used to train new seamen in submarine and destroyer tactics right before the Second World War. Now it was ground zero for the instruction of the next generation of CIA. Here, Davis found a new life in passing on what she'd once learned. Driving classes for evading threats and surveillance, getting in the black, effectively taking on an identity as well as qualifying with certain firearms and marksmanship, were all in her wheelhouse. It was the latter, however, the one she instructed recruits to be the ultimate last resort, which she most excelled in.

Much of her childhood had been spent taking target practice with her father and his .22 rifle. A CIA paramilitary officer, he instilled in his only child a hunger to know not only how to protect herself but also the value of perseverance. The hours were filled each weekend, shooting together at a paper target pinned to a tree on their farm. Those were Davis's fondest memories of him. Out there, she could talk to him about anything. *Always listening, always encouraging.*

One particular afternoon, she'd come home from school in tears. A Spanish teacher had berated her in front of the entire class for being unable to translate the sentence written on the chalkboard and then mimicked her less than stellar pronunciation. Her mother tried repeatedly and failed to get her to talk. Instead, the twelve-year-old wandered out to the target practice tree and continued to cry.

"Why the long face, Audrey?" he asked as he walked up and sat beside her. He held out a small bag of both their favorite candy, horehound. Taking a piece, her tears soon subsided as she looked up to him and retold what had happened.

"Teacher's probably too old to remember ever being your age. Middle school." He grunted before shaking his head and standing up. "Go get my rifle and the box of cartridges."

When she returned with it, he stood more than a hundred yards away from the tree.

"Where's the target?" she asked with a puzzled expression.

"It's there. Look closely. See the silver dollar? Taped it there against the tree."

"Are you wanting to shoot?" She handed him the rifle, expecting to see her hero impress her once more.

"No, you're going to."

"But I can't hit that small of a..."

"Yes, you can. Load up."

She took three shots, all misses before he stopped her and took the gun away. Suddenly the crying started up again. "There's more to this than a crummy Spanish teacher. Talk to me."

He waited patiently until the last tear slowly trickled down her cheek and she tried to summon the words. "You're leaving again tomorrow. You go for weeks, sometimes months. I hate it. I want you here, Dad. Why can't you stay? Why?"

The father pulled his daughter in and hugged her tightly. "I know. It's rough. The work I do, I can't explain but know I do it not just to protect this country but for you and your Mom as well. Honey, you can learn and speak fluently any language you put your mind to. You can be strong, even when I'm not here. That silver dollar down range, you can hit it. You hit a spot the size of that within a full paper target all the time. This is just a few more yards back. Now take a breath. Relax. Trust yourself."

Taking the rifle from him, she took a deep breath and exhaled. The tension and stress seemingly blew away with the easterly wind. Lining up the sights, she squeezed the trigger and fired.

"Stop! Let's go look." She thought he was crazy until they got closer. "Clean right through the middle," he beamed with pride for her. Audrey's eyes grew wide with disbelief before she found herself grinning as well.

"Here," he said, giving the silver dollar to her. "Wherever you go in this life, no matter how far away I am, when you think you can't overcome something, pull this out and remember."

"I love you, Dad."

"I love you too, Audrey."

In 1964, he went missing and was eventually pronounced dead in Vietnam. How, why, and what he was doing was never explained. Now, when she stepped onto the range and aimed at a target downfield, she felt a sense of being back there with him and hearing his words of instruction. All the while reaching into her pocket and feeling for that shot-through silver dollar.

The range sat at the end of the road past one of the driving courses. Its firing bays stretched out long with targets at varying distances, some even a mile away. The forest bordered its edges. Today, fourteen recruits would be training in the use of the Beretta M9 semiautomatic pistol as well as an M40 rifle.

She took time to inspect each weapon and the bay where each recruit would shoot from. Once Davis finished, she checked her watch. *3:15. Still got a few minutes before they arrive.* It only took a moment to decide what to do next.

Davis picked up an M40 and checked once more to see that the barrel was empty before inserting a magazine consisting of five rounds. She then laid down on her stomach and perched the rifle on a low tripod. Adjusting the scope, the instructor sized up the shot and paused.

The events of the night before had been swirling in her head all day. The very act of attending a party at the White House and then, while there, catching her date with his secretary had seemed surreal. *What is it with men?* Then there was the matter of the strange but familiar face she'd seen on the ride home. The mystery of who it belonged to baffled and left her concerned. Both encounters were weighing on her more than she'd cared to admit.

Davis looked through the scope once more downfield and exhaled deeply, realizing she had been holding her breath. The tension in her muscles relaxed. The unease began to subside. In that instant, she squeezed the trigger and watched as the bullet traveled at 2,550 feet per second to the ring just inside the bullseye. *Pure exhilaration.*

Checking the shot in the scope, Davis fired another round, this time hitting the edge of the bullseye—a near miss. Then a third shot that was dead center. She smiled to herself and admired her marksmanship. *Dad would have been proud of that one.*

Shot after carefully aimed shot reverberated out from the range as Davis put on an incredible display. Just as she fired her final round, the unease resurfaced once more. This time only the identity of the stranger lingered in her mind. She tried to dismiss it. *But those eyes. That scar.* She searched the recesses of her memory. *Maybe a face in a past file.* It would have to wait as the first of the recruits approached up the road.

It was a moment that, to some, had been two years in the making. For Cooper, it had been more like four and a half. There on the television, Mikhail Gorbachev walked side-by-side with President Ronald Reagan down a red carpet towards a crowded East Room while the Marine Corps band played *Hail to the Chief.* So much had happened since that cold day on the streets of Moscow when both he and Davis thwarted a plot against the now General Secretary's life.

What were the odds of this ever happening? Cooper couldn't help but wonder. He'd never met the President but knew of his faith and determination to reach this historic moment. The man known to many as "The Gipper" had faced an assassination attempt early in his presidency. He'd been hit by a bullet that ricocheted off his limousine, coming closer to death than most had ever realized. *One inch away from his heart. He was seventy years old. Most guys that age wouldn't have made it. But here he is, achieving a reduction in nuclear weapons with our fiercest enemy. How?* Then he remembered a story once told to him by a close friend who worked as an intelligence advisor to the President. During a morning briefing in the Oval Office, Reagan had recalled that time to those in the room. *"God was watching over me,"* he'd said. *The President spoke about how God had heard his prayers as he lay on a stretcher, staring up at a tiled ceiling, struggling to breathe. "I truly believe he was protecting me for a specific purpose."*

The General Secretary had also played a key role in reaching this moment. He'd taken steps no other leader of his country had ever achieved. A man who'd witnessed the atrocities of Stalin's terror as a boy, he'd instituted a new era of openness and opportunity in the Soviet Union. The first dominoes had fallen. It was only a matter of time before Eastern Europe would truly take hold of freedom.

Cameras flashed and the audience clapped as the two men stepped toward the podium. Reagan spoke first as a Russian interpreter translated off to the side at intervals.

"On the Soviet side, over 1,500 deployed warheads will be removed," the President stated. "On our side, our entire complement of Pershing II and ground-launched cruise missiles, with some 400 deployed warheads, will all be destroyed. Additional backup missiles on both sides will also be destroyed.

"But the importance of this treaty transcends numbers. We have listened to the wisdom in an old Russian maxim. And I'm sure you're familiar with it, Mr. General Secretary, though my pronunciation may give you difficulty. The maxim is: *Dovorey no provorey*—trust, but verify."

The General Secretary chuckled and smiled once more. "You repeat that at every meeting," he replied.

The room broke out in laughter upon the English translation. Cooper laughed as well as he sat in his recliner. *Neither Brezhnev nor Andropov could have come close to rivaling the President in his humor. It's like a match made in Heaven.*

"This agreement contains the most stringent verification regime in history," Reagan continued, "including provisions for inspection teams actually residing in each other's territory and several other forms of on-site inspection, as well. This treaty protects the interests of America's friends and allies. It also embodies another important principle: the need for glasnost, a greater openness in military programs and forces.

"We can only hope that this history-making agreement will not be an end in itself but the beginning of a working relationship that will enable us to tackle the other urgent issues before us: strategic offensive nuclear weapons, the balance of conventional forces in Europe, the destructive and tragic regional conflicts that beset so many parts of our globe, and respect for the human and natural rights God has granted to all men."

The podium was soon turned over to Gorbachev, followed by the moment everyone had come to see. The two world leaders turned towards the table to the right of the podium and sat down facing the audience. Two large binders lay on the table in front of each man. An official from each country came over to turn to the exact page and point out where to sign and then again several more times. They exchanged binders and began signing once more. Finally, it was over. The treaty signed, handshakes exchanged, and a roaring standing ovation from all who were present. History had been made for the world to see. Cooper, meanwhile, bowed his head in silent prayer, giving thanks. Even when he didn't understand why he was in Moscow during the twilight of his career, there was a reason. Now it was finally being revealed to him.

Just then, he heard a car pulling up in the driveway. *Must be time.* He turned off the TV and headed outside where Agent Holden was just now dropping off Nikita.

"You ready to work?" Cooper asked the boy.

"Yes sir," he said with a smile, eager to both make some spending money doing outdoor labor and spend time with someone he looked up to and saw as both role model and adopted grandpa.

"Audrey said to tell you she should be here at eight to pick him up. I've got to get back now and help Sergei get started on his homework."

"Sounds good," he acknowledged before nodding to Sergei in the backseat. "Math homework?"

"Yeah," the ten-year-old said, a bit downtrodden. "Multiplying fractions."

"Take care," Holden said with a wave as she put the car in drive and headed off. As she drove down the driveway and out towards the gate where the main road was, Cooper noticed not one but two vans parked just outside of it. A man stood in front of both cars with surveying equipment while another had a map he was reviewing placed atop the hood of the second van. Inside both vehicles appeared to be men sitting in each of the respective driver's seats.

It doesn't take that many people to survey a parcel of land. Does it?

"What are we going to do first, Uncle Carson?"

"We'll start with some work on the irrigation ditches. I got us some shovels in the truck over there. You go ahead and hop in. Something I need to get out of the house first."

He went back in and headed towards his bedroom closet. There he kept his prized possession, a Holland & Holland Royal Double Barrel Rifle, in a leather case. Also, lying on the top shelf was a SIG Sauer P226 pistol. Cooper began loading both barrels of the rifle and stashed a few shells in his pocket for safe measure. He then took the pistol and inserted a magazine before tucking it in the waistband behind his back and underneath his Barbour Beacon jacket. As Cooper returned outside, his heart rate increased. Never since he retired had he felt this alarmed. *But it could all be nothing. Suppose they really are surveyors? You really going to pack this much firepower around the kid? But what if... You don't want to alarm him, so just in case, carry them discretely. Nothing's going to happen.*

"I thought we might get a rabbit if we're lucky," he gestured to the rifle case he brought out as Nikita sat waiting in the truck.

"Great! Mom hasn't had a chance to take us on a camping trip yet this fall. I can't wait to get one." Though Davis had spent some time teaching her boys the basics of handling a gun, Nikita learned most of what he knew from his mentor and friend.

"Just might," Cooper replied as he set the rifle in the back of the truck. "Then you can fix rabbit stew for dinner tonight. We'll keep our eyes open for them while we tend to the trees." He looked out once more on the vans and the two men seemingly at work.

Trust but verify.

It was five minutes past four when the FBI-standard black sedan pulled up to the Davis residence. Almost before the vehicle had even come to a stop, Sergei threw open the door and bolted towards the house.

"What's the hurry?" Holden called out as she removed the keys from the ignition.

"*Ducktales* already started!"

"You know your mom would want you to knock out the homework first. Tell you what, I'll find something in the kitchen for you to snack on, and you open up that math book."

Sergei nodded as they headed on in. As they did so, there was but a lone jogger passing by the residence. Down the street, the ongoing construction was as loud as ever. Workers had been at it since noon installing new roof shingles on the house. Holden had already put the utility van incident from the previous week behind her.

In the kitchen, she put a kettle on the stove to boil water for lavender tea and began fixing sliced bananas with peanut butter for Sergei. There had been a time in her career, at the beginning, right after training at Quantico, where her assignments were anything but this. Busting drug dealers and human traffickers in South Florida had exposed the then-young field agent to a dark and grizzly world. She'd seen more than she ever desired and was more than thankful when the opportunity to move into a protection division opened up. It was after two years of guarding and protecting key witnesses, including a high-level Cuban defector, when the Davis family came into her life. Holden remembered that day as she finished the snack plate and set it out for the boy. Both of the kids had spoken little English, and Audrey was still trying to assimilate back to the life she hadn't known since college. As she kept a vigilant eye out for possible KGB illegals seeking to exact revenge, her job, in some ways, morphed into something even more important. When each of them needed a confidant or a word of support, whether it had been after a rough first day at an American public school or difficulty juggling the duties of a single-working-mom, Holden had been there. Over time she'd become more than a federal agent who carried a badge and acted as a watchdog: Holden had become almost a fourth member of the family.

She realized, however, that the day was coming when her work here would be done. In four years, not a single threat had been made, much less carried out against the Davis family. Whether by her director's orders or Audrey's choice, Holden would be reassigned elsewhere as needed. When that day arrived, she knew it wouldn't be easy, yet she would be glad to see the family finally out of the woods.

The last shots from a dozen or so M40s rang out through the clearing as the training class came to an end. Davis watched as each recruit carefully inspected their rifles to ensure both the chamber was clear and the magazine empty and dispensed with before returning them to their respective lockboxes. A dark green bus came by the range shortly thereafter to collect the recruits, leaving Davis alone once more. The nagging concern was still in the back of her mind.

She checked her watch. *4:32.* On the base was a landing strip for chartered flights through a dummy corporation established by the CIA. It was convenient, allowing employees to quickly return to the McLean, Virginia area. After a short forty-minute flight, Davis would be in her car returning home to pick up Nikita from Carson's and make dinner. The plane wouldn't leave, however, until 5:15.

Picking up the rifle, she reloaded it and began to line up the sights once more at the far-off target. A light mist had begun. Thankfully the shooting gallery had been built with a protective tin roof covering her from the elements. Pulling the trigger, the sound of two casings hitting the concrete floor resonated off the ceiling as the bullets hit the target more than 600 meters down range.

It wasn't in a file. Something about the gunfire was resurfacing a memory. She lowered the rifle and became lost in deep thought, blocking out everything, including her present surroundings. *You've seen that face in the flesh… There was the sound of semi-automatics being fired… There was yelling, screaming…*

Suddenly she gasped. Her body trembling. Never before had she been this afraid since that fateful morning four years ago.

The sound of afternoon cartoons was coming from the TV upstairs. Sergei had triumphantly announced five minutes earlier that he'd finished his assignment, setting his textbook next to the sheet of paper with the twenty completed math problems on the kitchen counter. As part of her job, Holden periodically would make a sweep of the house and backyard. She started upstairs checking the rooms.

"Doing good?" she asked as she opened the door to the family's makeshift game room where Sergei sat in front of the television.

"Fantastic!"

She nodded before closing the door and heading downstairs. Holden passed back through the kitchen and turned the doorknob leading into the garage. Some tools, given by Cooper, hung on the walls and rested on a workbench. A stack of boxes sat opposite the workbench. With Davis's car gone, it was mostly empty. Agent Holden quickly surveyed the area before reaching around and hitting the garage door button next to the entryway.

"What the…"

A pair of men's shoes appeared as the large door began to rise. Then, slipping underneath and standing up, came into full view the black pants, navy-colored jacket, and the coarse unshaven face of a bald-headed man holding an AK-47 rifle.

CHAPTER 7

The next second seemed like an eternity to Holden as she saw a sadistic-looking smile form on the man's face. Desperately, she reached inside her jacket for her firearm as the man raised and pointed the automatic, capable of firing bursts of a hundred rounds per minute. Using the door for cover, she got off a single shot before seeing the dreaded flash of light. A spray of bullets ripped through the surrounding walls and began to splinter the door. She ran back through the kitchen and grabbed the seldom-used handheld transceiver. "This is Holden. Davis house is under attack! Repeat, under attack! Request back-up at once!"

Entering the main hallway, she ran into the living room and peered through the curtain. Two more men were going through the side gate that led into the backyard. Both armed with automatic rifles as well. *And all I have is this handgun. Great.*

She'd noticed the suppressor mounted on the gunman's rifle. Contrary to many moviegoers' perceptions, such attachments truly didn't silence a weapon that produced a sound up to 185 decibels. The odds, however, of anyone hearing the terrorists over the noise of the nearby construction and hammering of shingles was less than assured. *Probably figured on that when they premeditated this.* Taking stock of the situation, she decided on her plan of action. Whatever was about to happen, Holden was determined to protect the boy at all costs.

Davis knew she needed to get to a phone—first to call Holden and then Ashcroft, who could see to an immediate boost in security for her family. The nightmare scenario, the one she thought might be long past them, was now at her doorstep.

She grabbed the M40 and two full magazines before heading towards a Jeep parked nearby that she used to get around The Farm. The nearest phone was two miles down the road on the spread-out and wooded installation, where an instructor's office and a small supply depot stood. Hopping in, Davis pulled out the key. She fumbled inserting it into the ignition before dropping it on the floorboard. *D—nit, Audrey, get it together.*

Just as she reached down to retrieve it, the sound of the windshield exploding into bits of glass caused her entire body to freeze. *But how? On a heavily secured base?* Never did she think it was possible, here of all places.

Taking a deep breath, Davis first tried to get a bearing where the shots were coming from before looking up to see a bullet strike the grey upholstery vinyl of the driver's seat. *Straight ahead in the tree line.*

Instinct now took over for the CIA instructor. Out in the open, the car was her only cover. With the M40, however, she had enough long-range firepower to hold her own. A blue jean jacket lay beside her. As the gunfire continued, it became clear from the sound that the shooter was slowly coming towards the vehicle. A plan of action formed in her head.

Picking up the jacket, she tossed it out the driver's side. Dirt was whipped up and the denim fabric torn to shreds while Davis rolled out the opposite side. Hitting the ground with barely any time to size up the target, she took aim and fired straight ahead underneath the vehicle. Five rounds left her rifle. Of those, three found their mark. The assailant, now out in the open, fell to the ground.

"Throw your weapon away!" Davis stayed behind the car with her sights aimed at the terrorist's skull. "I mean it," she yelled once more. "I'm not going to ask again."

The man looked toward her and nodded. His upper right leg appeared to be bleeding. He tossed the rifle ten feet away from him. "You got me," he said with a thick accent.

Continuing to aim the rifle, she stood up and slowly moved towards him. Davis made up her mind to make him crawl towards the Jeep where she'd tie him up and then race to that nearest phone. Time was of the essence. She knew the lives of her kids and those closest to her were in grave danger.

"Keep your hands where I can see them," she ordered him.

The man let out a strained sigh and did as he was told. It was clear he'd need medical attention sooner rather than later. Prison, however, wasn't an option for the man wanted by INTERPOL as well as Israeli Mossad for his part in several bombings. He didn't trust lawyers. If not the death penalty, then the inmates would see to his demise. No, he decided then and there. He would either finish the job or die trying. Tucked into the belt loop beneath his loose shirt and jacket was a Lahti L-35 pistol. His arm was still good. Once she came within point-blank range, then he would reach for it.

"That's it. Once you finish setting out those soaker hoses, we'll turn them on for a bit to test them out."

In less than two hours, Nikita had gotten more done than Cooper figured the twelve-year-old would've accomplished. As the sun dipped below the horizon, Carson readied two outdoor lamps from a small cabin he used to store tools and equipment. They would only need them for the last bit of work before calling it a day.

Nikita's hands were covered in soil as he laid out the last line of hoses. Getting up from the dirt floor of the greenhouse amongst countless potted saplings, he began to wipe them off on his jeans when he suddenly jerked his head up.

"Hey, Uncle Carson, did you see that?"

Cooper stopped in the middle of plugging in the connector cords for the lamp. "No. What was it?"

"Way down past the far end of this row of trees," he pointed out the greenhouse door towards where the brush began. "That bush shook. You don't think it's a deer?"

The sixth sense of a man who'd spent a lifetime learning to know when one was being watched kicked in. "You know, let's call it a night. Load everything in the truck, and let's head back to the house."

"What about the lamps? Are we going to put them back in the shed?"

"Leave them. I'll take care of the lamps in the morning." As Cooper spoke, the winds shifted, blowing directly from the direction of the brush. The whiff of a *Laika* cigarette reached his nostrils. He recognized the Soviet brand immediately and felt a chill down his spine.

He reached around and felt for his pistol. *Lord be with me,* was his short and silent prayer. He knew what was out there and recognized, even more so, that his expertise alone wouldn't be enough.

The two loaded into the truck. Cooper took the Royal double-barrel rifle and set it on his lap as they began heading down the dirt road that led back to the house.

"Why do you have your rifle out now?" Nikita asked with a confused look.

"Suspect that might have been a hog you saw out there in the brush. If we spot one as we pass by there, I plan on shooting him. Don't want it tearing things up or getting into the greenhouse."

He kept the truck's speed at thirty miles per hour. He couldn't lose his cool, not now. They'd have to pass by the brush. Only when they were clear of the spot could Cooper gun it fast. His heartbeat quickened and his hands began to sweat as he gripped the steering wheel firmly.

They were now twenty yards from the spot on the driver's side. Cooper rolled down his window and prepared himself. He pulled back the hammers on both barrels with his right hand as he kept the left on the wheel. Gripping the stock, he had his finger on the trigger, ready to fire. It was a sight which caused Nikita to begin to worry.

"Get down!"

The deafening sound of the rifle blast jolted the boy as a firefight began. A man in camo, clutching a handgun near the brush edge, fell and hit the ground. Immediately farther down, two more men in identical camo appeared, leveling their rifles as they took a stand in the middle of the road. Cooper quickly made a sharp J-turn, firing several rounds out the window towards them with his P226 pistol before speeding off.

Bullets began pelting against the truck bed. One hit the back windshield. "Keep staying down. We're going to have to turn the old cabin into a fort with them blocking the road."

Keep your cool, Mary. You've got to stay calm.

Holden readied her service pistol as she knelt down in front of an open window facing the backyard. *Take care of these two, then deal with Ugly around front.*

She watched as the fence gate slowly opened. A man dressed much like the one in the garage but with longer hair and a jagged scar along the whole of his chin. *Now!*

Two bullets struck the man: one hitting the protective Kevlar, the other a fatal shot to the temple. As he fell, a bearded squad member behind him unleashed a torrent of bullets, several barely missing Holden's head. She ducked for cover and continued to fire.

Holden knew pinning him down wouldn't be enough. She was reminded of that once more as the back door leading to the garage creaked open. Her heart now felt like it was about to beat out of her chest. Loading another magazine clip, she moved towards the sound. The thud of boots taking slow and heavy steps on the hardwood floors meant only one thing. Once he rounded the corner, the baldheaded gunman would face the stairway leading upstairs. *Sergei!*

Her mind was made up. Turning around the corner, she fired two haphazard shots and ran. The gunman ignored the stairs and followed as she headed towards the basement door nearby. As she reached for the door handle where a drawing of the fifty states was taped right above, a bullet tore through Holden's left arm. Groaning in pain, she kept moving. Only the rushing adrenaline kept her going. The bearded gunman was now at the open window.

"Musan!" the gunman yelled to baldy. "The boy must be in the basement!"

Holden leveled another round as she opened the basement door, this one striking the bearded gunman in the neck. Baldy fired a spate of bullets at her as she entered the basement stairway and took cover. It was then she finally noticed her arm covered in blood. *That cavalry better get here fast.*

Then came a second stark realization: there were no extra magazines on her. She had but one round left. Looking down the stairway and towards the main room of the finished basement space, it was clear there were no audibles left to call.

But one. Locking the door and racing down into the room, she turned left and headed back to an empty space behind and out of sight of the stairs. There next to the washer and dryer was the breaker box. Pulling open the metal box door, Holden flipped off the breaker switch for the basement. The room immediately descended into darkness as she took cover behind the dryer, clutching her pistol and hoping for relief.

"I don't care how you do it, walk or crawl, you're going to get over to that Jeep." Davis kept the gun pointed at the man still lying on the road. She stood but ten feet from him. "What's it going to be?"

A grunt came from him as he slowly reached for the ground in front of him with one hand and shuffled forward. The cold steel of the gun concealed underneath his clothes now pressed against his skin. His other hand flexed in anticipation of what he was about to do.

"I don't have all day. If you want someone to patch you up, you'll move faster," Davis barked at him as she feared what may be happening to her kids elsewhere. Instead, he began to move slower. Suddenly, his right hand swooped around his torso and pulled forth his last firearm. Three final shots reverberated across the gun range.

This was it, Holden was sure. The baldheaded gunman now stood at the top of the basement stairway, hastily loading another magazine. The FBI agent remained hidden behind the dryer when she saw the illumination of a flashlight.

"I know where you are, FBI," the man declared in a heavy accent. "You and boy are dead." He fired another burst only to draw out the sickening wait. Family photos that lined the descending stairway walls were shot to bits as broken glass and shattered picture frames fell to the ground.

Holden's arm was bleeding badly, and she began to feel faint. She shuddered as the sound of boots descended the stairway while the AK continued to fire sporadically. Finally, he reached the bottom step with the sound of crunching glass announcing his presence. He could not be seen, yet the sound gave away exactly where he stood. Then out of nowhere her pistol, readied just moments ago for this final chance, now began to tremble in her hands. She felt her mind begin to go foggy. An internal struggle just to stay conscious was taking place.

Why...did it stop? The automatic suddenly went quiet. She could see through half-closed eyes the light shift as if he were looking back for some reason. Whatever it was, however, seemed to be nothing of consequence. Letting out a petrifying laugh of a man who enjoyed cold-blooded murder, he took the last step, turned, and shined his flashlight towards the washer and dryer. Slowly he approached before stopping directly in front of Holden, who could no longer muster the strength to hold her own gun.

"What? Where you hide him? Answer me now!" He waved the end of the gun barrel inches from Holden's face. When she gave no reply, he slapped her across the face hard. Nearly unconscious, she hoped for a speedy end. She watched as he pointed the gun once more and readied to fire.

"Goodbye pathetic American police wo—" a force suddenly struck baldy, dropping him to the floor. But for a moment more, Holden's senses stayed alert. There before her, the man who was about to kill her lay still. His skull now nothing more than a pool of blood.

"Oh my gosh! Ma'am, can you hear me?" Just as she heard those words, police car sirens began to wail outside.

Cooper pulled the truck up as close as possible to the cabin. "Here," he exclaimed, handing Nikita his pistol. "You know what to do, Nikki. Time to use what you've learned practice shooting." The boy couldn't believe what was happening as he found himself thrust into a combat situation. He'd gone with Cooper to shoot at targets taped to old pine trees plenty of times and had slowly developed a skill set that he understood was to be used for hunting deer. Never did he believe it would be required in self-defense before the age of thirteen.

Cooper looked out into the open area between them and the brush and saw five men. Two appeared to be coming straight at them, providing cover while the others attempted a flank position on the cabin. The sun was gone now, and only a crescent moon provided light. The old man stayed behind his truck bed and fired both Royal .375 H&H Magnum cases at the two straight ahead before reloading within seconds. Hastily, he took aim and shot at the flank attack, this time taking down one of the men.

He paused to look over at the boy. Nikita held the pistol like he was taught with both hands. His body was trembling, and a grimaced expression marked his face.

"It's okay, kid," Cooper spoke loudly to him over the sound of automatics. "Self-defense. Just breathe. You can do this."

As bullets pelted the vehicle and the saplings in front of them, the boy summoned the courage and returned fired on the men who threatened their lives. Tears were now streaming down Nikita's face. He'd gone through exfiltration from the only country he knew, the loss of his own father, and the pains of culture shock. Through all of it, Audrey had done her best to shield him from outside perils and allow him to be a kid. Now, in this moment, the innocence and bliss of childhood were extinguished. The reality of a harsh and cold world was upon him.

CHAPTER 8

Davis threw the body into the back of the Jeep. As soon as he was in, she hopped behind the wheel and raced to the nearest phone as fast as she could. Intuition, a trigger finger, and two rounds left in the M40 had saved her.

The vehicle pulled up to a mobile building that doubled as an as-needed office. Another Jeep was parked out front. An instructor was leaving to catch the plane back to McLean when he saw the body and his frantic co-worker.

"Phone lines haven't been cut?" Davis asked as she rushed past him to the door.

"What on earth happened?" The instructor's face was a mixture of shock and concern.

She neither heard nor had the time to answer. Grabbing the phone receiver atop one of the desks inside, she dialed the one person she could trust at Langley.

"Ashcroft here."

"Sir, it's Davis. Someone just tried to kill me here at The Farm. I don't have time to explain, but my boys are in danger. Cooper and Agent Holden as well. You've got to get them to a secure location!"

"Audrey, we just got word of a shooting at your home."

"Sergei is he…" For the first time today, her voice was unsteady.

"We don't know yet," he said in a calm but firm voice. "FBI and the police just arrived. We've federal agents on their way to Cooper's farm as we speak."

"I need to get back there, now."

"Agreed. Get on that plane, Audrey. We'll talk more later."

"Yes sir."

The shooting intensified. One of the men now stood fifty yards away near the portable overhead flood light. Carson saw his chance to narrow down the enemy's advantage. Taking aim, he shot out the lamp. The man immediately became disoriented from the sudden darkness, wobbling around, before taking a .375 caliber round to the chest. Still the rest moved in closer.

"Get in the cabin now!" Carson yelled the order to Nikita and pointed to the cabin door as his voice became nearly inaudible over the shooting.

"But you need me!" the boy hollered back. The old man grabbed him by the arm and nearly tossed him inside. The strength of his grip jolting Nikita. "Don't open this door. Stay inside. If anyone enters that isn't me or the police, shoot 'em. Now stay in there." Cooper swung the door shut, leaving Nikita alone in the dark cabin with blackout curtains.

There were three left. All were within fifty yards coming from both the right side and straight ahead. Cooper wiped the sweat from his forehead and bit his lip. *God, let me hold out just a bit longer. If only to protect Nikki.*

Out of the corner of his eye, he saw a bright light on his flank. He shifted his head, trying to avoid disorientation from the shock grenade thrown near him, before firing both barrels randomly in that direction with his eyes shut. Cooper reloaded once more, staying down. *Wait until the next one is so close you can't miss.*

He got his chance. Another camouflaged man hurdled over the truck bed. Cooper got off a blast before the attacker fell on top of him. Blood dripped from the man's stomach, his vest ultimately defected. A deadly wrestling match ensued. A knife was quickly drawn and raised over the head of Cooper. Unable to move fast enough, the blade streaked across his left cheek and found its way into his shoulder. Cooper yelled out before kneeing the man in the gut and firing the second barrel, ending the assailant's life.

A white-hot pain traveled through his side. It took a moment for him to realize he'd been shot. He took the knife still lodged in his shoulder and threw it at an approaching figure in a desperate attempt to hold him off. Ducking, the terrorist fired at Cooper's upper right leg, causing him to yell once more.

"Ne strelyat."

Cooper barely heard the Russian order to hold fire as he became faint. Coming towards him was a tan-faced Caucasian man, well-built, carrying his own rifle with a small radio strapped to his hip. It was clear to him that this man was the leader of the group.

The man knelt down and stared Cooper in the eyes. "7,751 kilometers. That's how far I travel to kill you, Mr. Carson Cooper. Colonel Muammar Gaddafi sends his condolences in advance."

"I'm touched," Cooper dead-panned. "Never knew he cared so much."

"You're an enemy to the people of Libya," the man answered sternly.

"The trouble you caused has not been forgotten. Now, imperialist spy, you will pay the price for your transgression."

"If your Colonel is so upset with me, why did he send a Russian to do his dirty work?" Cooper asked. His breathing was now becoming labored.

"Because only I could wish to see you dead more than he. Do you know who I am?" the leader asked him in an accented voice.

Cooper shook his head wearily.

"Think back to your last time in Moscow. You should remember what happened."

"You," Carson spoke as he gasped for air. "One of the Spetsnaz conspirators. I...thought...they rounded up every last one of you?"

"Not all of us were captured. Allow me to introduce myself. I'm Konstantin Boytsov."

Cooper's mind ventured to that deadly morning. It was coming back now. This was no doubt the lone driver who escaped just as he and Davis thwarted the attempted assassination of Gorbachev.

Boytsov watched as the realization sunk in before placing the heel of his boot squarely on Cooper's leg wound. Cooper cried out in agony.

"Your interference that day cost my comrades their lives. Both those there on that street and others at the hands of executioners. I can never return to my *Rodina*. I'm forced to live in a barren desert. I'm a fugitive without a home. All because of you and that woman."

The writing was on the wall. This was the end and Carson knew it. His body ached in severe pain. However, he wasn't afraid.

Over the years, while on missions for the CIA, he'd come to hold fast to the words found in the Book of Isaiah: *Fear not, for I am with you.* Cooper knew who was with him. Afraid? No. Strengthened and at peace, understanding this wasn't the end? Absolutely.

Boytsov pointed his rifle and emptied his magazine. The sickening sound echoed throughout the farm and surrounding forest. When it was over, he started towards the door of the cabin. As his hand reached for the knob, a voice came on over the radio.

"Get out now," were the words in Arabic. "Repeat, get out now. They're coming down the road!"

The Russian shook his head in anger. *Take the win, Konstantin. You got the main target you came for.* Later he would find out if Audrey 'Tatiana Alexeev' Davis had indeed been terminated. Gesturing to his lone surviving team member, the two hurried off into the woods. The commando turned terrorist believed it was over. Revenge had been exacted both for the strongmen who sheltered him as well as himself. The price for injustice had finally been paid. *Maybe even the dreams will come to an end.* If only he knew it had, in fact, just begun.

PART TWO

CHAPTER 9

Konstantin Boytsov and his comrade reached the van parked at the edge of the woods, nearly two miles from the scene of their bloody shootout. The driver, a Lebanese recruit from the training camp, barely eighteen, gestured wildly for them to get inside.

"They just reached the farm," the driver told them as both men slid open the side door and leaped in.

"How much time do we have?" Boytsov asked in Arabic. He'd entrusted the young man with not only their transportation but their escape as well.

"Eight minutes until the roadblock goes up. State troopers are already on their way to the designated spots. I heard on the radio scanners," the driver replied, hitting the gas pedal, as the distinct sound of rubber burning on asphalt was notable to both of the commandos.

Boytsov checked his watch. They only had so much time at the safe house to change clothes and grab their fake passports before leaving to take the first of several flights that would eventually get them back to Tripoli. He knew returning to his country of refuge would be temporary.

He'd given his word to Director Ahmed Raza in exchange for leading the now completed operation. Whether he agreed or not with the dangerous scheme, supposedly the brainchild of Gaddafi himself, wasn't important, only his loyalty to Raza—the man who'd earned his trust long ago.

That, however, would be handled in good time. Boytsov sat back in his seat and closed his eyes. *You've been avenged, comrades. I did not forget.* He then began humming a tune no one in the van could place.

They were calling him a hero. Tucker Wallace had just pulled into his driveway after a long day at his public accounting firm when he noticed two men across the street entering the backyard gate of the Davis residence. He didn't think much of it until he noticed what they were each carrying. Then he saw one of them go down. That's when the former Army Ranger ran to get his hunting rifle. Following the trail of two bodies, he got to the basement in the nick of time.

Davis listened to the last details of the raids as she sat in the waiting room outside the ICU of Mount Vernon Hospital. A member of the FBI's counter-intelligence division filled her in as they waited for an update on Mary Holden's condition.

"What about the others?"

"According to your eldest son, there were as many as six assailants there on the farm. When we arrived, we found four bodies. Road blocks were put up several hours ago, and we've got police and agents at Dulles International ready to arrest anyone who fits the description we have."

"I see." Davis closed her eyes for a moment and let out a heavy sigh. The descriptions were cursory at best. It had been nearly impossible for Nikita to make out their faces well in the darkness of the night. *What that kid has gone through...*

60

She'd barely had a chance to see him when she returned from The Farm. Both boys were now under the protection of more than a dozen agents at an undisclosed location. Sergei had miraculously been spared from almost the entire ordeal due to Holden bravely leading the terrorists to the basement. Initially, the high volume of the TV with the door shut kept him from hearing most of it until, finally realizing something was wrong, he hid unharmed in a closet until the police arrived.

"Got here as soon as I could." It was Koufax, of all people, sitting down beside her. He took her hand and squeezed it in a caring manner. The FBI agent meanwhile excused himself and left. "Anything I can do for you, Audrey?"

"Koufax?" Davis found herself caught off-guard at the sight of her often quiet and reserved Soviet Select colleague. For the first time that evening, however, a half-smile, ever so brief, appeared on her face. "Thanks for coming. Oh, I don't know. It's been a whirlwind of a day. I haven't eaten since lunch, but I don't think the cafeteria is open at this hour."

"I'll go pick something up and bring it back. You waiting to see the Agent still?"

Davis nodded. "I'm not leaving here until they let me see her. She saved Sergei's life. I think it's the least I can do."

"Understandable," he noted. "Don't forget to take care of yourself, though. I mean it. You've been through a lot today. Not many could've handled that terrorist the way you did."

"You said terrorist."

Koufax gave a puzzled look. "Yeah. So?"

"Mary faced off with three terrorists today. Carson, six. All the while protecting the kids. Facing off with just one of the thugs while carrying an M-40 doesn't make me anything special. Not one d—n bit."

61

Koufax said not a word. A look of empathy was all he gave.

"I'm sorry," Davis finally said. "I...oh gosh. Tell me, I'll be honest, but I just didn't figure you to..."

"Have a heart? In our line of work, even on the 7th floor, it pays to keep up some sort of a facade. I guess I am a bit quiet at times. I know what it's like to feel like you almost lost someone." He paused for a moment as if he had trouble still accepting something. "And I know what it's like to actually lose that person."

"Your wife?" Davis asked.

Koufax shook his head before standing up. "There's a burger joint just across the street. I'll go over there now if that sounds good. Be back soon."

"Thanks, Koufax." Her co-worker turned and headed out the door. Several minutes went by before a nurse came over to her.

"Ms. Davis," spoke the nurse, a middle-aged Hispanic woman. "Agent Holden is awake now. She lost a lot of blood and is very weak. However, her condition has stabilized. The doctor believes she'll recover."

"Thank goodness," Davis said aloud. "Can I please see her?"

"Very briefly. Agent Holden needs all the rest she can get right now. No more than two minutes."

"Understood."

The nurse led her down the corridors of the ICU. "Remember, two minutes," she said to Davis once more as she opened the door to the hospital room. "Keep it light. Nothing too serious or upsetting right now."

Davis stepped in to find her friend lying in bed, staring straight at the ceiling. IVs and heart monitor wires seemed to run to and fro. Turning to face her, Holden spoke first.

"You never told me how your date went the other night."

Davis smiled. "I'm glad to see you're doing better, or at least have your sense of humor still."

"Hey now, I'm in charge of looking out for you," Holden replied weakly with a grin. "Important stuff to know."

"Let's just say I may need to start attending PTA meetings again," she said with a chuckle. "At least the venue was something special."

"Where did you go?"

"White House. A state dinner. Did get to meet a naval aviator."

"Hope it was a fighter pilot. They're always the best," Holden replied with a slight smile.

"Listen, Mary," she said before clearing her throat. "I know you need to rest. I just wanted to say, from the bottom of my heart, what you did today…." Davis stopped at that lest she started to tear up. "Thank you."

"Anything for Sergei." Her eyes started to close. "So tired."

"Get some rest. It's alright. I'll be back later."

Agent Mary Holden was already fast asleep.

CHAPTER 10

The safe house was an hour's drive away. Davis noted the heightened security all around the large chalet on the edge of South Mountain State Park in northwest Maryland. Her family would be safe here, for now at least, she told herself.

A male FBI agent standing out in the driveway opened Davis's backseat door and led her up to the front porch. Another agent, a woman appearing to be in her late thirties, opened and gestured for her to come in.

"Ms. Davis, your boys are asleep in a room we set up for them just down the hall off the living room. Yours is right next to them. We've someone assigned guard duty just outside their door. Anything we can get you?"

"Something to help me sleep," Davis replied. It was 2:15 a.m., yet her mind was still racing, asking questions when she knew the answers wouldn't come until morning or much later.

"Sure thing. I'll go get you a sedative and some water," the agent answered as she led the way towards the kitchen.

"One more thing," spoke Davis. She looked around the room and noted various family photographs. "Whose place is this?"

"Belongs to the Deputy Director at the Bureau. Vacation home of his. Doesn't come up here as much as he used to and on rare occasions has offered this place up to hide protected VIPs."

"I wouldn't consider myself a VIP."

"The Deputy Director does. He was shocked to hear what happened. He also greatly respects how you and your eldest son handled yourselves against those terrorists. Anyway, you can check in on your kids if you want and get ready for bed. I'll be back with the sleeping pill."

Passing through the living room with its stone fireplace and vaulted ceilings, she saw a suited man with a barrel chest guarding the boy's room. Nodding to her in acknowledgment, he stepped aside and allowed her to go in. Davis entered the darkened room and shut the door behind her. Taking a second for her eyes to adjust, she saw both of them resting in bunk beds. Davis found Sergei in the top one, no doubt having begged his older brother for it. Climbing up the first two steps of the attached side ladder, she watched him rest peacefully. *If it weren't for Mary…* She kissed his forehead and returned to the ground where Nikita lay below asleep on his side. Instead of kissing him goodnight like she'd done almost every night of his life, Davis watched her son.

"Why can't we go back home, Mom?"

The words spoken by her eldest son four years ago drifted back to her now. How do you explain to your son, born under the hammer and sickle, that you're actually an American working under non-official cover for the CIA? Or that his Russian father, a man he looked up to, had taken part in an assassination attempt on Gorbachev and died at the hands of his own murderous comrades.

"It's not safe anymore, Nikita. There's so much I want to tell you and yet so much I can't. This is our new home now."

"So we can't go back?"

"No, son, we can't."

"But will we be safe here?"

"Honey, look at me. You're safe here. Mom is not going to let anything happen to you."

"Does that mean you won't go? Nothing's going to happen to you...like Dad?"

She could still picture the look in her son's eyes: pain from all that he'd gone through and a fear of what might still come. He wanted to be brave. He always did, most likely due to being the oldest. Still, he was only a boy whose world had been shaken. In that moment, she got down on her knees and hugged him close.

"I will never leave you. As long as I have breath in me, I'll always be here for you."

Taking a step back, she watched them sleep for a moment more. These two children, after all was said and done in her career at Langley, were what mattered most to her. Now she felt she'd let them down and broken her promise. Their world had been shaken once more. She closed her eyes as the stress of it all only intensified. "Never again," she whispered softly but firmly. "On my word, no one will ever hurt my family again."

As she readied for bed minutes later, her thoughts shifted to Carson. He'd been on her mind throughout the evening but only now was it beginning to truly sink in. She remembered how it was him who'd encouraged her to leave Moscow, return home and live the life she'd given up for her country. When she was about to be killed by one of the Spetsnaz conspirators, it was Carson who had arrived at the last second and saved her life. Stateside, he'd become a trusted friend and family member. Then in his final act of kindness towards her family, he sacrificed himself in order to buy time and save Nikita. *Now he's gone. Shot down in retirement by terrorists.*

She took and swallowed the sleeping pill with the glass of water before turning out the light. Finally, Davis's head hit the pillow at the end of her nightmarish day. Closing her eyes, she drifted off with but one thing on her mind. *I owe it to you too, Carson. I will find these people, and they will pay.*

CHAPTER 11

They allowed her seven hours of sleep. Ashcroft gave the order that Davis was not to be disturbed until at least 9:30. At that time, there was a knock at her door. The rest had done her some good. She quickly dressed and went to the kitchen where the boys were already finishing breakfast. Sergei ran to hug his mother, who embraced him tightly. Nikita, however, remained in his chair with a distant expression.

After a bowl of brown sugar oatmeal and two cups of coffee, she headed out the door where a car was ready to take her onto Langley.

"Sir, I apologize for coming this late in the morning," she said to Ashcroft as she later entered his office.

"Audrey, there's no need for apologies. Sit down, please."

She took a seat across from his desk. Files lay strewn about. It was evident to Davis that the DDI had been reading extensively since he arrived that morning.

"First, I'm glad to see you're alive. It's madness what happened at The Farm yesterday, and I'm thankful your sons didn't get hurt. Cooper, though, his death is a tragedy. Our paths crossed more than a few times here at the Agency. There'll never be another like him. With that said, we've already begun hunting down the SOBs responsible."

Davis gave an appreciative gesture. "What have you found out?"

"The man who attacked you at The Farm has been ID'd as a Syrian bomber in Lebanon for an offshoot group of Hezbollah. Israel's had him on their wanted lists for quite some time. In order to enter the base, he killed a recruit strikingly similar in age, complexion and likeness earlier that morning. He drove the dead man's car to work and used his documents to get in. Made it through the entrance without any issues, unfortunately. The base is now going through a complete review of security. Big changes coming, no doubt. The attack on your home featured a similar crew: Middle Eastern, trained, and had at least one on a wanted list.

'The third attack, however, is where things get interesting. As your son noted to investigators on the scene, one of the men was overheard speaking Russian. The rest of those found dead, we're unable to make an exact identification of their nationality, although there are a couple educated of guesses.

"Sir, there's something you should know. I saw one of the Spetsnaz assassins that tried to kill Gorbachev. Last Saturday night, walking in my neighborhood. It wasn't until yesterday though that I realized who it was."

Ashcroft breathed in deeply, then exhaled. "I see." The significance of the detail was not lost on him as he pondered for a moment longer before continuing.

"We've traced the purchase of the van parked outside your residence yesterday. At least four additional vehicles were bought by the same man at a used dealership in Baltimore. The salesman was able to give a description and lucky for us, we spotted the guy trying to fly out of Dulles."

Davis's facial expression seemed to take on new life at the news of a lead. "What have they got out of him?"

"Nothing yet. He was picked up this morning about to board a red-eye flight to Miami. Carried with him two other fake passports— American, French and Lebanese."

"I want to be part of the investigation, sir," she stated flatly.

Whereas others might've quickly dismissed her as simply over-reactive or letting their emotions get in the way, the DDI chose not to. "Why, Audrey?"

"Two reasons. First off, we know that at least one of the terrorists was Russian. I'm not an expert in Arab affairs, but I do know the Soviets. What's more, I suspect as you do that somehow the foiled assassination attempt against Gorbachev plays a part in this. I'll just say it: I'm about as perfect an analyst for this as the Agency is going to find."

Ashcroft kept his cards close and gave but a stoic look. There was no need to reveal the details just yet, much less whom he suspected responsible. "And the second reason?"

"There's been a leak." Davis let those words hang in the air for several seconds before continuing. "Only a select few were aware I was ever Tatiana Alexeev. The boys have always been explained to anyone we ever meet as having been adopted. Even Reagan, when he called to thank me the day Director Casey presented me the Intelligence Star, only had been briefed that I foiled the attack and knew nothing of my NOC.

"Only six people know my full story: Koufax, Skylar, Shelby, Clark, Agent Holden, and yourself."

"You think it wise to be talking about this with me?" he deadpanned. "I'm a potential suspect."

"I'll take the risk and eliminate you, sir," she said with a slight smile.

"How very generous of you."

"Seriously, I have to trust someone here. We've known each other long enough for me to realize you're not the type to turn traitor. Besides, I've met your wife. Pretty sure Barbara would kill you if she caught you making a dead drop."

Ashcroft shook his head and laughed. "She would at that. There are two others you haven't considered, both archivists. One retired a year ago. His area covered your full Top Secret file. His successor is the other."

"So you've already suspected a leak as well?" she asked.

"As soon as I heard there were three simultaneous terrorist attacks involving your family. This won't be easy, Audrey. It's a two-part inquiry uncovering who the mastermind was, as well as the one who supplied him the intel. We can handle the archivist, but the Soviet Select, especially Clark, the Deputy Director of Operations, will be tricky. They'll all need to be kept in the dark about our search for a mole. And anything you find out on your own about the terrorists will only be released to the Select as needed. By the way, at least we don't have to worry about things getting complicated between you and Skylar."

"How in the...."

"My job is to know everything," Ashcroft answered as he stood up from his swivel chair. He walked over to a bookshelf where a picture frame sat between a biography of Wild Bill Donovan and a first-edition copy of JFK's *Profiles in Courage*.

"You know," he said, picking up *Profiles*. "They say Kennedy never actually wrote this book. His speechwriter Ted Sorenson was supposedly the man behind it all. Pulitzer Prize-winning work and no credit. Kind of like what we do here, only on a greater scale." He turned and looked at the picture frame. "That was Cooper, to a T."

Davis came over and saw the photograph. There, in black and white, was a much younger Carson Cooper standing atop the deck of a nuclear submarine in a drysuit. The fine lines that marked the face she knew were missing. Same distinct mustache and slicked-back hair, only no grey.

"Where was this photo taken?"

"Baltic Sea, 1957. Most of the details are classified to this day. Luckily though, you have the clearance to hear it. You see, we'd just exfiltrated an asset. Scientist. Weapons technology. That sort. Anyway, as soon as we got him out, he refused to talk. CIA was livid with him. He said he was upset with himself for not bringing his family with him and regretted it. Never mind there hadn't been time to arrange for the family, who lived in Latvia, to secure an escape when word came that the KGB was on his trail. So when a briefing was given with several of our top officers, Cooper immediately volunteered. They dropped him off several miles from shore in icy waters during the night. He swam in and ventured to the cottage the family kept on the outskirts of town. Somehow, he managed to convince the wife and two kids to come with him. Using an inflatable raft and collapsible oar he packed, he set out to take them back to the sub. His report detailed multiple close calls throughout the mission, including with patrol boats, but through his bravery, the scientist's whole family escaped alive. Carson didn't get any awards, applause, or anything resembling recognition. Nobody even knew who he was. He simply went home to his wife for three weeks and then went right back out into the cold. That's the life he lived for his country."

"He deserves justice," Davis thought aloud. She did her best to keep the whirlwind of stress and pain she was feeling from getting the best of her now. There would be no tears in her boss's office.

Ashcroft set the book back on the shelf. Too many times in his career, he'd seen what happened to others motivated by retribution. Often it led to faulty analysis and, in turn, tragic consequences. Now he was torn on what to do about his most gifted analyst. He could see the apparent danger. He also could not ignore the potential.

"Justice is separate from revenge. Never let the pursuit of the former become a soulless pursuit, resulting in the warping of the mind and the degradation of morals. If you do, you've found yourself caught up in revenge. Remember that, Audrey."

CHAPTER 12

Tripoli, Libya

It was the same dream again. Boytsov was back in the old dacha hidden in Losiny Ostrov National Park. The winds howled outside as he and five other men sat around a fireplace. Until this moment, he'd been forced to live in the shadows. Deep cover, in a fishing village on the coast of Estonia. No friends. No family. No confidants. Only the rare and fleeting encounters of a KGB handler and his own thoughts to keep himself company. But now he was here, among comrades. None knew the other's real name, but it didn't matter. These were men, maybe the only men it seemed, who could truly understand the weight he carried and shared in his zealous loyalty to the *Rodina*. For the chosen six Spetsnaz, each shared the same fate.

They spoke of the hardships. They spoke of mothers and fathers they left behind, never to see again when they first reported to their master. They spoke of the fate of the new Soviet Man. They spoke of the coming mission, laughing at the thought of death in order to give strength to one another. They spoke of hope: settle down, marry and raise children in a prosperous land. As the hours passed and the vodka shared, a friendship grew like none they'd ever known.

Just as Boytsov found himself at peace among these new brothers, the fire went out. The setting in which he was in became blurred. Suddenly the picture came into focus and he was jarred by the scene of combat. Here, on the streets of his *Rodina's* capital.

Sasha, get back in the car and be ready to get us out of here fast. There in the midst of the firefight, he dutifully returned to the parked Zhiguli and watched.

He could feel the bond he had with each of them strengthen even as he looked on. The courage he witnessed from each Spetsnaz moved him. The culmination of the mission was now at hand. All they had left to do was blow out the target's car door, end his life and escape.

But then out of nowhere, the tide turned. One by one Boytsov's comrades fell. Their lifeless eyes looking up at him from the cold concrete, seemingly begging him to come to their aid. *Sasha, get back in the car and be ready to get us out of here fast.* The order echoed in his ears once more. He had to stay, had to stick to the plan, lest he destroy them all.

Finally, the one who gave him the order stood alone, directly in front of the Zhiguli, before taking a bullet to the chest. Then a second and third. His body crumpled to the ground before Boytsov.

You said to get back in the car! Why didn't you let me stay? Why!

A mist formed around him. Indecision and fear swept him. He was lost without sense of direction. Adrift without his brothers in arms.

Suddenly he saw him. Coming through the mist, now standing at a distance. So often the recurring dream reached this point and each time resulted in the same outcome. The despised CIA Station Chief would look upon him in silence. What he was thinking, Boytsov could never ascertain. All he felt was a raging sense of anger at the American who'd taken all away from him.

This time to his surprise, there was a PSS pistol in his own hand. Boytsov raised the firearm, aimed and shot at Carson Cooper. He fired again and again until the magazine had emptied. *Revenge, revenge at last.* The nightmare would now come to a close. He could move on, at last.

Before he could examine whether his enemy was for sure dead, however, the mist returned. It seemed like ages before it finally cleared. When it did, the Russian looked in bewilderment as the American still stood. Somehow he was even bigger in stature and stronger in appearance than before. *Death is not the end, Konstantin Boytsov,* he spoke. *Death is not the end.*

The jostle of the French Air flight touching down on the tarmac at Tripoli International Airport finally awoke him. Fighting to catch his breath, he was relieved to see no one looking his way. *These dreams are only getting worse.*

It had taken a total of five flights to get here: Baltimore to Boston to Reykjavik to Madrid to Paris and now his city of refuge. The forty-four hours of travel time left his legs aching to move. What he wouldn't give for a stroll along the shoreline nearby to take in the saltwater air. However, a lone black helicopter awaited him on a nearby tarmac across from those used by the commercial airlines. Collecting his lone carry-on bag, Boytsov headed straight across the simmering asphalt as a stewardess and an airport official yelled in vain that he was heading the wrong way, the turbine engines drowning out the sounds of their voices.

The pilot, dressed in a Libyan Air Force uniform, sat alone waiting for him to climb aboard. Boytsov took his seat and sat in silence, enjoying the return of warmer air as the chopper took off. Despite the earlier nightmare, his mood was upbeat, still on a high from his hit on Cooper. Looking out, he could see Okba Ben Nafi Air Base. Once used by the Americans and named Wheelus Air Base until the coup, it was now a Libyan People's Air Force base that saw Soviet transport planes stationed there as well. The Russian noted where spots on the air base tarmac were still damaged more than a year after the U.S.'s retaliatory bombing raid known as Operation El Dorado Canyon.

Landing on the far side of the base, away from possible Soviet eyes, Boytsov was led to an empty hangar. There, Director Raza was waiting for him.

"It's good to see you again, my friend. I've already received word from our source of your mission's success," Raza greeted him as the hangar door shut behind his most trusted commando instructor.

"Da," he answered in Russian before returning to Arabic. *"Cooper has been eliminated. The Americans can now shake in their boots, knowing what it's like to feel the enemy's wrath on your own soil."

Raza gave a faint smile before continuing. "While the mission was a victory overall, unfortunately, he was the only target your team succeeded in taking out. The rest either survived or were unharmed."

Boytsov was taken aback. "And you heard this from?"

"The same source that revealed their identities and told us where they lived. They also say that one of your men was arrested at the airport. Fits the description of that young Lebanese you brought along."

The Russian rubbed the back of his head and looked down at the floor, wondering where they'd gone wrong. Finally, he looked up and spoke. "He is a good man. Was a reliable driver and spotter. We can trust him."

"He's also young. Can't you imagine what will happen to him in their prison system? An accomplice to the murder of an elderly man and the attempted murder of two children and a woman? We'll be lucky if he makes it to the trial without saying a word. Leave it to me. I'll see that he's taken care of…Now, that brings us to another matter."

"Yes, Director Raza," Boytsov readied himself for the request. "I'm prepared to honor my part of the agreement."

"Very well. Colonel Gaddafi will be most pleased when I tell him the news. Take a couple days to rest up. After that, you're to make contact with your old friend, General Zhukov. We have no doubt that you'll be able to persuade him."

Does he understand the risk if this fails? Another thought struck the Russian as he listened to the head of Libyan Intelligence go over the details. *What if Raza and the others know this but are just too afraid to tell the madman the truth?*

When the meeting was finally over, he bowed his head slightly. "It will all be done as you say." The two parted ways and Boytsov stepped out of the hangar just as a Soviet Ilyushin Il-76 airlifter took off. He looked up to the sky. A crooked grin began to form on his face. It amused him how he could literally be under the Soviet Union's noses yet utterly invisible to them. *All this time, diplomatic relations, using this airfield, and yet not even a clue.* It was for that reason he owed so much to Raza. The man had thrown him a life preserver when he needed it most and kept his secret airtight from the KGB. It wasn't by any means due to any trait of nobleness. Boytsov knew that well. In providing him refuge, Raza had gotten both an expert training consultant and a lead-in to a much bigger prize.

But now it was time to seek that prize, risking the safety the former Spetsnaz had known till now. His heart sank at the thought. There existed no alternative. His lone choice was painfully clear: dutifully serve his Berber master and the crazed Colonel who ruled over them all.

CHAPTER 13

Arlington National Cemetery – Washington D.C.

The winds blew hard from the east on the afternoon of the funeral. A large motorcade stretched along Eisenhower Drive coming from Old Post Chapel before turning onto York Drive. Up ahead, the Old Guard, known as the longest-serving infantry unit in the United States Army, escorted the procession. Both boys had insisted on coming, Nikita especially. Over the last few days, he'd become drawn in and closed off to those around him. He barely uttered a word to Sergei and ignored his younger brother whenever asked to come outside and throw the football around. Instead he sat on his bunk bed, sometimes reading a copy of *Treasure Island* that Cooper had once given him but mostly staring up at the bunk overhead. Only when he heard his mother tell one of the on-duty agents that the boys wouldn't be going that he became visibly upset, nearly yelling that no one would stop him from being there.

There were at least fifty mourners at the overcast gravesite, Davis noted as she exited the car with her sons. She viewed the caisson that carried Cooper's flag-draped coffin. It would be here at Section 60 where he'd rest forever amongst fellow veterans of WWII. *Why? Why like this?*

Trudging past their tombstones, she couldn't help but wonder. *Those men, they mostly died of illness or old age. Not a firefight on their own land at the hands of terrorists.*

The mourners finally gathered at the grave as the casket was carried to rest on the platform. Ashcroft, along with Skylar and Koufax, was there, standing a few feet away from the Davis family on the other side of an FBI agent acting as security.

The chaplain began to deliver his remarks. Even amongst family and close friends, much of his life story remained untold. Army Intelligence, service in both theatres during the War, and a general mention of his time with the CIA was all that was said of his career. His love for his late wife Cathy and desire to serve his country were the overarching themes of the words spoken.

When he was finished, the gravesite became quiet. Only the sound of birds chirping off in the distance could be heard. Then, an Army Captain came forward and saluted.

"Firing party, fire three volleys!" Sergei jerked his head at the order shouted by the nearby firing-party commander to his men. The sound of seven rifles firing in unison reverberated throughout the cemetery.

"It's okay, Nikita," Davis whispered as she placed a hand on her oldest son's trembling shoulder. Each time, the boy's face grimaced at the sound of the gunfire, his teeth grinding and his eyes shut in fear. For a moment, Davis thought she'd have to take him back to the car. *How could you not have thought this would upset him after everything?* She continued to silently scold herself until it was over. To her, it was but another instance of her failing to protect him.

A bugler stepped forward from the escort band's formation to play "Taps". Each sorrowful note reviving the painful memories of the first time she'd heard them more than twenty years before. The grief laid on her at an early age had not been easy. Empathy for Nikita, who'd already lost a parent and now what seemed like a grandfather, was real.

As the music ended, the casket team began folding the flag. A soldier known as the 'present man' handed the now folded flag to the Army Captain. Turning around, the Captain presented it to the next of kin, Maggie Stanwyck, Cooper's little sister and sole surviving sibling. Cathy Cooper had been unable to have children, making Maggie the closest living relative he had remaining. Tears trickled down the aging woman's face. Cooper had often spoken of her and would call once every week to visit. Giving a word of condolence, he then saluted and walked back towards the head grave.

A final individual approached before it was over: a uniformed woman known as the Arlington Lady holding the arm of an Old Guard soldier. She, like the Captain, offered her condolences as well as presented two letters: one from the Army Chief of Staff and the other from herself.

Davis looked down and saw her children's misty red eyes at the conclusion. It was now time to go. Looking out toward the coffin one last time, she felt no longer the need to cry. For her at this very moment, the time for mourning had passed. All she could do was pick up the pieces and never forget the Chief of Station.

CHAPTER 14

"Taking the afternoon off?" Deputy Director of Operations Pat Clark looked on with curiosity as Davis cleared off her desk in a hurried fashion and locked up the files she'd checked out.

"FBI just called and asked if I'd like to watch the interrogation. I'm heading there now."

"I see," he replied with a nod. "Hopefully he isn't too headstrong. Otherwise, it could be a while until they get anything useful."

"Same." She reached for her purse and headed to leave her windowless office before Clark stopped her, blocking the doorway. Towering six foot four with a large frame and Texas drawl, the head of Operations was known to be as imposing a figure as fellow Texan Lyndon B. Johnson ever was. "I do hope you'll let me know what you learn. Operations can't act without good intel. We'll need it if we're going to get those d—n terrorists."

"I'll let you know what I can, Clark. Not sure what will be classified and what…."

"Nothing's classified from me." He was now standing over, leaning out towards her face. Unlike the senators and subordinates LBJ once practiced such tactics on, Davis didn't step back.

"Then you won't mind if it goes through proper channels before reaching you then." Clark attempted to avoid reacting to the rebuttal, instead staring directly down at the young woman who was rising to the top faster than he or anyone else at the CIA ever had. Finally, he let out a laugh.

"Wouldn't have it any other way, honey." He stepped aside, allowing her to exit. "Take care now and stay safe."

"Goodbye, Clark." Walking away, all she could think was how glad she didn't have to directly report to that egocentric chauvinist.

Forty-five minutes later, Davis stood anxiously behind the glass of a two-way mirror. Seated at a table in a windowless room was one Baqil Karam. Thus far, he'd volunteered only his name and nationality, Lebanese. A thorough check of the databases showed the young man had never appeared on a watch list, been linked to a terror organization, or even received so much as a traffic ticket in Beirut.

"He's been kept in solitary confinement so far," a member of the FBI investigative team named Chip Murray remarked as he stood beside her watching Karam. "The kid is young. I don't think he realizes what'll happen if we have him around even some of the milder types in prison."

"Who's interrogating him?" Davis asked.

"Me." Murray kept his gaze on Karam. "If you'll excuse me," he said as he turned to head for the door.

Growing up, Calvin 'Chip' Murray Jr. had not always sought to be an FBI agent, much less a counter-terrorism interrogator. He'd dreamed of being a professional baseball player back when his dad coached his youth league teams and took him to games at legendary Tiger Stadium where Cobb and Greenberg once played. He was pretty good too, a pitcher with a low-90's fastball in his senior year of high school with a knuckle-curve that confounded both hitters and catchers alike. A scholarship to play ball for the Michigan Wolverines awaited him after graduation. Then tragedy struck. Late one evening as his dad came home from work at the auto plant, he was shot and killed at a stop light. The family was devastated. Chip ultimately chose to forgo the scholarship to support his widowed mom and instead go to community college at night. Meanwhile, investigators were stumped by the murder. Months later, after hours of questioning, a suspect confessed to being in the car that night with the man responsible for shooting the elder Murray. Justice was served and from then on, Murray grew enamored with a career in law enforcement. After college, he applied and was quickly accepted for training at Quantico. He made it a point to learn all he could from his instructors about the finer aspects of negotiation and questioning. Assigned to the counter-terrorism interrogation team upon graduation, he was considered one of the best in his field. Many a hardened criminal had sat across from him thinking he'd never talk, only to return to his cell dumbfounded by all he'd willingly confessed to.

Karam didn't bother to look up when Murray entered through the room's side door. As Murray sat across from him, he set down a plate of open-faced meat pies known as *sfiha*. The aroma caught the suspect's attention as he gazed at the warm dish and then at his interrogator.

"Thought you might be hungry. Go ahead," he gestured to Karam. "We can eat and talk."

The man looked puzzled, unsure if it were some kind of a trick. "It's alright, see," Murray reassured him before taking a bite. "If you're worried I cooked it, it's actually from a Lebanese restaurant a couple miles from here. Mmm, that's good stuff."

Pulling the dish slowly towards himself, Karam took a bite. Murray noted the tension in the suspect's face seemed to relax somewhat.

"Which part of Lebanon are you from?" Murray asked.

"Jounieh," was the reply in between mouthfuls. "You know where that is?"

"Yep, along the coast about fifteen miles north of Beirut. Some excellent cliff diving spots around there. You get out to the water much growing up?"

"My father and grandfather had their own fishing boat. I went with them often and drove the fresh catch to market afterward."

"You want something to drink with that? Water, coffee, *zhourat* tea?"

"*Zhourat*," Karam said with a pleasantly surprised expression. "You get that from this restaurant as well?"

"No. Made it myself, actually. One second."

Murray stepped outside before bringing back a piping hot cup and saucer. "Was hoping you'd ask."

The suspect took it and sipped slowly. "Quite good," he remarked, setting the cup back onto the saucer. "Thank you."

Murray nodded in acknowledgment. "So, growing up you helped with the family business. Sounds like you were all very close."

"We were," Karam answered. He was smiling now for the first time since his arrest as he recalled the happier times of his youth before the civil war destroyed everything he held dear. As Karam told his story, Murray asked few questions, instead mirroring the man sitting across from him while carefully noting his non-verbal actions.

It seemed clear that Karam's path to radicalization had started with the death of his parents and all but one of his siblings. The family had the misfortune of being caught in the crossfire of a shootout one day between Maronite and PLO forces. Their home was later destroyed in a bombing raid and the rest of the family scattered. Alone, unemployed and without any real ties, the young man began to search for some sort of meaning. It was when he'd drifted towards the southern part of the country months later that he fell in with Hezbollah.

"Could I please have some more tea?" the suspect asked after nearly two hours. By now, Davis had grown tired watching behind the two-way glass, wondering where this questioning was headed. Murray, though, was preparing to make his move. Slowly he created the illusion of control with Karam, giving the man a level of comfort in their conversation he'd not had with anyone upon his arrest. After bringing in a second cup, the interrogator started on a new track.

"Karam, you've talked about how you became a warrior and who you felt was responsible for the pain you suffered. What I still don't know is what would make you come to America."

"Sometimes, you help a friend in order to repay the help he's given."

"Repay the help he's given?" asked Murray.

"Yes. A friend of the cause."

"An Arab?"

Karam shook his head. "White like you."

"So, what were you doing to help this friend here in America?"

The young man pulled his hands, which had been spread forward on the table, inward. He looked down as he spoke. "My friend needed help with his fishing business," he said with a shaky voice before pausing to find the right words. "I help him with sailing to right spots and catching cod. He uses bad nets and his equipment is old."

"Karam, I'm hearing you say that you're just helping a friend fish but I also heard something in your tone of voice that made you hesitate."

"I...I have a friend that needed help."

"Needed help that required carrying multiple passports under different

86

names," Murray said nothing else, letting the somber fact hang in the air.

"That was a friend's passport from Beirut. We room together. It must have somehow got lost and ended up in my bag."

"From the look of his photo, it would seem he looks very much like you."

The suspect scratched the side of his neck. "It's the truth."

"You mentioned having a surviving sibling. Where is she now?"

"In Montreal. She married a French engineer about six years ago. I haven't seen her since she left home."

"Sounds like you miss her."

"Very much. She was the oldest and was like a second mother growing up."

"Then let's shoot straight. I want to help you. If you really want to see your sister again, you'll help me. The man you helped isn't going to help you in return. If he was, he'd be here now. Karam, you're covering for someone who doesn't care about your cause. You want your country liberated. Coming to America to attack a family who's never set foot in your homeland does nothing for your issue. He and whoever else he's with used you for their own gain. They don't care if you rot in a foreign prison for the rest of your life. I do care, though. Work with me, and I'll see you're treated with respect. You'll have the right to see your sister again. We'll let her know you want her to visit. We can arrange it."

Karam put his hands to his face and exhaled loudly. He hesitated several more seconds before giving his answer. "What do you need from me?"

"Start with this guy." Murray presented a rough sketch, based on the description Davis gave of the man she'd seen the day of the assassination attempt and more recently the evening she returned home from the White House. "Tell me what you know."

"His name is Boytsov. Eight months ago, I was sent for training at camp. Do you…"

"You said camp?" Murray interrupted for the first time.

"Far away in a desert in Libya. Many men like me were there for commando and paramilitary training. He was an instructor in marksmanship and other tactics. After six months there, I was taken aside by him. Said he was assigning me for a special mission to strike at some bad people in America that stood against us. He did not say more. Over time, I realized from how he spoke that he knew these people from somewhere else."

"From where else did you suspect?"

"Some said he was from Eastern Europe. Soviet Union was mentioned. There's much mystery about him. No one's really sure."

As Karam continued on about his instructor, Murray noted his relaxed manner, identical to when he talked earlier about his family. After another hour, the recording camera was finally turned off and the interrogation session was over.

"Quite impressive," Davis said as Murray returned to the viewing room. "How long did it take to learn how to get answers like that?"

"A little training and a lot of on-the-job practice. It's a good start. Plenty more we need to get out of him, particularly more details about the camp. I focused more on this Boytsov character. Tomorrow we'll start back again."

"I appreciate the work you're doing. Really."

"Thank you. It's just what I do," Murray replied as he noted the tension in her face. *What she's been through*, he said to himself. He couldn't imagine anyone trying to take out his wife and kids. There was more than just professional motivation for the FBI interrogator to uncover the details about the attack. It was one parent wanting to help another.

It was right before she left the prison her pager began to beep. Davis checked the area code. *717, Pennsylvania. Odd.* Stepping into an unused office, she called back the number.

"Hello?" answered an older gentleman's voice.

"Hi, this is Audrey Davis."

"Ms. Davis, my name's Don Wainwright. I'm an estate attorney up in Gettysburg and I'm calling because Mr. Carson Cooper was a client of mine. A good friend as well. Anyway, he named you in his will and I was wondering when, if possible, you might be able to come by my office?"

"Named in his will?" Davis asked in a puzzled manner.

"Yes, ma'am. Tell you what, I might be driving south your way next week, day after Christmas. Could I call you back later and we arrange a time to meet then?"

"Sure, that works for me."

"Great. Look forward to meeting with you. Merry Christmas," he replied before hanging up. Putting the phone back, Davis stood there bewildered as she had a sudden epiphany. *You never got to say goodbye.* At that moment, the thought tore at her. She felt the strong desire for five more minutes, as so many often have. Then the driving will to move forward returned. *Bury those thoughts, Audrey. Bury them and don't look back.*

.

CHAPTER 15

Sochi, Krasnodar Krai, Soviet Union

The setting seemed almost surreal to Boytsov. Standing on Soviet soil for the first time in over four years, he felt both a sense of triumph and fear. His cover was that of a sports writer following the Yugoslav soccer team here for a weekend match. It had not been easy getting a message through to the General, yet nonetheless, it worked.

Boytsov sat at a table in the back of a local bar not far from the stadium. Black and white photographs of the national team and local clubs lined the walls. Across the room, a radio played VIA, known as state-recognized pop music. A typewriter sat before him along with a full mug. His eyes periodically glanced out towards the main doorway, waiting for his man to enter.

He was writing a feature on one of the up-and-coming Yugoslav players when several revelers entered. Boytsov looked up and saw trailing behind them his man: Brigadier General Yakov Zhukov. The high-ranking member of the Red Army was in full dress uniform. Despite being in his fifties, he maintained a high degree of fitness, unlike some of his contemporaries at this stage of their careers who'd developed a gut. He only drank as the situation required and privately preferred mineral water to any alcoholic beverage. Nonetheless, he approached the bar and ordered the bartender to give him a bottle of vodka and two glasses. Then, he went looking for a seat.

"Comrade, will you join me in celebrating our team's victory today?" he asked Boytsov. "It's no good to drink alone."

"Unless you're covering the Yugoslavian team that is," Boytsov replied.

"Then you definitely need a drink," the General slapped him on the back. "Come, come, take a shot," he said as he began filling up the glasses and then took a seat. "To sportsmanship between fellow communist peoples," he bellowed with a hearty voice as he raised his glass.

Boytsov gave a resigned expression and chuckled before raising his own. "To sportsmanship."

The two threw back their shots and laughed. Seeing that the correct code words were given, General Zhukov began.

"It's good to see you again, comrade," he spoke in a whisper. "There have been many rumors since the plot failed. Some said you were executed. Others, you defected to the West. And of course, others that you became a hired gun."

"Rumors. They're about all we have left to grasp in the *Rodina*," Boytsov replied. "I'm glad the back channels worked and you got my message."

"Indeed. How have you been? You're taking quite a bit of risk showing up here, you know."

"I've been well. After the ambush failed and the roundups began, the Libyans offered refuge in exchange for training their next generation of commandos. How about you though?" ignoring the statement on his risk-taking. "How's guarding all those launchers and missiles?"

Zhukov's face turned to a sour expression. "Like being an old *loshad*' waiting to be sent to the glue factory. You know, when they showed Gorbachev on television signing that Treaty, the young officers at the base just laughed. 'Guess we'll be busy disassembling tomorrow,' remarked one idiot. 'Hopefully we get transferred somewhere more exciting than this *svalka*. Maybe Budapest?' Fools! They can't see what's happening to their way of life. At this rate, we'll all be decommissioned and retired on a pension of worthless rubles in no time. Maybe the youth will stand a chance in the next era. But what will become of us, the old guard?"

"What did you do to the officer who made the wisecrack?" asked Boytsov.

"Had him transferred to Afghanistan," Zhukov replied without missing a beat. "Thirty years. Almost all spent handling these weapons of destruction. They won't have any use for me once they dismantle them. They'll cast me aside. All for what? World peace? There will never be peace. Peace is an abstract idea. A dream that is only awakened by the bright blast of reality."

Boytsov watched and listened carefully. Months before, Gadhafi's personal wish might have been ill-fated. Now, the conditions were right. Circumstances, motive, opportunity. Zhukov would no doubt be a willing participant and accomplice for what he had in mind.

"Ah Konstantin, the world has changed much since our paths first crossed. You remember those times? Much simpler."

"I do in fact, Yakov. It seems like only yesterday I was on a training exercise in the Caucasus Mountains, and you were a Colonel on your way to becoming a General."

"You saved my life that day. I've never forgotten."

"That green officer!" Boytsov remembered his Spetsnaz division resupplying a base when a stupid lieutenant got lost leading his platoon during a war games exercise and began attacking the base's security patrol with live ammo. If it had not been for Boytsov's quick thinking in which he ran through live fire and rescued Zhukov from a ditch where he was pinned down, the General would not be sitting there now.

"I refuse to accept this as the end. I say to myself, 'Yakov Alexandrovich Zhukov, you will not let them discard you. You've given too much to your country for that. You deserve more, your fair share for the service you've put in.' But I don't know how to go about it. It's like I'm living in a Tolstoy novel."

"What if I can get you your fair share?" Boytsov watched with quiet anticipation as the wheels began to turn in Zhukov's mind.

"What do you mean?"

The former Spetsnaz almost began when a group of young students took a table nearby them. Both remained silent until another student came from outside, calling for his friends to join them at another bar down the street.

"Why not sell what's about to be destroyed?"

"You mean…"

"Comrade, I already have the buyer ready and willing."

Zhukov's mouth dropped open in disbelief. It remained so until he picked up on Boytsov's concern that he was drawing attention. "How much?"

A barely audible whisper was given in reply. It took but a second for the General to respond.

"If I did agree to this, how would it be done? Off the base, out of the country, and across the sea? All without anyone finding out?"

"You mean without anyone finding out *in time*," Boytsov noted. "And what they did find out wouldn't be enough to pin it on my buyer. I give you my word. I wouldn't have come all this way to speak to you if I didn't already have a plan ready. A thought-out plan, I should say, that will not fail."

"Before you explain it to me, I have another question: what's in it for you?"

"Repaying a favor. That's all I can say, really. A favor that was well worth it."

Zhukov stared at the man before his eyes, who was soliciting him to commit treason against his own country. The rewards for success would be great. So would the consequences of failure.

"Okay then, comrade. How will we commit the greatest heist of the century?"

CHAPTER 16

Restless—that word described Davis to a tee. Unable to sleep, she arose and wandered about the house, noting the two FBI Agents on-duty, before discovering a small wine cellar in the chateau. Selecting a Napa label, she poured a glass and noted the tinge of brown. An older red wine. No doubt expensive. Taking a sip, she tasted the dark fruit and the perfect amount of acidity. Respite. It wasn't until a couple glasses later that she finally returned to bed late. Late enough that she found it a struggle to get up at the sound of her 5:45 a.m. alarm.

Wearily, Davis made her way to the kitchen and turned on the drip-cup coffee maker. Copies of both the *Post* and the *Wall Street Journal* lay on the counter. She picked up the *Journal* and began skimming the headlines. For all the intelligence gathered by the Agency, there was always some tidbit a journalist had gotten before an operative. Davis sipped her coffee slowly as she read about the latest from the INF Treaty, including reactions on the feasibility of the required missile dismantling inspections for both sides. At 6 a.m., she pulled out the comics and sports sections for the boys, then went to shower and got dressed. Half an hour later, the former spy turned analyst headed out to the waiting car where she soon dozed off in the backseat.

She'd been at her desk for not even ten minutes when her office phone rang. "Audrey, this is Ashcroft. Be at my office in three minutes." Davis didn't even have time to respond when he abruptly hung up. As soon as she arrived, it was clear that an urgent meeting of the Soviet Select was underway.

"I just briefed the Director," Ashcroft began as he looked down at the carpet in disgust. "Our lone suspect from the terror attack is dead."

Davis looked up from her coffee in shock. "How?" How did it happen?"

"Suicide?" George Shelby asked with a perplexed expression. Koufax and Pat Clark leaned in closer, eagerly waiting to hear more. Skylar nearly spit a sip of his green tea across the room.

"The FBI is saying the cause of death appears to be strangulation. They say his bedsheets were used."

"So it was a suicide then," Skylar remarked.

"Initial evidence would point to that. However, there are a couple irregularities. Particularly the times when the guard shifts changed and when three convicted felons were walked down the hallway at the exact moment. It's going to take them some time to investigate."

"That puts us at square one," said Clark. The Deputy Director of Operations shifted in his chair, seemingly frustrated by the situation. He then turned towards Davis. "Unless they were able to get anything out of him before he kicked the bucket." Davis wasn't sure if the intense stare he was now giving was a look of concern or another power play.

"We're hoping to get a transcript of what their investigator was able to learn sooner rather than later. Besides that, nothing new at the moment," Ashcroft interjected while avoiding eye contact with her. "What has been established is that one of the attackers was Caucasian and at times spoke Russian." Whatever Soviet connections there are, I expect this team to track them down and, if necessary, upon approval from higher up the chain, craft a response to neutralize the responsible party. Toby, I want you to begin looking at lists of known operatives and commandos that have either gone rogue or are working under a deep cover."

"I'll get you the files on what we've come across out in the field," Clark affirmed to Koufax. "Until we have something more concrete and Shelby can make hay of where in the world these guys are, we'll have to sit idle on operational plans."

"Understandable, Pat. And Skylar, you'll be working with Toby. Do all the digging you can." All the while the DDI made no mention of Davis. *Probably too shaken up*, Shelby assumed, like the rest from where he sat. *Who could expect her to work on this? Too much for a woman to handle, separating emotions from unbiased analysis and investigation.*

"Everyone know their marching orders?" Ashcroft grunted.

"Affirmative," Koufax answered.

"Yes, sir," Skylar and Shelby said simultaneously.

Clark turned again towards Davis, this time with a look of empathy as well as something else on his mind. "We're going to find these bastards, Audrey."

"Thank you," she replied softly.

"Yeah. If only we get all the information we need," Clark added sharply.

"Well then, everyone's dismissed," Ashcroft said as he stood up from his swivel chair. "Audrey, do you mind staying for a minute?"

The Deputy Director of Intelligence waited until they were the only ones left in the room before he pulled open his desk drawer and removed a file. "Here, it's everything you need," he said as he handed it to her. "I spoke to Murray, and the complete Karam interrogation material will be kept confidential until after New Year's. That should give you a head start."

"You really think one of them is the mole, don't you?"

"Like I said, can't rule out the archivists, but smart money is it's one of the Soviet Select. There is something else, however." Ashcroft shifted in his seat before continuing. "You recall during the interrogation that our suspect was training inside Libya. The regime there has been known to provide sanctuary to a variety of terrorist groups. It's possible the Spetsnaz you recognized was part of one of these organizations operating there. It's also possible, I might add, that he works directly with the Libyan government."

"So you're saying, sir, Muammar Gaddafi himself might be the mastermind and this was his answer to Operation El Dorado Canyon?"

"A scenario we can't overlook."

"But if the Libyans are behind this and it is retaliation, why go after us? I've never had anything to do with the country, much less even visited the African continent. Also, I thought Cooper spent his career focused on the Soviets?"

"That's where you're wrong." Getting up from his desk, Ashcroft walked over to his bookshelf and removed several volumes on the History of WWII by Churchill to reveal a rectangular safe. Entering an eight-digit code, the electric lock opened and he withdrew a large nondescript file. Davis's eyes grew wide with curiosity as she eyed it.

"Ten years ago, Cooper was sent to Benghazi on orders to make contact with a man named Omar. By that time, our diplomatic channels with the country had been severed and so Cooper operated without official cover. It was dangerous but with great risk came great potential reward. You see, Omar was in charge of Colonel Gaddafi's official bodyguard and protection detail. He'd come in contact with an American businessman, took a risk and passed him a note. What it said, in short, was that he was secretly a sympathizer for the former King Idris and wanted to do whatever he could to return him to power.

"Cooper made contact with Omar and a plan soon developed to infiltrate the security detail with those who could act as additional intelligence assets, as well as be ready to strike against Gaddafi should the ideal opportunity arise. Finding the right people would be a challenge. That's where Cooper brought in Mossad."

"The Israelis were involved?" Davis asked.

Ashcroft gave a nod. "He knew one of their case officers on the ground there and got the green light from here on the 7th floor to proceed. Mossad was already invested in the region and knew who we could use to join the Gaddafi bodyguard. Some say they even had their own people go undercover protecting the tyrant. No one, not even Cooper, knew for sure. The arrangement, however, proved effective for both the Israelis and us. For a time that is.

"Eventually, Cooper was transferred back stateside and a new case officer was sent to replace him. Three months later, it all hit the fan. Omar had failed to make multiple scheduled dead drops. Mossad then gave us the news the head of Gaddafi's detail had been arrested. Over the next few weeks, several Israeli agents' who were part of the operation disappeared. That was a dark time for both of our country's intelligence services. There was a bit of finger-pointing as to who was responsible. In the end, we lost our closest sources to the Colonel."

"So, it's conceivable Libya would have a motive to take out Cooper. Including those he was closest to," Davis noted. "Do we know what, if at all, they found out about him?"

Ashcroft shook his head. "It's believed while under torture, Omar revealed some details about his case officer. To the old spy's credit, Cooper took his cover seriously, made use of the disguises provided by the Office of Strategic Services and would have kept personal details in conversation to build trust to a minimum. That's where, again, someone had to have been passing information from this building to the responsible party. I've gone over the records of everyone who's checked out this file before I confiscated it. The archivists and the Select all had access to it or have been in proximity of someone that did. I want you to go through this file as well, Audrey. Study everything he was involved in there and see what connections and possible leads you can find."

He reached out and handed her the enormous trove of CIA history. As Davis held it in her hands, it seemed to weigh several pounds. *Who knows what we'll find in here.*

"One last piece of business I'd like to discuss," his voice taking on an icy edge. "Your drinking problem."

"Drinking problem? You've got the FBI snitching on me or something? I may have had a glass before bed but that doesn't make me a slush."

"You look hungover and lousy to be a matter of fact. Doesn't take a rocket scientist to deduct that though I heard about your sleeping problems through my channels. I've never known you to have this issue before. You spoken with anyone?"

"I apologize, sir. I had a lot on my mind after the interrogation yesterday. But really, I'm fine."

"Nobody bats a thousand, not even you, Audrey," he answered while reaching into his desk for a pill bottle. Davis had seen her boss reach for it before. She had noted the medication's name and learned it was blood pressure medication. *Well, if you had worked in this gig for as long as he has, who wouldn't be on prescriptions?*

He reached for a glass of water and swallowed a pill before continuing. "You're an adult. Do what you like. What I'm saying is, having this job while coping with what happened barely two weeks ago, you can't carry your burdens alone."

"Sir, I spent a decade alone in the Soviet Union spying without official cover. I can take care of myself."

"You're forgetting whom you eventually confided in." He leaned back in his chair and let that sink in for a moment. "We all have a breaking point, Audrey. It comes down to who or what we turn to."

He hoped he was getting through. Ever since Davis arrived back in the states, Ashcroft had seen something special in her. It was evident from her record that she'd mastered the tradecraft of a successful spy, but through her debriefs he'd learned she possessed a gift for analysis and decision making. Men like himself were nearing retirement. Now was the time to ready that next generation of leaders at the CIA. But if she were to go far, she needed to learn this lesson and realize no one is invincible, much less alone.

"Sir, I'll cut the late-night drinking and think about what you've said. You have my word."

"Good," he replied with an air of resignation. "I'll let you get to work then. One last thing. Take tomorrow, the 24th, and Christmas completely off. Don't come into the office for even an hour. I know just how much drive you have, but take care of yourself and rest up. Spend time with those boys."

"I will, sir," she nodded. That was something she hadn't done enough of since the attack. It would be much needed for sure.

Davis shut the door and took a seat behind her desk. Opening the Karam interrogation file, she reviewed his initial confession. *Boytsov. Believed to be in his early thirties. Green eyes. Caucasian. Often dresses in traditional Bedouin attire. Skilled in marksmanship and commando activities. Instructor at training camp.* No physical description of the camp nor mention of its location inside Libya was available. That line of questioning had yet to be delved into and now would never happen. She'd need to review all satellite intelligence on known and suspected paramilitary training camps in the country. Anything up to date would require going through Shelby. If so, he'd be an early candidate for surveillance. *Long nights tailing in a car. Great. Guess I should've asked for a thermos for Christmas.*

Even if they found the camp, however, it wouldn't be enough. They'd need to know for sure Boytsov was still there. If they were wrong and even worse civilians were there instead, their failures would make CNN and be broadcast the world over.

Matching his description from Karam with what we can see on satellite is the logical first step. Having another set of eyes on the ground is another. But who? That would involve going through Clark, another even trickier person to investigate along the way. She'd have to get with Ashcroft on that one. *Doesn't matter. We'll figure it out.* For now, she'd work to connect the dots. No matter how long it took.

CHAPTER 17

"How was your trip?" Director Raza shook Boytsov's hand as the commando entered the car parked alongside the shores of the Gulf of Sidra. Though it was late at night, the Russian had been summoned by his master to give a report.

"Successful," answered Boytsov. "Zhukov took the bait. The necessary preparations have been made."

"Excellent! Gaddafi will be most pleased to hear this. Will it all go off as scheduled?"

"It should in the coming months. I expect no delays."

Raza leaned back in his seat and looked out at the sea through the passenger window. *Soon, we will be a real power. No longer intimidated by the United States. No longer plagued with retaliatory bombings or sanctions. Then we can achieve what the Colonel speaks of so often: a United Arab Republic stretching from here to Syria.*

"You have done well for us. When this is over and we can finally reveal our new source of strength to the world, you can expect to be rewarded. No more will you need to stay hidden in the desert."

Boytsov merely nodded. *Fools. They still haven't wrapped their minds around the risks involved, much less the fallout if the weapons actually reach these shores.*

"You may return back to Al Jadid for now. A new batch of recruits and freedom fighters should be arriving later this week. Rest until then. Later, I will call you when the second part of the plan is ready to be implemented."

"Thank you, Director." The meeting over, Boytsov got out of the car and watched as it drove off into the night. Turning towards an SUV parked down the street, he noted the young intelligence officer sitting behind the wheel waiting for him. It would be a long night's journey to the southern desert region. The former Spetsnaz pondered the trip for a second before shaking his head and bowing it in resignation. He'd no doubt sleep most of the way while suffering again the dream of his fallen comrades and the *Rodina* that was no more.

The boys were smiling for once. Davis watched from the chateau's living room window as Nikita pulled his younger brother around on their new sled through the two inches of fresh snow they'd gotten Christmas Eve. Torn wrapping paper lay strewn all around the Christmas tree, the same tree that had come from Carson's farm. A seasonal album sung by Tony Bennett played over the stereo. Davis sipped on a mug of warm apple cider dressed in a red turtleneck and jeans. It all would have seemed straight out of a Hallmark card except for the three FBI agents posted in and around the house.

She tried to ignore the family's situation and be present in the moment. This, at the end of serving her country on Soviet soil, was what she'd wanted. *Peace and normalcy. Why is that so hard?*

The sled hit a rock, causing Sergei to go airborne. Hitting the snow face first, his older brother gave a look of genuine concern, soon followed by laughter when he realized he was okay. A snowball fight soon ensued. Davis watched but for a minute before heading outside.

"Hey!" Nikita exclaimed as a snowball from his right caught him off-guard. "What are you doing out here?"

"Free for all!" Davis threw another, this time at Sergei. All three were laughing now as a full-scale snowball fight was underway.

"Truce!" Sergei held his hands up finally after a while. "Let's all build a snow fort and then start again."

"Good idea," Davis replied. "Nikita, help me roll some snow over towards that hill."

Just as they started, a silver sedan pulled up in the driveway. An older gentleman in an overcoat got out with a leather briefcase. The FBI agents on duty outside seemed to know who he was. Quickly, Davis realized who it was. "Guys, keep working on the fort. I'll be back."

"Ms. Davis? Don Wainwright, lawyer from Gettysburg who called recently about Mr. Cooper's will."

"Yes, sorry, wasn't expecting you. What are you doing here on Christmas? How did you find where I was?"

"Well, my family moved up their schedule a day, and we're driving to Norfolk now to celebrate together. Also, as his lawyer, my path has crossed that of the intelligence community more than a few time which has resulted in me getting a security clearance. I had some matters to attend to with them for his estate and in mentioning your name, they said where I could find you. Since you were on the way...."

"This really isn't the best time. No offense, but...."

"I can make it quick. Five minutes, I promise."

"Okay," she demurred. "We can talk up there on the front porch."

A row of cherry wood-stained rocking chairs each separated by a small, round side table lined the expansive covered portico. Taking a seat,

Wainwright pulled out a single sheet of paper.

"Per Mr. Cooper's last will and testament, 'I hereby leave to Ms. Audrey Davis a selection of my personal library. This includes, for your enjoyment, as well as Sergei and Nikita's, the complete collections of Sir Arthur Conan Doyle, Jack London, Jules Verne, and C.S. Lewis, as well as my King James Bible and journal. I'm also leaving you my late wife's collection of Jane Austen novels so that you'll never need to borrow them again.'" This last line elicited a chuckle from Davis, who'd borrowed the Austen books more times than she could count.

"Lastly, I leave you this envelope containing a key to my safety deposit box at the First Owings Mills Bank.'" Wainwright pulled a nondescript white envelope out of his briefcase. "Before you ask, I haven't the faintest idea what he left in the box. The books are in the trunk of my car. I can get them now if you don't mind."

"Sure. Do you need me to sign for any of this?"

"I do." Wainwright pulled out another piece of paper and extracted a pen from inside his coat pocket. "Here you are. I'll go get those books then."

She wrote her name on the bottom line before picking up the envelope. Feeling the key inside, a mixture of curiosity and grief arose in her. *It can wait till after New Year's. You'll be in a better place by then.*

The lawyer returned with a large box. "The man sure liked to read," he remarked with a strained voice. "It's heavy now. Would you like me to set them inside for you?"

"He did at that," she replied, taking the box. "I got it. Really appreciate you bringing this by."

"No problem at all. I'd best be on my way then. You and your boys have a Merry Christmas."

Davis gave a nod, then smiled. "You have a Merry Christmas as well."

With that, Wainwright turned and left.

Just as she started to pick up the box, Sergei hollered at her. "Hey Mom! What's in the box?"

"Books. Mr. Cooper left them to us in his will. Be careful with them."

"Sherlock Holmes! Cool!" Sergei thumbed through the pages eagerly. Nikita stood aloof, not sure it was okay to handle the old but well-preserved editions.

"It's okay," Davis told her oldest. "He wanted you to enjoy these."

Nikita moved toward the box, reaching inside to pull out a copy of *20,000 Leagues Under the Sea*. He looked at the front cover for a moment before tucking it under his arm and heading inside without saying a word.

"He's so sad. Always whenever Uncle Carson comes up," Sergei said to her.

"I know, son."

"Isn't there anything we can do?"

Davis's mind immediately went to her search for Boytsov. All she wanted was to catch the monster who'd brought so much pain to her family. *To bring closure, to bring justice, and to simply avenge what they've done to my son. If only I didn't have to wait until after Christmas...*

"Mom?"

"Be there for him," she said, returning from her thoughts. It was all she knew to do for her oldest son. "Just be there."

CHAPTER 18

February 8th, 1988 8:08 pm MSK (Two Months Later)

Caucasus Mountain Region – Soviet Union

"Good evening, General Zhukov. You said there was something urgent?" Major Pashin asked as he entered the base commander's office.

"Message from Moscow. Just received a few moments ago requesting that the respective commanding military and political officer read simultaneously. I believe this is your copy."

KGB Major Igor Pashin, the political officer of the base, glared at the General in such a way as if he were trying to see right through him. Though lower in standard rank, his status as the eyes and ears of the secret police allowed him to exercise a certain level of power here, where some of the Soviet Union's most deadly missiles were stored. Zhukov often found him obnoxious.

The General handed a copy to his colleague and went to shut the door. He made sure that his assistant, just outside, had heard everything up to that point.

Pashin read the words slowly as the harsh winter winds howled outside. "This seems rather sudden. Why tonight, do you suppose?"

"We don't question orders, Major," Zhukov answered as he turned on the radio, setting it to a station playing Russian folk music. "We only follow them as good servants of the state do."

The KGB officer nearly rolled his eyes. It was his job to spout propaganda, not this soldier's, and especially not directed at him.

"True. But we must be careful of those wishing to spread disinformation. Those disloyal to the Party."

Zhukov went ahead and signed the order. It would take both their signatures, though, for the action to be authorized.

"General, I'm going to make a direct call to the Kremlin to confirm," Pashin said as he reached for the phone.

As much as he'd hoped the Major would sign the order without trouble, Zhukov was prepared to do what was required. "Very well then. You must do what you must, just as I shall do now."

It all happened in under fifteen seconds. The result of Systema martial arts training years ago as a much younger man, which the General still practiced religiously each day. Pashin never even finished dialing for the operator.

"Lieutenant! Summon the base doctor at once. Something terrible has happened," Zhukov exclaimed swinging open the office door.

The young officer speedily made the call which brought the doctor there at the scene of death in less than two minutes.

"How did this happen?" the medical officer asked, leaning down to examine the lifeless body. The Lieutenant stood to the side of them with the door shut once more.

"We'd just finished signing off on new orders from Moscow when Major Pashin turned to leave and collapsed. He said not a word, doctor. Almost as soon as he fell, he was dead."

Opening the deceased's eyelids and unbuttoning his uniform to examine his chest, the doctor shook his head and sighed.

"I believe I already know what happened, General Zhukov. Lieutenant Alekhin, you should hear this as well. Upon the Major's most recent physical, it was discovered that he had a somewhat high heart rate. He explained that he'd just been on a ten-mile run earlier that morning. The blood vessels in both his eyes were enlarged, and the skin color of his chest was very red. Other than that, he seemed healthy, but I suggested to him that he monitor his symptoms and return to me if they persisted. It's a rare condition for a man less than forty. In short, he suffered a massive heart attack. I will do a further examination in my office to confirm, but all signs point to what I've suggested."

"Terrible, simply terrible," the General gasped.

"Lieutenant," the doctor spoke again. "You're a witness. If anyone should ask, you shall repeat as I have said. There should not be needless gossip and misunderstanding here. Is that understood?"

"Yes, doctor."

"Very well. Now please call for one of the medical orderlies to come and assist with removing the body."

The young man saluted and hurried out. The doctor waited until the door shut again.

"I never cared for the weasel. Always poking his nose into everything and using "for the sake of the party" as his excuse. It's good what you have done here."

"Thank you, doctor."

"I will take care that no one checks the neck. According to records, Pashin had no family, so we can bury him here on the base and avoid anyone having a chance to verify my report."

"Very well. If you'll excuse me. I have to see that these orders get carried out."

Finding a bored corporal sitting in a UAZ-469 known as the Soviet's poor man counterpart to the American's Jeep, Zhukov hopped in and ordered the soldier to drive towards the east side of the base. Five minutes later inside a highly secured hangar, the General stood beside his most trusted officer and looked everything over.

"Lieutenant Tamarkin, it's time."

Grigory Tamarkin felt a sudden chill, almost forgetting to breathe. For two months, ever since General Zhukov first approached him with the most sensitive of plans, he'd been preparing for this moment. He'd follow this man anywhere. He trusted him with his life. Still, the immensity of the moment and what was about to follow weighed on him greatly.

"Yes, General," Tamarkin saluted fiercely. "We will begin moving the trucks shortly."

"Very good. I will meet you all at the gate."

Zhukov turned and walked out of the hangar. There was a confidence in his step now as he headed for the gate. A gleam in his eye. *We will pass through those gates. We will make it to the sea undetected. And we will finally get our due.*

Treading through the snow, he felt a frigid gust of wind come from the west. The cold air stung the cheeks on his face. He looked up and noted the base's main Soviet flag, hanging from a flagpole nearby. The General watched as it violently flapped in the wind. Barely clinging to the pole, it seemed ready to rip away at any moment and disappear into the freezing winter night. *How fitting on an evening like this.*

Finally, he reached the main gate. "Sergeant, I'm presenting you with orders signed by both Major Pashin and myself to move three OTR-23 Okas as well as their corresponding 9M714B missiles tonight. Please verify them. Ah, here they come now. Prepare to open the gates."

A hundred yards away, three large amphibious launch vehicles lumbered down from the hangars towards the main entrance. Zhukov could see his loyal lieutenant now in the lead one. The sergeant, meanwhile, barely glanced at the papers. He noted both the signatures. Whether poorly trained to spot a forgery or too timid to question a superior, he quickly returned the papers. Nodding to a corporal, the gates began to open.

The slow-moving launchers creaked to a stop. As it did, the sergeant then began making a quick walk around each one.

"You're good to... General, I'm sorry, but I didn't know you were going with them. Should I summon a car to follow along?"

"*Nyet.* I will ride along," Zhukov replied as he climbed up a side ladder and atop the Oka. "These weapons which have silently kept the peace will soon be retired, comrade. I should very much like to oversee their final transit. I'll return in a few days. Colonel Anisimov shall be the interim commanding officer for the time being."

With an exchange of salutes, the General dropped through the roof hatch and ordered the convoy to roll out into the night. As they did, Lieutenant Tamarkin turned around to look back at the base once more.

"There is no looking back, Lieutenant," deadpanned Zhukov. "Turn around. We are now traitors to the state that's failed us."

CHAPTER 19

February 8th, 1988 1:10 pm EST

Langley, Virginia

Disappointment. That's what Davis sensed in Ashcroft. The Deputy Director of Intelligence told her all was fine, that there was only so much one could do with analysis. His face however betrayed him.

Immediately after Christmas, Davis pored over Cooper's Libya file. The intelligence network he created in his time there was astounding. It became easier to understand why the Libyan government might despise him enough to exact revenge. The agents he ran within Gaddafi's protection detail, known collectively by the codename of CALEB, were of high value. The same could be said for the agents he worked with outside of the detail. Motive was there. The smoking gun, along with Boytsov's exact location was another matter.

What could be clearly ascertained by all, including the Soviet Select, was that Boytsov had been a member of the Eastern Bloc's special operations, confirming Karam's abbreviated confession. Whether an actual Spetsnaz who got caught up in the attempted assassination of Gorbachev or a hired mercenary from a Soviet ally was anyone's guess.

Surveillance satellites used by the CIA underwent changes in their positional schedules. The goal was to identify any fair-skinned individuals found in various suspected paramilitary/terror group training camps in Libya's southern desert region. Ultimately, the results had narrowed it down to three potential sites. A suggestion had been made by a more hawkish analyst to bomb all of the camps. "Better clear them out for good," he'd chirped as the satellite footage was disseminated. A sharp retort to be silent and remember operations wasn't in his wheelhouse was given by Shelby, Davis recalled. Operationally, it could never happen that way. While helpful, skin color wasn't anywhere near enough for a positive ID. They'd need more, much more.

Boytsov seemed like a ghost to Davis. No results matching his physical description could be found in the CIA's computer system. The FBI tried in vain to track down any footage of him boarding a flight at Dulles International or even a scan of a used phony passport matching his likeness elsewhere at suspected connecting destinations. In the field, the Agency's assets came up empty on details. Koufax floated the idea that maybe the terrorist attack hadn't been approved by Tripoli, and Boytsov was now either in prison, dead or been given up to the Soviets. While plausible, it was generally agreed that it was just as likely Tripoli approved the attack.

But you should be able to find him, Audrey. Of all people! She continually beat herself up over the failure to connect the dots. *My boss, my sons, Carson's memory. I'm letting them all down.*

The late-night drinking had stopped, *for now at least.* The stress which hadn't dissipated was only increasing in intensity each day. The pain and sadness she felt remained unspoken. On edge and exhausted, Davis knew she was approaching her mental limit.

Now seated at her desk, a myriad of maps, files and satellite photos lay strewn about. One particular file lay before her titled "Mossad Cable Traffic: 1987".

Davis scanned each page slowly. She pondered the reaction of friendly governments if they knew an ally was reading their communications. Canada, Great Britain, and Australia alone maintained the trust of America's intelligence services and avoided this sort of surveillance. The risk of any diplomatic fallout could not be taken likely. For that reason, only a select few at Langley had clearance to read the traffic of various allied and friendly nations. Some, if they ever found out, may object to the practice. The spy turned analyst, however, knew this was a necessity in an ever-dangerous world.

It started as a hunch. Finishing Cooper's Libya file in late December, she was struck by a puzzling question: *what if Mossad continued the intelligence operation inside Gadhafi's security detail even after Omar was arrested? What if they managed to keep at least one agent from ever being found out? What if it was still going on to this day?*

Yes, Israel said they didn't have any intel to help find Boytsov when we first asked. But they'd have more than a few reasons to be coy. If there is someone, however, who's still on the inside…

So she began. Starting with the 1980 file when Omar was arrested and then on to the following year, Davis poured over intercepted cables sent by various embassies and consulates in the Mediterranean region to Tel Aviv. Though by no means complete, she discovered them to be both extensive in detail and laborious to read through. Every day for the last week, she sat hunched over her desk, eyes looking for a reference, a clue eluding to knowledge that could only be attained from someone close to the Libyan dictator. The hours of each day ticked by from morning to dusk. Sometimes she lost all sense of time in her windowless office, only reminded of the hour whenever the need arose for another cup of coffee or the janitor came by late to collect the trash. No matter how long it took, Davis was resolved to believe the lead she so desperately needed lay here in the cables.

Wait a second. She stopped herself from turning to the next page. Rereading the last paragraph, Davis's excitement grew. "*Libyan coast guard patrol ordered to concentrate presence 30 kilometers west of previous position. Order given by Colonel Gaddafi during meeting with Defense Minister at Bab al-Azizia.*

Continued extraction of Jewish people fleeing country by sea recommended at...."

Bab al-Azizia. Gaddafi's compound! Someone was on the inside. She noted the origin of the cable, Rome, as well as the month. From June '87 onward she focused on the communication traffic between the Embassy at Rome and Mossad headquarters. Ten minutes later, she struck gold.

"Tensions are still high four months after the American's Operation El Dorado Canyon bombing raid. Colonel Gaddafi's security detail continues to increase in size. Movement outside the compound is limited. Background checks by Mukhabara el-Jamahiriya intelligence are being conducted of everyone on the detail no matter the length of service."

"Bingo!" Davis exclaimed aloud knocking her full coffee mug off the table. *This is the breakthrough you've been looking for. Star of David right under that anti-Semite dictator's nose.* As she felt the wave of elation, a hard reality hit her. There was still the issue of getting Mossad's help. Where they'd worked with the CIA both in the past and now, this source, this valued agent whose life would be on the line if any leak occurred, was clearly being protected and off-limits to them. *Unless...*

Looking up at the clock, Davis noticed it was already one-thirty. She still hadn't had lunch. She'd already skipped it twice this week in favor of work. *You've got to take care of yourself, Audrey. Just go get something.* Quickly she stood up and gathered the files, locking them in her desk drawer before leaving her office and locking the door as she left.

CHAPTER 20

They were less than 450 kilometers from Sochi. At the diesel engine launcher's top speed of just over 65 kilometers per hour, they would arrive shortly before five in the morning. *If all went as planned. But why shouldn't it?* Zhukov ran over everything in his head. The tracking transmitters had been removed from each of the warheads. The doctor could be trusted. The papers, including the signature, would pass muster with any low-ranking soldier they might cross at a checkpoint.

But what if the ship isn't there? What if a patrol boat should see us? What if there's an unforeseen mechanical issue? Fear and worry couldn't be completely extinguished. Showing it however wasn't an option. *These men are brave, Yakov, but also nervous. You have to keep confident if you're going to make it out of this alive.*

The driver was caught off-guard at the sound of humming from behind him. He was even more surprised upon checking the rear-view mirror to see it was his General, humming *Esli Zavtra Voina*, the Soviet war hymn *If the War Should Come Tomorrow*. He shyly joined in, then Tamarkin, followed by a fourth soldier in the main cabin. Their nervous humming soon turning into full-throated singing.

Hours passed by. Finally, Zhukov could see the checkpoint just up ahead. A small guard hut that appeared to be new. The General shook his head as he double-checked the map he carried in the right breast pocket of his uniform jacket.

"What shall we say to them, General?" Tamarkin asked.

"We will present them with the paperwork documenting our journey, Lieutenant. The base we're supposed to be taking these to is just north of here and hasn't been passed up. I imagine my presence will calm any concerns as well."

Three Red Army soldiers stood at the freshly minted checkpoint with a red and white barrier pole. *We have no need to fear them. There's more than enough of us to force our way and continue our journey. It's the pesky phone drilled inside that hut wall, ready to be picked up. Ready to give us and our location away. Ready to end our journey and any hope of reaching the sea.*

"Papers please," hollered a young private, not even nineteen years old.

The papers were passed to the driver, who opened the side window hatch and held them out to be inspected. The soldier, climbing up the side and reaching for them, read slowly, trying to do his best on this initial assignment in his early military career.

"Having any trouble, Private?" A sergeant stepped forward from the hut just as snow began to fall. He took the papers from the boy and read them himself.

"Rather late to be transporting warheads and launchers at this time of the evening?" the more senior soldier asked the driver pointedly.

"Sergeant, I'm General Yakov Zhukov," who was now up out of one of the top cabin hatches. "I believe in carrying out orders promptly no matter when they're received. I also have business with the base commander listed in those orders. I demand that we be let through at once."

The sergeant gave a quick salute. "My apologies, General. Forgive me, but the timing of this transfer is most unusual. You must acknowledge that."

"I'll acknowledge that you are holding up orders of the State being carried out by men of much higher rank than you. Let us pass, Sergeant. That's an order!"

Even for a non-officer, the sergeant knew of the OTR-23 Okas. He knew as well from what he'd read in *Pravda* that Okas were included in the recent weapons treaty signed between his country and the United States. He'd been sipping his tea in the mess hall when he overheard a pair of high-ranking officers mention plans to send the missiles to Sonya, *two hundred miles east of there*, to be destroyed soon. None of this was adding up.

"Following protocol in these circumstances, General, I will call the base commander to verify these orders. If you'll excuse me."

As he marched off to the guard hut to place the call, the driver, acting without orders, instinctively reached for his pistol. Behind him in the second Oka, two men were already out above their hatch, guns ready. They too did likewise. It all happened in a flash—bullets whizzing through the air, tearing through the cheap plywood walls of the hut and breaking the stillness of night. The sergeant was dead before he could pick up the receiver. His two privates sprawled out on the ground with barely a chance to get off a returning shot.

"What do we do with them, General? Should we leave them here and set fire to the hut?"

"And bring attention here? The road would be swarming with KGB investigators in no time." The whole situation frustrated Zhukov. He looked over at the hut, now torn to shreds with the blood of the sergeant marking its bullet-holed walls. This wasn't how it was supposed to go. Whether he wished to admit it or not, the reality was that they'd be onto his trail sooner rather than later. "Take and load them in the back," he continued with exasperation. "At the very least they'll waste maybe an hour looking nearby for them."

The Lieutenant looked down at the boy who'd first approached their vehicle. At least a dozen shots riddled the body of one not too much younger than him. *Most likely conscripted. He never asked to be here. Only did his job. And for what, to be gunned down by men wearing the same uniform as him?*

Tamarkin recalled an early lesson his grandmother had given him as a young boy. A pious member of the Eastern Orthodox Church who refused to accept the state's stand against religion, she'd taught him the Ten Commandments. He recalled in particular how much she touched on *'You shall not murder'*. Killing in war was one thing. But what about killing while stealing weapons that were only to be sold to an unsavory client?

Carefully, he picked up the private with the driver's help, stuffing his body into a side compartment within the vehicle. As he did, a splotch of blood stained the olive-colored left arm sleeve of his coat. *That stain won't ever come off, Tamarkin. Not now, not ever.*

CHAPTER 21

The wheels were turning inside Davis's head as she sat in the commissary eating a chicken salad sandwich for lunch with a fruit cup and an Arnold Palmer to drink. She looked out of a window facing onto a small courtyard. *There has to be a way to convince Mossad to help us. Something we could trade?* Finishing her lunch ten minutes later, she headed back toward the elevators.

What do we have they'd want that we could realistically offer them? Hardware, intel, sources? Her mind then went to the content of the cables. She began mentally working through the recent Israeli intelligence needs mentioned in them like one shifting through a Rolodex. *Help locate terrorists on their most-wanted lists? Maybe…but we already keep the lines of communication and info pretty open on the matter as it is. Developing assets within enemy states and organizations?*

By now, she was back in her office. Removing the files from her locked drawer, a light went on in her head. *That's it!* Five minutes later, she'd hurriedly bypassed Ashcroft's secretary and made a beeline for his desk. Davis quickly explained her analysis behind the idea of an active Mossad asset within Gaddafi's protection before moving on to her epiphany.

"Sir, the only way Mossad will give us intel from this agent is if we not only keep what they pass on close to chest but also offer something up they desire equally as much. Going through the cables, I think I've hit on it.

"An off-shoot of Hezbollah has been making some noise and the Israelis are trying to track down where they're getting weapons. Mossad's Rome Station has ascertained that the hardware is being shipped out of a port in Sicily. However, they're always transported using vessels owned by different entities appearing, at least on the surface, to be clean and unaware of the cargo. Tel Aviv wants to cut off the source but can't find the seller. Based on intel reports we've gone over during our Soviet Select meetings, I recall one of those ships belonging to a shell company owned by a weapons dealer known to sell arms to the Red Brigade. We have a source close to the dealer, as you know, that we've been running for months now."

"That's allowed us to know when the arms get sold to the Brigade, which in turn has allowed us to tip the Italians on their location and have them raided shortly thereafter," Ashcroft finally interjected. "Highly valuable source that has saved us and our NATO allies quite a bit of trouble. Code name, DOMINO."

Davis readied herself for the ask. "What I propose, sir, is we either have DOMINO start informing us when arms are sold to this off-shoot group so Mossad can seize the shipments or..."

"Or wrap up the operation and have the arms group shut down. You know both the Brigade and this off-shoot would likely just find other sellers. Sellers, we have zero sources in."

"But we'd disrupt their weapons supply lines for quite a while and put fear in anyone who thinks of selling to them. More important though, we gain a source close to Gaddafi that's desperately needed."

Ashcroft sat in his chair for several seconds, both hands interlocked underneath his chin while deep in thought. Then he looked at her and spoke:

"Audrey, if you wouldn't mind stepping outside my office for a few minutes. There's someone I need to call."

"Understood, sir." Davis stood up and went out into the small reception area. Taking a seat on a couch, she briefly made eye contact with Ashcroft's secretary, a veteran of the Agency for nearly twenty-five years, who gave a polite smile. Davis smiled back before focusing on Ashcroft's office door. The minutes drifted by painfully slow as she waited, wondering just who her boss was speaking to.

"Audrey, Director Ashcroft says you can come back in now," the secretary said with that same smile."

Please say yes. Davis headed back with a tinge of nervousness. Never before had she made such a bold proposal based on her analysis. When she entered, Ashcroft looked up from his desk and gave her the answer.

"Approved. We'll have our Chief of Station in Tel Aviv communicate the idea to Mossad. If this works, we just might get the breakthrough we've been looking for in this Boytsov business."

Davis did her best not to appear too excited before asking one last thing. "I was thinking I might instead speak to their COS here in D.C. about it if that would be okay?"

"You want permission to talk to Benny?" Ashcroft jumped to what he knew was about to be asked.

"Going through the head Mossad officer out of their embassy here could be the best play. I've met the guy a couple times at official state receptions and read up on him. He knows his line of work and is on good terms with most of their intelligence hierarchy. Let me meet with him and have him communicate our offer."

Ashcroft double tapped his desk with his West Point class ring. "Do it."

"Thank you, sir," Davis replied as she began to get up from her chair. "I'll put a call into the Israeli Embassy now and schedule the meeting."

CHAPTER 22

In but one evening, a full range of emotions had been exhibited by
Zhukov's band of renegades. Anxiousness, confidence before now a
subdued and muted mood. The recent murders, however, had little
effect on the General who was on edge to reach the shore ASAP. For
the rest of the trip, neither road block nor another soul was seen. Only
darkness and an unknown future lay ahead.

It was in the early hours of morning that the sound of waves crashing
could be heard. "We've reached the Black Sea, General," the driver
declared as he turned onto a dirt road that overlooking a beach and the
vast body of water. Where shall we go to now?"

Zhukov's eyes scanned the horizon. Nothing. He reached for a pair of
binoculars packed underneath his seat. *It's too dark to see anything. If they're
out there, they must be mad to run without their lights on. Unless that Cypriot
captain is trying to avoid patrol boats.*

"General?" The Lieutenant prodded his commander after a minute went
by without a reply.

"We're right where we're supposed to be. However, we lack a secure
radio channel with which to communicate by. The only way we can be

sure they're out there is to signal by light."

"And what will the message be?"

"I will handle that," he replied, holding out his hand waiting for a flashlight.

Tamarkin reached for and handed Zhukov one he carried in a bag. *If he's wrong, we're all dead. Arrest. Speedy court martial. Swift execution. You've trusted him this far, Grigory. No reason to start doubting now.*

The top hatch was opened as the General climbed up and stuck his head out into the salty night air. Pointing the flashlight out toward the Black Sea, he began flipping the switch on and off, signaling in Morse code.

"What did you say, General?" Tamarkin asked in between repeated attempts to reach the unseen vessel. The Lieutenant received no answer. He looked up and saw the muscles in his commander's face tighten. The deep exhale. The eyes scanning the void seaside horizon.

"There! Over to the left! Did you see it?" The driver yelled excitedly.

"Drive down to the beach. We're about to go for a swim."

"General, do you suppose they will move their ship any closer to shore?"

"The operational capabilities of the Oka was built for amphibious activity. As long as they lower the ramp leading into the cargo hold as planned, we should be good. It's too risky for them to come much closer lest they be seen too close to shore at daybreak. By the way, to answer your question, my message asked what kind of *kreatopita* Elena was making next month."

"What?"

"The captain's sister. For his birthday, if I recall. The code phrase, Lieutenant."

The three olive-colored launch vehicles soon reached the shore. It was now 4:50. Sunrise wasn't too far away. They'd have to move quickly if they were to avoid being seen.

Oka missile systems, built to replace the launchers for aging SCUD missiles, were unique in both their effectiveness and mobility. Whereas older models were limited in their ability to navigate even small bodies of water, these latest vehicles were propelled by two waterjets positioned in the rear. The original Soviet designers visualized them being used on lakes and rivers. *But out on sea? This, however, was possibly a first*, the General reckoned.

The sound of the jets starting up could be heard just as the driver flipped a switch a few meters offshore. As they did, a dark blue cargo ship, with a red stripe on the bow one and a half kilometers off-shore, came into view.

The lead Oka splashed into the water, followed by the two other launchers in the convoy. The sea soon rose above the tires as the amphibious vehicles headed for their destination, moving at a speed of eight km/h. The whole scene seemed surreal to Tamarkin.

Twelve minutes later, a hinged door from the bow of the ship opened, and a ramp lowered into the waves. "Steady now, Corporal," Zhukov said in a direct manner as they prepared to carefully drive up the ramps. "Best to take our time lest we slide off or crash into the ship."

It was as if they were entering the mouth of a giant steel whale with a ramp as its tongue. The ship was, in fact, a decommissioned (and now repurposed) WWII-era landing ship, an LST capable of carrying more than 2,000 tons.

The lead launcher slowly exited the water, reaching the top of the ramp and into the cargo hold. A rough-looking sailor directed them to drive forward into an already cleared spot for them. The other two Okas followed right behind. Before they exited their launcher's cabin, the General addressed his men, including those in the other to vehicles over a secure radio frequency.

"I will do all the talking, comrades. Your duty now will be to guard these launchers. None of the crew shall come anywhere near them. Is that understood? This may be a Cypriot flag vessel, but we Russians will guard what is ours. You all have trusted me so far. I thank you for that. Now, we must continue onward to claim our reward."

"Yes, General!" Tamarkin and the rest said in unison with a fierce salute.

Stepping out onto the cargo hold, Zhukov moved with a cool calmness towards the front of the launcher. Four deaths, desertion, theft of three nuclear warheads and their corresponding missiles and launchers. *You've crossed your Rubicon, Yakov. There is no turning back.*

He could see the captain walking down the stairway at the other end of the expansive cargo hold. The man looked exactly the same, from the clothes he wore to the distinctive pipe he smoked, as he did at their one brief meeting in Sochi a week ago. Captain Pavlos Nicolaou was a man of simple tastes and habit. The only attributes that stuck out about him to his crew were his strange fascination with Shakespeare's *Othello* and his loud distaste of the Turks occupying the northern part of his ancestral home island.

"General Yakov Zhukov, welcome aboard the *Phaedra*. I take it that you and your party are all here?"

"Thank you, Captain. Yes, and we're ready to get underway."

"Very well. I will give orders at once to make for the Bosporus Strait. Before I do, you did bring…."

"It's all here," Zhukov said as he held out a large burlap bag. "Half up front, as we agreed. You'll get the rest for providing us passage at the end of our voyage."

The Captain peered into the bag, thoroughly examining the gold and ruble notes. He verified everything was there before looking up at the behemoth missile systems. It didn't matter their fearsome capabilities or that they were meant to be destroyed but would soon be sold to a third-world nation bent on nuclear power. *All that matters is timely payment and a good bottle of whiskey to help me forget what I've just done.*

CHAPTER 23

"Here to see Benjamin Wiesel." The posted guard at the Israeli Embassy checked his list before allowing Davis to proceed through the main gate and find a parking spot. Once inside the main lobby, a receptionist escorted her to a secure basement office where the Mossad Station Chief was waiting for the CIA analyst.

"Audrey, it's good to see you again," the boisterous middle-aged man greeted her with a handshake.

"Benny, thanks for meeting me. I have to ask, though, why no to lunch? Christopher's is the best spot in town and the Agency was buying."

"What is it President Reagan says...'trust but verify'?" Wiesel chuckled. "It never hurts to take necessary precautions, lest there be unwanted surveillance."

"We always take every precaution. But if it makes you feel any better, then by all means."

Wiesel gave a polite nod before gesturing to a chair by his desk. "Please, sit. What is it you wanted to speak with me about?"

"I take it you're aware of the attack against my family a couple months back?"

"Including the untimely death of your friend, Mr. Cooper, I am."

"The CIA is now trying to locate the man responsible. Our source points to a guy from the Soviet bloc that's operated out of Libya. He works as an instructor at one of their commando, or should I say terrorist, training camps. While we think we've got it narrowed down to a couple locations, we haven't been able to make a positive ID. Our intelligence assets on the ground there are limited."

"And you need to ask a favor?" Wiesel asked.

"Not necessarily a favor." Davis took a moment before diving into her offer. "What if I told you I not only know that your country has been trying to pinpoint where a certain off-shoot of Hezbollah has been getting its weapons but also the identity of its arms dealer."

"I would say that would be of some interest." Wiesel eyed her carefully. "Not to mention how you came about that knowledge. Where's this going?

"If there's even a single asset in Libya under Mossad's watch, we could use their help about now." Davis then proceeded to break down the full details of the trade as instructed by Ashcroft, who'd received direct orders from the Director of the CIA himself. She desperately hoped that she was getting through to Wiesel.

"These guys are a threat to both our countries, Ben," Davis added as she finished making the offer. "Gaddafi has already sponsored attacks and hijackings on your people...."

"I know that," he answered, somewhat annoyed. "No history lesson needs to be given. Mossad and the Israeli people must deal with threats from those of his ilk on a daily basis. For the record, I'm not at liberty to comment on anything you've just mentioned. However," pausing to decide carefully what to say next. "I will make your request known to Tel Aviv. I will also put in a good word for you. Know this, Audrey, I have two daughters back home. What happened to you, we live in fear of each day."

"I won't forget it, Benny. Thank you."

"I make no promises. If I should hear anything, I will let you know at once."

"Regardless, I still thank you."

"Anything else I can help you with, Audrey?"

"Lunch at Christopher's? Shop-talk is finished as far as I'm concerned."

Wiesel immediately got up from his desk and grabbed his coat. "I was hoping you'd ask again."

Four hours. That was the time it took for the decimated remains of the checkpoint left in the General Zhukov's wake to be discovered by a passing convoy later that morning. It then took top Soviet army brass some time to put the pieces together. At first, they were dismissive. "What were the odds someone would be mad enough to steal a missile system, much less three of them? A thousand miles from the nearest border, where would he even go?" The possibility, though, could no longer be ignored once they'd learned of Major Pashin's ultimate demise. An investigation of the base was quietly launched by the GRU. Zhukov's assistant soon confessed to the strange circumstances surrounding the KGB officer's death, including the last order he'd signed. No record could be found for the order, nor General Zhukov for that matter. While tracking systems showed all warheads accounted for and resting in a vaulted bunker beneath the base, an audit showed three were in fact missing. All this had left the Kremlin hierarchy up in arms about what they should do and just who they could tell.

"Does anyone even realize what's at stake? We just signed a treaty with the Americans which will have these missiles and their launchers destroyed! What am I to tell the General Secretary?" the Defense Minister bellowed to a roundtable of officials.

"That his own Soviet military can't be trusted," the Chairman of the KGB said coolly but with eyes trained on the face of his rival, the head of the GRU.

"We are investigating possible foreign government connections Zhukov may have. If it does prove true," the GRU head remarked, "then it would seem that the KGB, as much as they pride themselves on supervising us in order to protect the *Rodina*, should have picked up on this."

A shouting match nearly began before the Defense Minister stretched out his hands out in the direction of each. "Enough. Security and the watchful eyes of the KGB failed just as much as the GRU did to pick up on the signs of this man's intentions and prevent him from escaping. Redeem yourselves by finding out Zhukov's whereabouts. Do you even have any clues?"

"*Nyet*," replied the KGB Chairman anxiously. "If he traveled south, he hasn't successfully left our borders. Should he have escaped by sea, then he's out of our surveillance scope and now the responsibility of the Soviet navy.

The Commander-in-Chief of the Soviet Navy didn't too much care for being pulled into this. He'd run a tight ship so far in his tenure as the most senior member of his nation's fleet and hadn't lost a warhead. He wasn't about to take anything from that shifty career bureaucrat.

"I assure you, Defense Minister, all vessels of the Soviet Black Sea fleet are accounted for and the strictest of measures have long been in place for any ships coming and going from our harbors."

"But can you guarantee they didn't board a ship outside of a port? The Okas are amphibious. There's no need for a ship to dock too close to shore."

Stiff silence was his response. For as long as anyone could remember, the old Admiral refused to tell his Kremlin superiors simply what they wished to hear, a rare virtue if ever there was one in Moscow. It had earned him some disapproving remarks in some quarters, yet he'd survived (so far) the tumultuous seas of drama and backstabbing. Now, he would make no such promise to the Minister.

"In that case, Commander, just how far would you suspect a vessel, perhaps a cargo ship, would travel in the time between early morning two days ago and this very moment?"

"Twelve knots an hour, fifty-plus hours straight. They could have well cleared the Straits and made their way past Istanbul."

The Minister's blood began to boil. "Maybe some of you understand the significance of the ridiculous situation we're in. Some of you though, by the pathetic expression on your face and the lack of security you had in place to prevent this, clearly don't comprehend. To put it in terms you would understand, I've asked a member of the INF negotiation teams to appear here today to explain what's at stake. Lavrentiy Gagarin, the floor is yours."

The GRU spy and weapons negotiator slowly rose from his chair. The effects of jetlag were having their way with him right now. There was also a sense of fear—a fear to be speaking before some of the most powerful men in his country now looking to him for information and understanding.

"Comrades," he said after clearing his throat. "Over the last two years, the United States has paid particular attention to our Oka missile system. They've expressed that even while we publicly say our Okas have a range of fewer than 500 kilometers, they believe their capable range is much farther. Their Secretary of State wouldn't budge on the deal unless they were included on the chopping block. Everyone here, I believe, is aware of their true capabilities. That is all I will say regarding that. The General Secretary believed, along with consultation from the Politburo and the negotiating team, that it would be wise to give up these weapons in return for a reduction in arms from the Americans. If they were to find out that we have lost even just one of these, the consequences would be dire. Their longstanding distrust of us could lead them to assert we're lying about what has transpired and are breaking the treaty. That would all undo the hard work to secure this historical moment of peace. At worst, we put their missile defense systems on edge, overly fearful that a preemptive strike of some sort in West Germany is forthcoming. That is not a situation we can accept. If I may be so bold, I second the Minister's concerns and believe all resources must be used to track these weapons down at once."

The Minister nodded in approval. *He's an effective communicator who knows where to put his chips, that's for sure.*

CHAPTER 24

Aegean Sea

The first mate aboard the *Phaedra* couldn't help but laugh. A storm system arriving from the southeast was rocking the boat hard. No damage had been reported, and he'd seen much worse in his many years at sea. The same couldn't be said for the Russian guests. Presently, a young corporal who had tried in vain to reach the railing on the top deck had ended up vomiting all over himself. *Probably his first time out at sea. Probably the first time for nearly all of them, for that matter.* Taking cover inside the hatchway, the first mate pulled out a pipe and a small packet of tobacco from the inside of his yellow rain jacket. The young renegade, no longer a soldier, was letting the rain wash the mess from his clothes as he began to recover. As he turned back towards the open hatch, the instant smell of the pipe sent him racing to the railing once more. The first mate began choking on the smoke as he laughed uncontrollably.

"That's the fourth one in the last hour," said another sailor passing by to watch. "What are they on the ship for anyway?"

"Best mind your own business. You don't want to get involved. Next time we pull into port, forget everything you saw. You understand, Stavros?" The sailor could see the grim look in his eyes and dared not speak more. He left the first mate alone to smoke his pipe and watch the sick Russian with amusement.

The sailor continued on his way up to the bridge where he was needed. An intercom connecting to the engine room had apparently shorted out in the midst of minor repairs, and he was given the task of messenger. Hurrying up to the brain center of the ship, he suddenly crossed paths with General Zhukov.

"Where is your captain?" the General asked.

"He's in his quarters." The seaman recalled orders to avoid conversation with their guests. "I...I can go let him know you wish to speak with him."

"No," Zhukov answered, holding up his right hand. "I shall go pay him a visit instead."

"But..."

The General was already halfway down the passageway. A few moments later, he was knocking on Captain Nicolaou's cabin door.

"Come in," was the groggy reply. Entering, he found Nicolaou sitting up on the edge of his bed. "What can I do for you, General?" he asked, rubbing the sleep from his eyes.

"I would like you to set for a new course," Zhukov announced.

"No longer sailing to Tartus?"

"*Nyet.* You shall sail to Tripoli, where we will dock."

"Your friend is the one who pays me. All you've given me is a small deposit in comparison. We continue to Syria unless you can come up with the money."

The General did his best to hide his frustration. "The agreement you made with my comrade was that you'll receive the rest upon arrival, Captain. If you wish to be paid, you'll do as I say."

"But…"

"The coordinates we gave you were a ruse, lest someone be on to us," Zhukov spoke forcefully yet not quite raising his voice. You'll be compensated for the longer journey. You have my word."

"And if I don't believe you?"

"Then my men will commandeer your ship and throw you overboard in this very storm." As he spoke, the Captain looked over at the revolver lying on his desk. He'd only pulled it out two days ago, after several years of gaining dust, when he took on his Russian passengers. "Do you really think you'd stand a chance?" Zhukov asked point blank.

The Captain shook his head and reached for his intercom. "This is the Captain. Set new course for the port of Tripoli immediately."

"There, that wasn't so bad," the General said with a smile.

"Don't push it, General. Shall my crew expect any more surprises?"

Zhukov headed for the door. He paused as if attempting to think of a clever response before giving up. "Just do as you're told, Captain," he answered without turning back. "Do as you're told, and you'll live to spend what we're paying you."

Gagarin's head hung low as he left the Kremlin that evening. *How could they be so foolish? Two and half years of work for what? To be wasted, no doubt.* Word had come from the Politburo. In short, the whole mess was to be swept under the rug. Yes, the directive had been given to pursue any leads on the whereabouts of the missiles. But none existed. All that could be ascertained was that the traitors either left through the southern border or escaped via the Black Sea. There would be no mass search required to have a real chance of finding them. The military, seeing it as a lost cause and fearful of failing their masters twice, convinced the brain trust of the Soviet Union that it would be a fruitless effort.

Riding in a chauffeured car back to his hotel, the weapons negotiator and GRU spy continued pondering the situation. If Zhukov's men left the country by sea, then the warheads and launchers most likely would have been sold to a non-nuclear nation looking to hold its own against the U.S. or the Soviet Union. *Syria, Iran, Libya, or maybe even Yugoslavia for all anyone knows. There's a danger there that neither of our nations would sanely want to risk.*

As the wheels continued turning inside Gagarin's head, he began to rethink his initial position about telling the Americans. *They have the resources we lack here. But you know how they'd really react to the news, Dmitri. The fallout would be disastrous.*

The black GAZ Volga, a standard car used by the *nomenklatura*, pulled up in front of the Leningradskaya Hotel. Entering the recently updated lobby, he decided he'd need a drink. The bar was just off to the right. He entered and ordered a double whiskey Coke. His time spent in Washington had introduced him to a new favorite libation. How much had changed in so short of time. Only two years ago, Coca-Cola wasn't even available in Moscow. *This country is changing, Dmitri. Changing in ways not seen before in your life or the lives of your forefathers. From glasnost to perestroika. We can't afford to let things return to the way they once were.*

The bartender handed him his drink. As Gagarin took a sip, he thought through two options. The first: do nothing. Consequence: the U.S. eventually finds out the Okas are missing and jumps to their own conclusions, or a reckless third-world country, desperate for attention and power, gets ahold of them. The second option had great risk not only for the INF Treaty but also his very being. He could tell the United

States himself.

But who to trust? There really wasn't anyone he could completely trust. Whoever he choose needed to have the least likelihood of being an agent of, or spied upon, by the KGB or GRU. They'd also need to know how to handle sensitive information the right way. Anyone remotely possible of taking this to their media or a congressional committee was out of the question. Sadly, there were too many like this in Washington. Those having a high degree of wisdom and discernment were few and far between.

That's it! Gagarin nearly said it aloud in satisfaction of coming up with such an idea. *He could be trusted. I'm sure of it.* He felt a sense of relief. There was no second-guessing, the man had made up his mind.

Gagarin threw back the rest of his whiskey and set the glass down. Checking his watch, he saw that it was already after nine. His return flight from Sheremetyevo to D.C., where his work for the GRU would continue, was in less than eight hours. *He will help you, Dmitri Gagarin. He must. The future of our country depends on it.*

CHAPTER 25

"But you were gone last night too! Come on, Mom. You can be the shoe this time." The disappointed look on Sergei's face as he'd just finished setting up the Monopoly board wasn't making it easy on Davis. *One more night, Audrey. You've got to be sure about this archivist.*

"I'm sorry, guys, but this is for work. Tomorrow evening, I promise, we can play a board game together. Okay?"

"Okay," Sergei answered somewhat dejectedly.

"Come here and give me a kiss before I go." She drew Sergei in, kissing her son on the cheek and giving him a hug.

"Mom, are we ever going to move back to our house?" Nikita asked.

"This is only temporary, and it's for our safety. We might move back, or we might get a new house. We'll just have to see," she answered before kissing her oldest on the forehead. "Don't worry. Now, I've got to go. Love you guys."

She nodded to the FBI agent in the kitchen who, though not Mary Holden, had taken on a very similar day-to-day role. *I really need to check and see how she's doing.* Until recently, Davis had visited Agent Holden twice a week in the hospital. Once the surveillance runs had begun, however, that had changed. Davis had heard only the day before that she'd finally been released and sent home. *I'll visit her soon. Maybe bring the boys with me to say hello.*

The drive to Reston was a long one. Once she exited off the highway, she changed vehicles at a used car lot where she'd made a deal with the owner to 'test drive' a new one each night for two weeks. Tonight's ride would be a white Pontiac Firebird with 220 horsepower. From there, she drove to the two-story brick home belonging to one Stephen Banks.

Davis loathed these stakeouts. Though trained in the art, it was a piece of spycraft she'd put to little use back in her Moscow days. She knew however that it was necessary if one were to catch the mole. After beginning with a thorough vetting of the recently retired Archives Director at the CIA, which included renting out a townhouse across from him to run surveillance, Davis moved next to his successor. The forty-one-year-old Banks, divorced with no kids, had been in the job for over a year now and at the Agency for fifteen. His criminal record was neither without blemish nor one that would require dismissal from his post. There'd been a reckless driving charge when he was younger in which the officer reporting on the scene of the accident noted the smell of alcohol on his breath. Banks passed the field sobriety test, however, and later pleaded no contest. Fast forward to six months ago, a 911 call was made by a next-door neighbor regarding a possible domestic dispute. When officers arrived, Mrs. Banks refused to press charges but asked still if they'd stay until she finished packing and provide her an escort to her mother's home.

Amid personal strife and soon-to-come alimony payments, it struck Davis strange that the new Archives Director had purchased a $30,000 red '87 Chevrolet Corvette. Payroll records showed only a modest increase in his salary upon promotion, tripping a wire all investigators have when looking for a traitor.

Thus far, Banks's routine had been predictable. Right before eight, he'd leave his home and either go to Gentry's Sports Bar or the liquor store.

If it were the bar, he drank alone and never interacted with other patrons. Always, his focus was on the TV set showing a basketball game or one particular female bartender that seemed to catch his eye, though he wasn't quite brave enough to flirt with her. On runs to get liquor, he never deviated from going down the same aisle, selecting two-fifths of his favorite whisky and was out of there within three minutes.

He can't be it, Audrey. She was growing tired of this. *No visible exchange, no conspicuous notes left out, no brush passes, much less a meeting. It's the same story every night.* Yet somehow, that same sixth sense was speaking to her again. One more night, she promised herself, and then she'd move on to the next suspect on her list.

What the... A car was parked in the driveway as she pulled up alongside the curb several doors down. *So you have a guest tonight, Banks.*

Davis almost wished she'd planted a bug in the house. It would've beaten waiting to see who came out. It was a line she wasn't ready to cross in her own off-the-record investigation, though. *DC8-953. I'll have to run those plates through the system.*

Turning on the radio, she sat back and waited, eyes glued to the home. Then, at a quarter past ten, it all broke loose.

The garage door opened revealing Banks with a man dressed in all black following close behind. The night made the stranger's face indistinguishable. The two got into the parked Chevy Corvette with the CIA's head archivist in the driver's seat. Backing out of the driveway, the car turned and drove opposite the direction where Davis sat parked. Quickly, she put the Firebird in drive and kept her distance.

The Corvette passed the sports bar, then the liquor store and continued towards the older district of town. *Where to?*

The entire time she stayed back. Always out of the street lights, lest they realize they were being tailed. As she drove, Fleetwood Mac's *Tusk* played over the radio, with its rhythmic beat of drums and opening lyrics sung softly.

Suddenly, the sound of burning rubber drowned out the music. Davis instinctively hit the gas as Banks and the stranger sped off in the night.

The Corvette took a hard right at the corner up ahead. *How did he see me?* It would be a question that would have to wait. She turned the corner and continued the pursuit as traffic began to appear ahead. Banks weaved recklessly through the pack of cars. Out of view, Davis hurried to catch back up.

Where'd he learn to drive like this? The sounds of trumpets coming from the music blared in sync as she shifted gears with precision. Adrenaline was now racing through her body, just as it had that day at The Farm two months ago and on the streets of Moscow years prior. Finally, she managed to get ahead of the traffic and back in view of the Corvette.

They were now coming towards a two-lane bridge that crossed the Delaware River. Beyond the bridge, a sharp turn sign reflected light from the oncoming cars. The Firebird was closing the gap, and Banks clearly new it, crossing over the double yellow line in an attempt to pass a Volvo.

Davis let off the gas pedal as she neared the bridge. She knew from scouting the area that beyond the turn, the lanes went back to three on each side. *Then you can try and force him off the road.*

Two bright lights suddenly shone up ahead. The sound of an eighteen-wheeler's horn roared as it pulled onto the bridge. All Davis could do was watch as the Corvette pulled hard to the left and then went airborne over the railing and into the night sky. Traveling a good twenty yards, it dove into the icy waters below. Davis turned off the road and raced out of the car. It was too late. By the time she reached the water, the Corvette was completely submerged.

CHAPTER 26

"I'm telling you the truth, lady. There's only one body in the car." Davis was growing frustrated with the police lieutenant, who was, in fact, doing his best at what was initially just a traffic incident. Reston County emergency services had sent in a trio of trained divers to search the water before they extracted the vehicle from the river. Only the body of Stephen Banks, behind the wheel, was found upon initial examination.

"And I'm telling you, there were two people in the vehicle!" she exclaimed in frustration.

"You never told me why you were following them. I need more than just you showing me an ID badge for the CIA. For all I know, you're partly to blame for this."

Davis shook her head. "The why is classified. Sorry, but that's how it is. Is there a phone I can use somewhere?"

Within half an hour, the FBI was on the scene, much to the lieutenant's chagrin. A call to Ashcroft, who'd been asleep when his bedside phone rang, did the trick. Davis's story of events, at least as much as she could tell, was taken down. The lead investigator then allowed her to examine the totaled Corvette, sans the body which had been transported to the county mortuary.

Not a sign of him. She looked into the soaked interior, examining the shotgun seat. The seatbelt hung along the bent right interior siding without any damage. A pair of sunglasses lay on the floor alongside what remained of a *Rand McNally* road map.

"We'll track down witnesses who might've seen them on the road tonight," said an FBI investigator as he came over to the car. "We'll also bring our own divers to check the water once more. Do you recall the Corvette ever being out of view?"

"Yes. Took a corner fast when they caught wind of me. Would've been plenty of time for whoever was riding with him to get out." *Only a spook could've gotten out and disappeared that fast though.* Davis figured it was no more than five seconds from when Banks made the turn and when she reached the corner. *But who?*

CHAPTER 27

Tripoli, Libya

Over three tours in the Middle East and North Africa, Daniel Meir had become an expert in his own right at both geology and petroleum engineering. It amazed him to think he'd gotten a C in geology and earth sciences in high school. Now, the Mossad intelligence officer could hold his own with the best of them.

It had been a long day for 'Mssr. Jacque Macron' of Pierre Standard Oil. As part of his cover as an exploratory petroleum geologist, he'd spent the afternoon out in the desert to the south conducting surveys and taking samples. Now, as the sun set on the desert landscape that stretched out for miles, he drove a Land Cruiser back into town, eager for a cold drink and a hot bath. First though, he had work to do.

There was a hotel across from the old medina quarter where the shopkeepers sold their wares and produce in the open-air market. While respectable and frequented by Europeans on business, its exterior had aged considerably since the coup of nearly twenty years prior. The former King had once been friends with the original owner, a wealthy Italian from the colonial days. Since then it had changed hands several times. It had even on two separate occasions been the site of riots and demonstrations against Western policy.

Meir pulled the Land Cruiser up to the valet desk and handed over the keys. Collecting a single duffle bag, he started towards the medina quarter. He'd come to look forward to purchasing fresh fruit and *Maghrebi* mint tea found here.

Passing through a narrow stone arch, he entered a quiet pink stucco corridor lined with stone cobble. Overhead from towering arches hung centuries-old brass lamps which had guided men from all walks of life through this narrow street. The old-world charm was not lost on the Israeli spy. In his downtime, he often found himself creating sketches of the varied architecture he discovered here. *One day, if I leave this business before I'm too old, I'll return to Bezalel Academy in Jerusalem and get my degree.*

Some of the shopkeepers had come to recognize him, giving a smile and a wave as he passed by. Meir politely nod but said nothing to them, instead keeping on the move, buying what he needed and continuing on.

For he couldn't keep Bar Dayan waiting.

He could see her now. Standing beside a busy stand covered with baskets of flowers. Unrecognizable was the bodyguard of Muammar Gaddafi in a full black niqab and matching chador cloak but for a thin blue beaded bracelet she wore on her right wrist.

"Do they not have any coffee beans from the Azira Valley?" the spy asked in Arabic as he approached, standing alongside Dayan in front of the crowded merchant shop.

"I prefer those grown east of there," the woman replied. *We're in the clear.*

"Tel Aviv sends its regards. How've you been?"

"Keep getting rotated back and forth between the main detail and doing advance work the last couple weeks," Dayan answered in a low voice as they walked alongside one another to another stand. "He's paranoid. Even with his own guard. Never the same since the American's retaliatory bombing."

"A matter of building longstanding trust. I might be able to help you with that."

"How?"

"We got a tip about another underground group. I made contact with them and we just might be able to put something together. Give the Old Bedouin a good scare and you a chance to shine. It will only go off, though, if you're seen with the detail."

"And just how will I know it's for show and not a real shootout?" Dayan asked with concern.

"Keep your eye out for a man with an orange shoulder band near the gate of the compound when you leave with Gaddafi. If you see him and he makes eye contact with you, then you'll know. All I can say for now. What else have you gathered lately?" he said, shifting gears.

"It would appear he's making another purchase." She came close to the slightly unzipped duffle bag he carried and slipped a discrete envelope inside. "I wish I had more on it. Whatever it is, they're keeping it hush."

"Possibly more MiGs for his Chad campaign?" Meir had recently been near the south border and heard reports of stiff casualties. A lightbulb went off as he remembered the orders sent from Tel Aviv only the day before.

"There is a subject we need you to keep an ear open for. A man called Boytsov. Possible ex-Spetsnaz. If you hear any mention of his whereabouts, get word to me at once."

Dayan picked up and examined a pear from a vendor's basket as she listened to her handler repeat the order. "I'll see what I can learn," she replied softly. Then, without even a goodbye, the woman mixed into the crowd and disappeared. Meir, meanwhile, continued his shopping for some time. Later, with the curtains drawn back in his hotel room, he opened the envelope. The single sheet of double-sided, single-spaced writing painted the picture provided to the spy by the closest source to Gaddafi. The hot bath and drink would have to wait.

What was that passcode again? 53807 or 53837? The second-guessing always seemed to take place during the first month of wherever he was stationed with the compact satellite transponder. Tucked away in a suitcase no doubt searched by the police when he was gone, it was glued perfectly inside a backup miniature metal detector. He carefully slit the metal detector open along the glued ends and then pulled out the transponder. Meir then switched the device on and set it to the correct frequency before remembering to move to the bathroom and turn on the bath water to muffle out the white noise. No more than a hundred and fifty characters, he sent out the coded message.

The Defense Minister and the Intelligence Chairman both involved? Meir thought to himself. *Whatever Gaddafi's buying sure is sensitive.*

Evening was the only time Zhukov allowed his men atop deck, lest the Soviet or American satellites identify them. Lieutenant Tamarkin leaned against the railing, looking out on the now cloudless, starlit sky. It wasn't until he left Moscow and started his military career that he saw the full constellations. Stargazing was one of the few pastimes that allowed him to find peace and relaxation in the world of weapon systems and constant orders from superiors. *So much wrong with the world, yet there's still beauty to be found. Now you're off to dampen that beauty with the mercenary sale of these missiles. For what? Money? The orders of the General?*

It was these inward thoughts that he often contemplated but buried inside. He couldn't disappoint General Zhukov. In the him, he saw both a brilliant soldier and leader who'd taken care of him throughout his short time in the army. He'd graciously made him part of a heist that would allow him to live well beyond the means of his parents or whatever they could've dreamed for him. *Always taking care of us. The General rewards loyalty.* It wasn't in his nature to question, to step out of line. Somewhere in his youth, perhaps Young Pioneers or elsewhere, he decided once and for all to walk in step with the most charismatic. Thus far, it had benefited him greatly.

But at what cost?

This wasn't Dennis Hudson's first time at the Agency. As a member of the FBI's counterintelligence division, he coordinated as needed with the CIA brass. It was, however, his first inside the Deputy Director of Intelligence's office.

"After we got the search warrant, our guys uncovered about $250,000, all cash, hidden in a safe underneath a washing machine in the basement of Bank's house. In that same safe, we also found copies of Agency personnel files of up to forty different employees, including yours, Ms. Davis. Those copies have been turned over to your Agency as of this morning."

"And the second suspect?" asked Davis sitting opposite Agent Hudson and Ashcroft.

"Not a trace nor of the car you reported being parked out front," the head of the counterintelligence division answered in a frustrated manner. "It really would've been nice to have at least gotten a call. We could've been all over the guy you saw well beforehand. Run a proper sting operation. But no, you guys…."

It was Ashcroft's turn to interject. "Dennis, you know why we couldn't have done that. I get it, not a perfect situation, but the matter was and is sensitive."

"And you still can't tell me who the other suspects were, or still are?"

Ashcroft shook his head. "I appreciate your help returning the files to us. The Director asks me to thank you as well." The DDI stood up to signal the meeting was over and see Hudson to the door. When he'd left,

Davis spoke first.

"I don't like it, sir. Not one bit."

"That makes two of us." He closed his eyes and rubbed his forehead with his right hand. "Your meeting with Wiesel. Anything from him?"

"No word yet. He said he'd put in a request on our behalf to the heads at Mossad. Too early to tell if they're willing to trade intel and use their asset to get what we need."

"Well, we've not a single shred of evidence that indicates who Banks was working for or with. That's got me worried."

"And we still don't know if Karam's death was actually a suicide. It's too convenient, sir. Someone had to be pulling the strings for that to happen."

Ashcroft returned to his desk and reached for a bottle of anti-acids. Davis watched with some bit of shock as he threw back the bottle. She took a hard look at her boss. He was approaching sixty-five and, as of late, seemed to already be past that number. He'd put on at least twenty pounds over the last year and a half. Beneath his eyes were now dark circles. Ashcroft, by all accounts, was limping towards retirement. He wasn't getting more than five hours of sleep a night and hadn't seen the inside of the on-campus gym at the CIA in some time.

It isn't all his fault, though, poor guy. She recalled all that the last two and a half years had brought on him. In the midst of the highs, such as the intelligence gathering for the INF Treaty, he'd been forced to navigate much more troublesome waters. The arrest and execution of Adolf Tolkachev, Director Casey and his involvement with the Iran Contra Scandal, and most concerning of all, a steady stream of agents being arrested in the Soviet Union. No one knew for sure who was responsible for that dilemma. Some blamed security flaws at the U.S. Embassy in Moscow, while others spoke in hushed tones of an agent within the Soviet Division of the CIA. Regardless, the stress was taking its toll on

Trent Ashcroft.

"Keep at it. Dig deeper into Banks. Look at every possible contact he may have had, no matter how innocent it seems on the surface. Whatever it takes. Until then, we're still in the woods."

CHAPTER 28

Tripoli, Libya

"Jawahir, patrol the outer walls until relieved. At 1400, Colonel Gaddafi will be making a trip to Mukhabara el-Jamahiriya headquarters. You'll go along as part of the detail."

Standing at attention, Bar Dayan saluted her commanding officer before being dismissed. The Amazonian Guard member's appearance stood in sharp contrast to the conservative attire worn during the recent meeting with her Mossad handler. Fitted with boots, combat fatigues bearing blue shoulder boards and a crimson red beret, Dayan had every look of a special forces soldier. If one wore makeup, lipstick, and had their long jet black hair done in a ponytail flowing in the wind, that is. The overwhelming fear of assassination had led Gaddafi to the practice of using female bodyguards. Some said his theory was that a man would have trouble shooting at them. Others speculated that it had nothing to do with safety, rather sinister intentions for some of the women whom he eyed like a wolf.

Dayan often wondered with amusement what her commander's reaction would be if ever it was found out that her first name wasn't Jawahir and neither was she an Arab. Should anyone within the compound learn the truth, she'd be mercilessly tortured and executed immediately. It was a risk, however, that she willingly took.

The northern walls of the compound known as Bab al-Azizia stretched out towards a roadway leading to Tripoli International Airport. Encompassing six square kilometers, the base was first used by the Italians during World War II before being rebuilt by King Idris during the short period of the monarchy. In recent years, however, it had undergone a transformation under the orders of Colonel Muammar Gaddafi, making it more than just the Libyan leader's private residence and a military barracks. Now it contained a vast field dotted with trees, roads, a communications center, offices, a site for rallies, and even a Bedouin tent where the Colonel slept. Beneath the grounds lay a vast network of tunnels. Very few knew where all those tunnels led to.

Looking out from the wall, Dayan pondered the path she'd taken to end up spying on one of the world's most dangerous men. She hadn't always planned on the life of a spy. Born in Haifa to a Jewish couple that had immigrated from Morocco shortly after Israeli independence, Bar Dayan was fascinated by all things aviation. At an early age, she watched the skies with fear and fascination as F-4 Phantoms and A-4 Skyhawks defended the homeland against the Syrians and Egyptians. The sight of these planes soaring stirred up feelings of excitement, adventure, and patriotism. From then on, she knew what she wanted.

Years later, as a teenager, Dayan was taking lessons from a family friend at a private airfield. Dedicated and obsessed with learning, she slowly became an accomplished flyer. The dream was alive and soon within her reach. Or so she thought.

At eighteen, rather than wait to be conscripted, she joined the Women's Corps. Everyone tried to warn her, including her parents. Dayan, with passion for the skies and a heart full of patriotism, stubbornly and naively refused to believe, thinking it would all change. The reality, however, soon set in: women were barred from flying for the Israeli Air Force. She was to stay on the ground and train as an aviation mechanic.

But when one door closes, another opens. She reflected on that day, a year later, when a call went out at the Haifa Air Field. Volunteers were being sought for a special activity requiring critical thinking skills. Desperate for a change, she signed up and received a call from the base commander soon thereafter. The young woman dutifully reported one early morning to the commander's office when she noticed a gentleman in a suit there as well. The man arose then from his chair, appearing to take stock of her. Dayan stood at attention for more than a minute before he spoke.

"How would you like to serve your country elsewhere? Here, complete this," he said as he shoved a paper containing an aptitude test. "You have ten minutes."

The next day, she found herself in the employment of the Mossad. Dayan quickly learned the spy agency had been keeping tabs on her piloting skills. The Israel intelligence organization put her through an intense round of training before sending her out into the field. Her first assignments involved posing as a tour guide pilot while gathering intel and running agents in North Africa and Italy. The bright young woman from Haifa quickly proved her worth, catching the attention of all who were privileged to reading her reports. It had all culminated in this pinnacle mission, possibly the biggest risk-reward cover ever by an Israeli.

There was nowhere else Bar Dayan would rather be. Here she had a chance to thwart the schemes of a dictator who despised her people and orchestrated terror attacks on both Israeli and American alike. In addition, as part of her training in the Guard, she'd received instruction in flying several fighter jets primarily used by the Libyan Air Force. Listening and reporting back to her handler, she was providing valuable information that kept her country one step ahead of the Colonel.

The patrol shift seemed to stretch on for hours as she walked along the wall. Finally, at noon, a regular Army private came to relieve her. Dayan returned to her quarters to eat a midday meal and rest for the afternoon ahead. Lying on her cot, she recalled what her handler had mentioned at their last meeting. *But will it be today?*

At exactly 1400, a black limousine with small Libyan flags flapping in the breeze on each side of the front hood pulled up at the entrance of the Bedouin tent. Following the limo as part of the entourage were several security vehicles. Dayan, along with fourteen other female guards, stood at attention, their AK-47s held out in front of them.

Then he appeared. In full military uniform complemented by aviator sunglasses, Colonel Muammar Gaddafi strolled out of the tent onto a red carpet. His chin held arrogantly high, the leader of the Libyan people conveyed to everyone around him that he was the man who called the shots. One of the female guards opened his limousine door. As she did, the Colonel stopped and lowered his glasses, giving a ravenous grin. He winked before getting in. The woman, meanwhile, was expressionless.

The drive to the Ministry of Intelligence would take just under twenty-five minutes. Ten Amazonians followed in two separate SUVs while Dayan rode in the limo, alone up front with the driver. The privacy window rolled up, she could hear nothing of his conversation with his staff from the shotgun seat.

How long had it been? Two years since she'd snuck into the country and caught the attention of a personal assistant of the Colonel. When interviewed, she'd told the story that she'd been orphaned at a young age before being taken in by a relative who traded in all manner of things with other Bedouins. In defending against bandits, wild animals, and an irate customer or two, she claimed to have quickly learned how to handle a gun and protect herself. That was enough to convince the assistant. After several months of rigorous training, she took her vows and began life as a bodyguard. Thankfully, she'd avoided the unspeakable abuse some Amazonian Guards had faced at the hands of the male Army soldiers or the Colonel himself. She prayed every day that she'd continue to do so until the day came when the mission was complete and orders came to return home.

The motorcade passed through the compound gate and onto the street.

As it did, Dayan suddenly tensed up. There, outside the gate on the right side of the road, just as her handler had said, stood a ruddy-faced man with an orange shoulder band. Instinctively, her grip tightened on the AK-47 as the man watched her and the motorcade go by. Dayan's thoughts went back to her last meeting, desperately trying to remember anything said about just how this would go down. That only led to frustration and anxiety, for the lack of details provided. She could only wait for the moment and be ready to 'save' the anti-Semite she despised whole-heartedly.

The motorcade continued on before approaching a street corner. The Mossad agent, meanwhile, scanned the streets and upper building windows. *This idea better not get us all...*

The limo swerved hard to the right. The driver yelled in fear as Dayan looked to her left to see a bright flash barreling towards them. Suddenly the limo was rocked by the force of a rocket-propelled grenade slamming into the concrete ten feet from their vehicle. Dayan's shoulder thudded against the side door and glass window. Gritting her teeth, she steadied herself while taking note of three rifles peering over the top of a stone wall twenty yards away, between a shop and an apartment building.

All ten Amazonians rushed out of their SUVs, taking up a defensive perimeter around their Colonel's limo. Before the last of them could get into position, one of them hit the ground with a bullet wound to the leg as the shooting began.

"Drive! Drive!" The driver began to turn the car around, returning to the compound, as they heard the screams from the back. Before he could, a second mortar struck in the direction he was about to go. A look of terror was in his eyes. Dayan was almost sure he'd never had training as a formal soldier. Regardless, the man now sat stunned in his seat. His hands in a death grip on the wheel.

"You've got to keep moving," she yelled as she shook his shoulder in vain. The man was in shock, unable to be awakened.

Just then, a third mortar struck. This time even closer than either of the first two, the windshield was covered in a thick blanket of debris. Dayan knew it was time to make a move lest the *attackers* miss and actually make a direct hit on the limo.

Opening the shotgun door, the young spy ran towards the closest SUV used by the Amazonian escort. The sounds of bullets whizzing by all around caused her to curse under her breath. She found herself almost doubting the real intentions of the ambush when several rounds landed several feet in front of her kicking up dirt. Finally, Dayan reached the driver's side of the empty vehicle. The keys were still in the ignition as the guards continued acting as a buffer between the assailants and Colonel Gadhafi. Shutting the driver's door, she swiftly put the car in reverse and swung around sharply so she faced opposite the limo. Then she hit the gas, checking her rearview mirror and right side as she angled between the driver's side of the limo and the empty sidewalk. Once backed up alongside the rear limo door, Dayan jumped out and headed for the Colonel.

"Colonel Gaddafi, you must come with me!" Dayan yelled as she banged on the blackout tinted bulled-proof window. "There's no time to waste. We must return to Bab al-Azizia."

Seconds went by. The door didn't open, nor was there any reply from inside. *Does he doubt if I'm on his side? Please don't let this all be for waste.*

Just as she was about to bang against the window once more, the Libyan leader finally unlocked the door and exited onto the scene of a fierce firefight. Two members of his staff followed behind, but they were not her focus. Protecting her charge and getting him back to the compound safely was all that mattered. Quickly she led him hunched over, out of the sight of snipers in the distance, and pushed him into the backseat of the SUV. The other two staffers hurried to join him as Dayan returned to the driver's seat and put the car in drive. The vehicle tore out of the street at a mad pace.

"What is happening? Who were those barbarians?" Gaddafi pounded his fist down into his seat in a mix of horror and rage. Dayan ignored the outbursts, focusing instead on getting out of the fixed gunfight alive without becoming a fatality.

Oh great! Meir, what did you agree to? Dayan spotted a man with an RPG launcher standing in a lone doorway up ahead, possibly preparing to fire yet another projectile straight their way. She prayed it wasn't locked onto their vehicle as she made a U-turn and cut down a different street, not waiting to find out.

"Where are we headed now?" Gaddafi asked, still panicked but now lowering his voice.

"I'm taking you a different route to the Ministry of Intelligence. They knew we were headed back to Bab al-Azizia and likely had a second ambush waiting."

The Colonel sat in disbelief. For the remainder of the drive, all remained quiet.

Upon arrival, a large number of armed soldiers were moving about. It was clear that word had reached them of the ambush. Dayan got out first as security rushed forth surrounding them. She looked up and noted the snipers belonging to Mukhabara el-Jamahiriya positioned atop several nearby buildings lest a second attack occur. She opened the rear passenger door and let Gaddafi out, following closely behind with her automatic rifle still held in front of her as men all around saluted the Colonel. Entering the Ministry, they headed up to a third-floor room with a sweeping view of the Gulf. There the Colonel was greeted by Director Ahmed Raza.

"Colonel Gaddafi, it's an honor to welcome you here, but I must ask, are you alright?" Raza said with an arm extended and just a bit too much enthusiasm, Dayan noted.

By now, the Colonel had regained some of his composure. He gruffly shook Raza's hand and took a seat. "There is not a scratch on my body,

Director. I demand to know what just happened and what we're doing to bring these cowards to justice."

"Every resource is being used now to uncover the perpetrators. We've learned your security detail suffered two casualties. Both will survive. None of the assailants have been taken into custody, nor have any bodies been found at the scene. That is all I have, for now, I'm afraid."

"That's it? I expect you to work harder to track down these men! Is that understood?"

"Yes, Colonel. It will be done," Raza said bowing his head. Gaddafi changed gears abruptly.

"I want a status update," he ordered. Raza's eyes shifted to Dayan standing guard at the door before answering. "I suggest we speak privately, Colonel."

"Nonsense, this brave woman just saved my life. She's protected me far more than your own Intelligence Ministry has today.

"Very well. Boytsov's operation has gone splendidly so far."

"Where is that Russian now? Isn't he with them?"

"No, he's returned to our training camp south of Al Jadid."

"He should be given a medal! Such heroism for what he's done. I demand you reward him properly on your next visit out there.

"It will be as you say."

"When will the ship arrive?"

Raza was now beginning to perspire. "Colonel, I strongly suggest we reserve this discussion to just the two of us. A matter of national security. I insist"

"Very well," Gaddafi replied before giving a backhanded wave for his female bodyguard to depart. Maintaining an expressionless presence, Dayan left the room. Taking up a post outside the door, she breathed a sigh of relief, the tension easing a bit for the first time since they left the compound. *It really worked. Almost got me killed, but it worked.* The trust she'd just gained paid off sooner than anyone could've expected. Now, she carefully began to consider her next move.

CHAPTER 29

It was already past seven when Ashcroft pulled out of the parking lot at Langley and headed onto the freeway. Though eligible for receiving his own protective security, he often shunned it, preferring the space, solitude and privacy. His mind, weighed down by the day's problems, did its best to focus on the road and stay awake. Dinner, CNN, and bed were what he had to look forward to. His wife, who would be out tonight at a women's bridge club, left cold chicken in the fridge. He didn't blame her for having plans. His schedule had been particularly unpredictable for a while now. It had been at least a couple weeks, however, since the two had gotten to go on any sort of a date or even spent quality time talking at home. He knew this job was eating him alive. *Just a little bit longer until retirement. Then it'll all change.*

With little traffic at the late hour, he soon turned into his upscale neighborhood in Alexandria. The Ashcroft home, a two-story Colonial with a wide front porch, lay at the end of a cul-de-sac. As the DDI pulled into the driveway, he missed the black sedan parked two doors down marked with diplomatic plates. All he wanted to do now was to get inside and finally rest. *Maybe I'll skip the headlines and watch a movie instead. A rerun of The Magnificent Seven is supposed to be on tonight and...*

Ashcroft's heart nearly jumped out of his chest. He stopped midway up the brick-laid steps leading up to the porch. A solitary figure stood on his doorstep.

"Director Ashcroft, it's good to see you again."

He almost didn't recognize him. It wasn't until the man stepped out of the shadows and into the winter moonlight. Ashcroft did his best to steady himself before he spoke.

"Mr. Gagarin?"

"*Da*. My apologies for showing up at your home in this manner," Dmitri Gagarin began. "I hope I didn't startle you. The reason I'm here is of great concern." His eyes scanned both ends of the street, like a scared animal fearing its predator. "May we speak inside?"

Nodding his head, Ashcroft headed up the porch stairs and unlocked the front door.

"Come on into the kitchen. I need a drink. Want anything?"

"Whatever you're having, thank you," said Gagarin, needing something to calm his nerves as well.

The DDI made sure all the blinds were closed before turning on the kitchen light and finding a bottle of scotch in the cabinet. Pouring two shot glasses, he set them on the table and took a seat opposite the GRU officer.

"Before I begin, you should know I'm devoted to my country. I'm not here to defect or sell information. After this one meeting, I should hope never to come anywhere near you or your intelligence apparatus again."

"Understood," replied Ashcroft. "I'm listening."

"The INF Treaty was not an easy thing for our two nations to come to an agreement on. Much work and build-up of trust were required. I'm proud of what we've achieved. All that, however, is now in danger of being destroyed.

"A few days ago, at a facility northeast of Sochi, three OTR-23 Okas went missing along with the base commander, General Yakov Zhukov. We believe he and a handful of men loyal to him went rogue and were responsible for the theft. Unfortunately, by the time we realized what'd happened, it was too late. It's assumed they made their way to the coast and found passage on a ship. The Soviet Navy is on alert in the Black Sea and eastern Mediterranean. However, my nation is full of questions and lacking in any meaningful intel."

Ashcroft, despite the lecture he'd get from his wife later when she smelt it in her favorite room of the home, took out a carton of cigarettes from his jacket and lit one up. A haze of smoke hung over the table as he attempted to let the nicotine calm him where the liquor had already failed. "So have we heard from this General Zhukov yet? Holding the weapons ransom, selling them to the highest bidder, or a threat made out of sheer lunacy?"

"*Nyet*. We're without a trace to work with. The Kremlin has decided against asking any of our Warsaw Pact allies for information, nor are they willing to alert your country of this. It's my opinion, however, that this is all a mistake. We've failed by our own means to track the weapon systems down, and should the United States find out on its own, I fear the ramifications. Does this need to be broadcast across your television and printed in your newspapers? I think not. Yet, the subject should be breeched discreetly, as we're doing now."

"Agreed. If what you're saying is true, we have an unprecedented situation that must be acted on quickly. But just what assurances do I have that you're telling me the truth?"

"If your Navy comes into contact with our surface ships, they'll note a heightened alert status in the regions I mentioned. However, to validate where my information comes from, I'll do you one better."

"And what might that be?"

"There is a mole within your closest circle handling Soviet affairs. Through our East German friends, we've obtained some of the intel he sells to the highest bidder. Your meetings, Soviet Select, I believe you call them, he attends. Codename POTOMAC.

"I've come to you only because this mole has specifically identified you, the committee's leader, in past reports. No other member of your Soviet Select does he speak of."

Ashcroft's hands struggled now to hold the burning cigarette, Gagarin could see. Carefully, the Deputy Director of Intelligence took one more long drag. Closing his eyes, he slowly exhaled the smoke as it drifted across the kitchen table before looking back at the Russian. "What else can you tell me about him?"

CHAPTER 30

The sight threw Davis completely off-guard. There in the driveway waiting behind the wheel to take her to work that morning, was not the usual FBI agent but rather her boss.

"Sir? What are you doing here?" Davis leaned down and looked inside the passenger's seat window at Ashcroft.

"Employee appreciation day. Get in."

Doing as she was told, Davis waited until they passed the main gate of the residence before speaking again.

"So are you going to tell me or just make me guess for the next hour or so? Sorry sir, but this is out of the norm."

Ashcroft remained silent until he'd pulled the vehicle off to the side of the road.

"What I'm about to say, doesn't leave this car. I was paid a visit by a certain friend of yours: Dmitri Gagarin.

"Gagarin? But why would…."

"Your analysis on him back in December was spot on. The man won't betray his country. He's loyal to the Kremlin, but the situation is grave. The Soviets have lost three Oka missile systems, including three warheads."

Ashcroft took several minutes explaining to Davis the situation before she spoke again. "How do we know this isn't some sort of a set-up?"

"Because of the other bit of information he gave up to prove his credentials. Audrey, there's a mole at the CIA, and it wasn't Banks. In fact, based on the intel he gave, I can number it down to four individuals: Koufax, Skylar, Shelby, and Clark.

"But I thought you said Gagarin won't betray his country?"

"He isn't. Or at least not in his eyes. You see, the mole, codenamed POTOMAC, once worked for the East Germans—the Stasi. The Soviets only ever got the intel from him secondhand. That was until about a year ago. The operation running POTOMAC ended unexpectedly when the Stasi could no longer meet his financial demands."

Davis's head was spinning. "Okay, so to summarize, there's a rogue Russian general who's stolen three nuclear missiles. Where they are is anyone's guess. We also know that the mole, according to Gagarin, who we can confirm is a GRU spy with access to cable traffic between their Embassy and the Kremlin, is not only alive but within the Soviet Select, hampering all our operations and analysis for the worse."

"That's about the sum of it. That last part, though, we keep quiet."

"Why? Tell the Director himself or the National Security Advisor. This is too big to leave them in the dark."

"And cause hysteria or maybe even return the CIA to the dark ages? You know just how many people in D.C. would love to see that? No way. You and I investigate the Soviet Select on our own. Keep it all airtight until we have enough evidence to move in on someone."

We're playing with fire, was what she wanted to say. Her most recent observations of Ashcroft were becoming more painstakingly apparent. To Davis, the man was brilliant yet worn out from the burdens of the Agency. The load he carried was only fueling the fear and paranoia in his eyes. If he insisted though on handling the mole this way, she'd do what he asked. Her loyalty to her boss ran deep. Keeping the mole situation airtight would probably be okay for now. Besides, she'd already been doing her own private investigation for two months.

"Well, in that case, let's discuss the suspects," said Davis. The DDI pulled back on the road, relaxed now that Davis was still on board. "Koufax. Motive? He's a recent widower. Been through some tough times and all without grown kids to have his back. Always keeps you guessing about what he's thinking. If he hit a mental low and nobody noticed, he'd be a prime candidate for recruitment."

"He's a hard nut to crack. Smart enough though to pull it off if he wanted to," Ashcroft noted. "Now, Skylar. There's someone who could be caught in a honey trap these days. What do you make of him?"

"Oh, he's a saint." Davis's thinly veiled sarcasm didn't escape her boss. "Besides that concern, his record's pretty spotless, but...."

Ashcroft interjected. "The analyst in you says...."

"He only moved up a single pay grade two years ago after sitting stagnant the previous seven. And, well, we all saw his place at the office Christmas party he threw a couple years ago. He has expensive taste in how he decorates. Pulling that off wouldn't be easy even on his new salary."

"Good observation. He did have a father, however, who was well-off. His parents split when he was young, and it appears a great deal of his wealth was gone by the time Skylar graduated from the Naval Academy," Ashcroft added.

"I don't know what to make of Shelby," said Davis moving on to suspect number three. "He's incredible at his job, but you know it, I know it, and half the seventh floor knows after hours he's a bit fast and reckless."

"He's young."

"Yes, and all it takes is for one accident for him to be put in a compromising situation. Women, booze... Blackmail is well within the realm of possibility for him."

Ashcroft sighed. "Clark's the one I'm worried about most. Don't get me wrong, I'm not saying I think he's the one. Rather, if the Deputy Director of Operations is an agent for hire, then we're all screwed. Plain and simple."

They continued on the subject for the entire drive, devising their plan of action before reaching the gate.

"You really think we can do this, sir? All on our own?"

"I do. Is there anything I missed?"

Davis shook her head. *It could work. It had to.*

Leaving the Bab al-Azizia compound was no easy task for an Amazon, much less a Mossad spy. Rare exceptions, such as visiting immediate family only twice a year, were few and far between. For Bar Dayan, the friendship of a cook was her saving grace. An older woman whose culinary skillset had allowed her to transition from the former King to the man who'd dethroned him, she looked forward to Jawahir's visits to her kitchen. Often Dayan would bring gifts. Other times she acted as a silent protector when other servants would physically bully her. With the cook's help and their similarity in size and height, Dayan was able to create an identity transfer. Adorning an identical full niqab and cloak while the cook remained out of sight in her private quarters, she'd leave the compound in the evening to either meet her handler or make a dead drop.

Walking alone down the streets that night, she contemplated the meeting between Gaddafi and Raza the day before—a mixed success in that she'd obtained the intelligence sought after by Tel Aviv but also suffered a lost opportunity. *What could they have been discussing that required me to leave? What's on its way?*

Not far from the old medina quarter, she turned into an alleyway that often remained deserted in the late evening. It was here that she'd make the drop. Reaching into her garment, Dayan took out a milk carton smeared with tomato sauce, curry, and coffee grounds. No one would pay the rubbish any mind. Without stopping, she tossed the soiled container into the alley, then headed to the market where she'd get the vegetables she'd promised the cook.

It was two hours later when Daniel Meir passed through the same spot. Carefully stopping to turn down the dark path between the buildings, he looked from the corners of his eyes lest he was being watched. The Israeli was now confident that no one was around. Meir casually strolled down the alleyway. Approaching the dead drop, he swiftly collected the discarded carton and then disappeared into the night.

CHAPTER 31

South Mediterranean Sea

Commander Kyle Billingsley peered through the canopy of his F-14 Tomcat, surveying the dark blue waters below. The squadron commanding officer had received orders to run reconnaissance throughout the region and make note of any and all cargo ships coming from the east. For two days, the men of VF-107, known as the Knights, and their fourteen Grumman-built jets had run countless sorties over the region near the Gulf of Sidra. The purpose of this task was unknown to all, including Billingsley. Seven hundred miles east from their carrier, the U.S.S. *Nimitz,* and five thousand feet above the sea, he wondered just when, not if, his squadron would get to see any action on this tour. He'd been aboard the *Nimitz* six years prior when the Reagan administration first decided to challenge Gaddafi over the disputed waters by conducting exercises in the Gulf. The pilots, mostly too young to have participated in Vietnam and experienced combat, faced for the first time the task of escorting enemy aircraft away from the exercises and were given updated rules of engagement to fire back if fired upon. The encounters nearly took a deadly turn back then when a Libyan Su-22 was overheard radioing its intentions to fire on a Tomcat it was zeroing in on and then firing a rocket which missed the tail of the American fighter jet. The Tomcats moved into action fast, shooting down two Libyan planes in a move that told not just Gaddafi but the world that the United States' fighter pilots were back on top and had orders to hit back if attacked.

"Birddog, I have a sighting forty miles out and about ten degrees to the east," radioed his wingman flying trailing offset.

"Roger that. Let's take a look," replied Billingsley, who relished his call sign. It beat the one a bunkmate of his had earned on his first tour: Stain, after his F-14 had a rough landing on the air carrier deck and got a little too nervous in his flight suit.

Both planes slowed speed as they approached, allowing for a good picture to be taken of the ship. The wingman moved into position. Attached to the belly of his plane within the forward camera bay, a nearly 2,000-pound camera known as the Tactical Airborne Reconnaissance Pod System captured it all. Meanwhile, Billingsley kept watch lest a surface-to-air missile come flying from the deck.

"Alright, I think we got it. *Phaedra.* Must be a Greek or Cypriot ship. That's the second cargo ship appearing to head toward the coast."

Billingsley took a look out of his cockpit window. "Only a couple of the crew seem to be on the top deck." He wondered again what it was all about. You can follow orders, but you can't help but guess the reasons behind them.

The patrol continued for another hour. There was little to see except the vast waters below and the morning sun rising in the east. His Radar Intercept Officer, Ned Landry, seated in the rear, was almost always talking unless an order was being given. Now though, he was silent, for there was little to be seen, and no traffic was coming over the comms channels. Even in moments of tranquility, the Squadron Commander was ready for anything. It was an attitude that had taken root in him long ago, back in his days at the United States Navy Fighter Weapons School, better known as TOPGUN. Unbeknownst to many before Hollywood catapulted it to popularity, the school was founded during Vietnam in the wake of heavy aircraft losses by opposing MiG aircraft.

Initially, the blame was placed on better turn ratios of enemy fighters and the need to upgrade the American F-4 Phantoms. The problem, however, went much deeper. A study issued by the Navy revealed inadequate training for air crews. Soon the school was established in '69, run by instructors determined to mold the next generation of top fighter pilots. They chose only the best, targeting those with a prowess in airmanship, discipline, expertise, and the ability to lead by example. Seventeen years later at Naval Air Station Miramar in San Diego, Billingsley honed his skills in air combat maneuvering.

The training there had been by no means easy or intermitted with beach volleyball. Rising every morning at 0430 for five weeks straight, Billingsley went through rigorous training in the classroom and out in the skies. The Squadron Commander found the nighttime training particularly fascinating. In fact, his class was the first to partake in a night ops training mission in order to better maneuver close-in dogfighting without clear visibility.

"Alright, Birddog," Landry spoke up finally as they neared their carrier. "Looks like the Rear Admiral wants to see you when we land."

"Bridge?" Billingsley asked.

"His cabin. Just wants you, not me. What did you do?" he asked with a chuckle.

"I just toe the line, Stetson. Well, I guess I'd better see what it's about."

Billingsley's F-14 hit the deck of the 1,092-foot carrier first. As the wheels touched down, he shoved the engine throttles to full power as was customary, lest he miss the landing wire known as "the trap" and need to make a touch and go before trying to land once more. Without missing a beat, the aviator's tailhook caught the third wire and quickly came to a halt. He then withdrew the hook, taxied out of the landing zone and parked the Tomcat.

Speedily, he headed down below to the gallery deck, one level below the flight deck area. All around him, the crew of over four thousand men and women were busy at work aboard the nuclear-powered ship, making it difficult at times to navigate the narrow corridors. He moved past the Maintenance shops and Command Operations space before reaching the stateroom of Commander Task Force 60, Rear Admiral Martin Truett.

"Come in," was the voice Billingsley heard as he carefully knocked on the door. When he entered, he found his Air Wing Commander, Captain Beau Chamberlain, there as well.

"Sir, Commander Billingsley reports," the pilot said with a salute to the Rear Admiral.

"At ease, Billingsley. I'd like a report on your most recent reconnaissance mission."

"Admiral, we encountered at least a dozen ships in the assigned search vector. Of those, five were cargo ships, but only two appear to be heading toward the Libyan coast. Both have a few more days at sea before they reach Tripoli or elsewhere. Our personnel are removing the TARPS now and should have the film reviewed soon."

Rear Admiral Truett turned to his Air Wing Commander before facing Billingsley once more. "Any foreign aircraft encountered?"

"None, sir. It was clear skies for us all the way."

"Aboard the cargo ships you saw heading toward Libya—could you make out what was on the top deck? Any specific cargo, defensive, or counter-measure weapons?"

"None that I was able to see, sir. Parts of the deck were obstructed by various canvases and such. If there was anything visible, the TARPS will pick it up." Suddenly, a thought swept across the young Squadron Commander's mind. One which caused him to take pause and consider the situation. "Sir, may I ask a question?"

"Go ahead."

"Should we be expecting hostiles on these reconnaissance flights? If so, I'd like to request permission to arm the Tomcats with one to two more sidewinders and request refueling to cover maximum distance on this search."

"I couldn't say. However, permission granted, Commander. You may go now."

It wasn't until Billingsley had left the room that Captain Chamberlain spoke.

"Told you he was sharp. Birddog doesn't miss a thing."

"I read his service record, Beau. Flew at the tail end of Vietnam. Shot down one MiG and later took part in the last battle that rescued the container ship *Mayaguez* from the Khmer Rouge. Faced MiG's again when we started challenging Gaddafi on his idea of 'sovereign waters' and held his own. Graduate of TOPGUN. The man is something special, that's for sure. What's much less sure is whether or not we have anything to fear right now. Chain of command is keeping tight-lipped about this reconnaissance operation."

Getting up from his chair, the Admiral moved toward a map of the Gulf of Sidra pinned to a wall opposite his desk. His eyes zeroed in on a dark red line marking the contentious 40-mile point. "But if there is trouble afoot, at least those Tomcats will be ready for them."

"I've read the logs of ships spotted by the Sixth Fleet over the last two days. Of those that could possibly conceal three Okas within its hull, seventeen originated from the Black Sea." Shelby held the list in front of him.

"What's our search radius?" asked Ashcroft.

"Mediterranean Sea from the coasts of Libya in the west to the Suez canal and the Syrian coast in the east," answered Shelby. The unsaid fact, that it was impossible to keep tabs on all suspect ships, was clear to all.

"What are we hearing from our assets on the ground?"

Clark fielded that question. "All's quiet throughout the Mediterranean region. None of our agents based in the ports of the usual suspects have heard a thing."

"There's just too many variables to consider right now," Skylar lamented. "I say we blockade the ports of the usual suspects, and if a nation throws a fit, we accuse them of attempting to obtain the weapons."

Davis saw Clark and Shelby roll their eyes in frustration. When she looked over at Koufax, his expression was as indifferent as ever.

"Toby, what do you think?"

The head of the Soviet Division looked up from his green tea and adjusted his glasses. "I think it'd be helpful to know where exactly the source of this bombshell intel is positioned."

"That's not happening," Ashcroft replied as he glanced around the room, checking for any signs of what the rest were thinking. "The source is sensitive and could potentially be compromised."

"Sir, that's why we have this group. We're airtight. You asked my opinion, and I need to know more about where the intel came from before giving my opinion."

"Privileged, Toby. Even to you." The answer left a chill throughout the room. Davis worried Ashcroft was coming on too strong. It was unclear to her if his remark was directed at the four suspects or just Koufax.

"Fine," Koufax replied before continuing. "First, we can't look for immediate answers from our sources in the Kremlin—at least the ones everyone here within the Select is privileged to know of—unless this General pops up to demand ransom from the Soviets. Second, naval reconnaissance is our biggest asset. Push to have it expanded and the number of sorties increased. I say we keep making note of any possible ships, look for anything suspicious, have our agents on stand-by in the ports like Latakia or Beirut, and when one of these ships drops anchor, we move in. Other than that, I don't know what options we really have."

Rubbing his temples profusely, Ashcroft looked over his copy of the data as the room waited in awkward silence for him to speak. "Alright, Toby, I'm going to run with your idea. We'll see what the Director says. Audrey, what do you have on that Lieutenant? Supposedly Zhukov's one-time personal aide and trusted confidant?"

The job of detailing the identities of the renegade officers and men who'd taken part in the weapons heist had fallen to Davis. One of the men, twenty-four-year-old Lieutenant Grigory Tamarkin, was, in fact, the son of a *nomenklatura* who'd worked with Boris Alexeev in the Kremlin. Tamarkin's parents had then been casual friends of the Alexeev's. In her non-official cover at the time, Davis occasionally dined with the Lieutenant's mother and heard a great deal about the young man. The past history was significant enough that Ashcroft wanted her take on his mental make-up. Sitting on the edge of the couch looking at the picture copied from the man's military file with both the DDI and Skylar opposite her, she looked up with confidence.

"He's a follower with a rebellious streak, Tamarkin—ideal candidate to get behind a madman like this if there ever was one. I'll break it down. The kid's mom used to talk about how she was concerned about him going along too much with the wrong crowd. Not with stuff like Young Pioneers, but just with whoever was the most charismatic at school. Blind loyalty, no matter what trouble that person got him into. She was also concerned for his relationship with his dad. The two didn't get along. Father wanted him to go into government service and was ready to pull the strings, but the son eventually chose the military to spite him. If this Zhukov got his claws into this guy early on, there's no doubt he'll go down with him to the end."

"Intriguing," Clark said with a hushed whisper before taking a sip from his mug. It appeared to Davis that he was fashioning an idea in his head.

Skylar added to the analysis as he adjusted his golden monogrammed cufflinks. "Which means we're dealing with a group of radicals. Maybe more so for money and selfish pursuits, but that can be used to our advantage."

"Maybe," remarked Ashcroft as he poured himself another cup of coffee. "You ever meet the kid in person?"

"Once or twice. When he was a boy, his mom brought him along on a shopping trip. Another time when he was older we had seats beside the entire Tamarkin family at the Bolshoi Theater. Seemed quiet. I was more focused though on the parents than him."

"Well, we first have to find the ship before you can use the psychoanalysis on the Russkies," Shelby deadpanned. The comment annoyed Davis—particularly the way he said it. *It's true, though. If only we knew their destination.*

"It's good to have you back, Konstantin. The new men badly need your instruction on the shooting range." Saeed could hardly believe the words that had just left his mouth. As much as he despised the infidel who marked his camp, he couldn't deny his value to the training of his men. For the last month, Boytsov had constantly been going back and forth between Tripoli and the training camp. The reason he knew not.

"From Tripoli," Boytsov said as he presented him with a gift. If only these were easier to come by here in the desert."

Saeed opened the box packed in ice and smiled. "This is a surprise. It's good to finally get fresh pomegranates and apples here."

"There's another crate just like it with grapefruits in the back of the truck."

"Thank you. I only wish I could return the favor and get you a bottle of your preferred drink. Perhaps your homeland's famous vodka." *What am I saying? Well, when you have a young recruit nearly shoot off your foot trying to learn how to use an automatic…Oh these last few weeks…*

Boytsov nodded. "That I wouldn't say no to." Saeed could see it was one of the rare moments when the Russian would, if only for a moment, allow himself to show his former identity. The former Spetsnaz had adapted well over the last few years. *Where he'd once had to contend with frostbite, orders from his KGB superiors, and a nation facing a supernova-like shift, here in Libya his greatest concerns now were avoiding sunburn and ensuring the commandos knew how to fight well,* Saeed thought to himself. Boytsov had served him and Libya well. He decided then that he'd somehow obtain a bottle of spirits for his best instructor, regardless of the laws.

"Are you back now on a permanent basis?" Saeed asked as they headed into the main structure on the base.

Boytsov wiped the sweat from his brow and reached to pour a cup of tea from the kettle lying on the table. "For as long as it pleases Director Raza."

"You don't sound too sure."

Boytsov hesitated to answer lest he give a reply beyond the training commander's clearance. Something else lingered in his mind, though. The mission, being carried out against his better judgment by orders of Gaddafi, worried him more each day. Whether at sea or on this nation's shores, he feared a disaster the likes of which the world had never seen. Another disaster he'd be witness to. *Just like Moscow.*

"I'm sure of nothing, Saeed. Only to be on hand at our darkest hour."

CHAPTER 32

Davis dropped everything when she got the news. Racing up the highway to the Israeli Embassy off Van Ness Street and International Drive, she was soon seated in front of Wiesel's desk.

"Good news from Tel Aviv," he began. "We've received word where Boytsov has been staying."

"And?"

"He recently returned to a training camp south of Al Jadid."

"Returned? Returned from where?"

"We don't know if he's been gone since his infamous visit here back in December or just returned from another mission abroad. What we do know is that he's back training commandos."

Davis wanted to ask how they'd obtained this information, but she knew better.

"Ben, this means a lot. I can't thank you enough for sharing this, and whoever was involved in obtaining his location, I...."

Wiesel raised a hand. "Like I said, I have two daughters back home. Besides, this man is a common enemy. It's Mossad's view that if your people should take action, it will mean maybe a few less trained threats that Israel has to deal with."

Returning to Langley, Davis' hands held the steering wheel tightly. A part of her was on auto-pilot, her mind transfixed on the image of a map of the Libyan Desert that hung in her office. She recalled the pins marking each of the suspected camps. A small blue one denoted the site west of Al Jadid with a label attached. *Camp 47*. The man who'd wrought pain and death to those she loved and cared for was hidden no longer. *Justice is coming, Boytsov. Justice you can't escape.*

.

PART THREE

CHAPTER 33

"Captain Nicolaou, should we anticipate another delay?" Zhukov was growing frustrated. It seemed as of late that the *Phaedra* was nothing more than a rusted tub. Already a storm had caused damage atop the deck. Now engine trouble threatened to slow them further.

"General, I have my best engineers working on it now."

"How long?"

"It all depends. They could have it fixed within the next six hours according to the chief engineer. There might also be a stress issue requiring us to slightly reduce our speeds, at which I'd expect to arrive three days later than expected, at most."

"Unacceptable. You will see we arrive on time."

"Don't forget that I have a stake in arriving in Tripoli too. If we push our luck, the engines could go out and it would take forever for us to make port. This is my ship. I make the calls. Is that understood?"

Zhukov was growing sick of the ego and pushback from Nicolaou. However, he wasn't ready to take command of a ship for the first time. "Three days then, Captain. No later."

"You've got it down to one?"

"Yes, sir," Davis explained to Ashcroft. "This is the only one east of the town Wiesel mentioned."

"Are you sure? If I go and get approval from the powers that be, are you confident we have solid intel here?"

"I do."

"Based on?"

"The word of a friendly nation's intelligence service along with what we've already obtained through our own satellite surveillance."

"By chance any details on Mossad's source?"

Davis shook her head. "Whoever it was that got word back to them is a sensitive source they're protecting."

"I can't make any promises, Audrey. I'll present this to the Director."

"If it's approved, will I…"

"You'll know when needed."

Ashcroft shifted in his chair before changing subjects. "I borrowed the key to Clark's safe."

"You what?"

"Calm down. I know all the security measures around his office space. We both have keys to each other's side door, and his secretary was out for lunch when I did it."

Davis's concern for her boss had now reached new heights. The haggard-looking man's paranoia was clearly causing him to take reckless action. Ashcroft noted her facial reaction and tried to ease her fears.

"He left his coat in here during our last meeting with the key in it. I was going to return it when his secretary let Julie out front know he'd gone home early with a cold. It only took five minutes."

"Okay. So, what did you find?"

"A file on an operation called FIELDGOAL. A year and a half ago it appears he made a trip to Rome to meet with the chief of station there, as well as an agent who needed the reassurance from a member of the top brass that he was valued. Well, turns out he met with someone else: a man from the East German Stasi. You know what else was there in the safe? Several envelopes of Swiss francs."

"You're not saying…."

"It's plausible. Could be nothing, but either way I'll get to the bottom of it. How about you? How's the deep dig on Shelby and Koufax coming?"

Her boss's brash behavior or the contents of Clark's safe, Davis wasn't sure which was more shocking.

"Shelby is a conundrum. On one hand, he could be a dead end. There was a DUI he got last year while on vacation at Huntington Beach. Some women, yes, but nothing to tie him to selling secrets. What I can't get over is the man I saw with Banks. To have pulled a bit of spycraft like that and escaping from the car that quick during the chase isn't something I could see either an out-of-shape Clark or Koufax do."

"Clark could've contracted someone to meet with Banks."

"Valid point. Speaking of Koufax, though, I did learn he likes to take drives out to Norfolk Beach on the weekends when he's not working. Seems to stay at a beach house the whole time. You didn't mention Skylar, by the way."

"Haven't got to him just yet. When I do, I'm going to make a thorough review of his most recent financials."

CHAPTER 34

The clock read 3:15 a.m. as Davis turned back from her bedside table and stared at the ceiling. *You're overthinking, Audrey. Why won't you just go to sleep?*

The more she tried, the more in vain her efforts for rest were. There were two reasons for this, of course. The first stemming from the attacks in December. Tonight, however, there was a second cause for her insomnia. *You said you were sure about the training camp site. What if you're wrong? What if you got bad intelligence for one reason or another? What if it's bad and they launch a strike on that camp? What if there are innocents there? Women, children? What if? What if?*

She turned on the bedside light and sat up. The questions she was asking were the same ones that had plagued strategists and spymasters for longer than she'd been alive. It was about taking a source of information, judging its authenticity, and then acting on it without second-guessing. Many had stumbled in this position: station chiefs, heads of intelligence, generals, even presidents. Had she as well?

"No," she uttered aloud with a sigh. *Trust your gut, Audrey. Mossad is a reliable source. It's not just you who thinks so, but also Ashcroft. That camp had already been suspected. The Israeli's intel aligns with your own analysis.*

But am I sure just because I want revenge? I mean justice. The thought popped up in a near malicious manner, causing her to doubt once more.

Off in the corner rested the cardboard box that contained the books belonging to Cooper that the boys had begun reading. Davis had avoided it like the plague, yet now she was drawn to it. Walking across the cold hardwood floor, she pulled back the cardboard folds and looked inside. *What would you do, Carson?*

Davis picked out from among the books at the very bottom of the box a worn-out brown leather journal. She carefully opened it up. Inside, the pages were yellowed, aged by time and the roughness of travel. Starting on the first page as moonlight came through the windows and illuminated the corner of the room, she read the date written in blue ink: May 23rd, 1949. Cooper had spent the day boating on the Chesapeake with his wife Cathy *and a son?*

A black-and-white photograph fell from behind the next page into her lap. There in a small sailboat, was a much younger version of her mentor and friend, holding his boy of about three with one arm and his other wrapped around the love of his life. All smiles, enjoying the sunshine and post-war bliss. *But what happened?*

She skimmed the next few pages before noticing a sizeable date gap between entries.

'Came back from Berlin. It's too late. Chris is dead.' Oh, Carson. There was grief in the words written down. Words expressing regret for being away, most likely on another mission, not there to do something and avoid the car accident which changed the young couple's life forever. He questioned how he could move forward and pick up the pieces.

The next three days of entries were all mournful. About to give up and close the journal, she looked over at the next page. The first sentence. *I've found peace.*

Continuing to read, there was no sign of further sadness or regret. *You found peace, Carson. But why?*

She went back to the entry. *James 1st chapter*, was all that was written below that single line. Davis then pulled out Cooper's King James from the box. It was even more worn than the journal. Carefully, she turned the pages, finding handwritten notes scribbled on nearly every bit of the margins. The words he clung to with hope were underlined in the same blue ink which marked the journal pages.

Davis read the short chapter slowly. It had been a long time since those years in a Catholic prep boarding school, where she'd been required to read much of the New Testament. Whenever she'd read this section back then, Davis figured her mind was likely on boys or the next equestrian tournament. This time, it seemed the words sunk in much deeper. She then turned her eyes to her mentor's myriad of notes.

Even in the midst of all those trials over the years, this is what kept him going. There was one note with an arrow drawn to a circled verse. "If any of you lack wisdom, let him ask of God, that giveth to all men liberally, and upbraideth not; and it shall be given him."

She closed the book and placed both the Bible and the journal back in the box. For Davis, the subject of faith was not one she dismissed, but rather held a great degree of passivity. At some point in those years following her dad's death, she simply chose to rely on her own strength to get through the challenges. The aftermath of being a twelve-year-old without a father, the danger and loneliness during her ten-year assignment in Moscow, she'd willed herself through it all. Yet now she was spent—mentally, emotionally, and, now, physically too. This time, Davis knew she needed more than self-determination.

For the first time in years, the spy, instructor, analyst and mother all rolled into one found herself kneeling in prayer. The words, neither poetic nor smooth, were difficult to utter. Yet they came out. When she was done, Davis lay back down and drifted off to sleep—a sound sleep, for the first time in months.

CHAPTER 35

Undisclosed Location

They'd been given forty-eight hours' notice. James Washington O'Neil, however, wasn't caught completely off-guard. It was these kinds of missions for which he constantly trained for.

Three Blackhawk helicopters took off from a secluded base in Chad under the darkness of night. Flying low, they were well under the defensive radar of the nation they were entering. O'Neil sat strapped into his seat alongside four other men, not counting the pilot up front. Twenty years. That was how long he'd been serving his country in one form or another. First as a Marine in Vietnam, gaining attention for his marksmanship skills in combat, then at the CIA in a variety of capacities. He'd most recently been posted in Moscow Station before requesting a transfer back to black ops missions.

Checking his weapon, he took a deep breath and closed his eyes. O'Neil visualized the layout of their target. *Seven structures, including a garage covering two trucks and a Land Cruiser. All clustered together. Terrain: flat desert. Only one road led in and out. Nearest town, seventy miles east of there.*

They would be required to act fast and with precision. If something went wrong, there would be no immediate backup. Any trace of their presence left behind was not acceptable.

"Fifteen minutes out," the pilot announced over their wireless earpieces. O'Neil silently nodded in acknowledgment. Having heard the rumors about their target, he felt no remorse for what was about to befall the man.

"Audrey." It was Ashcroft standing inside the doorway of her office.

"Sir. You need something?"

"Yeah," he gestured for her to get up from her desk. "Need you to come with me."

"Okay, where are we going?" she asked with a confused look. "The rest of the Select has only now been informed. They won't have a chance to mess this up," Ashcroft replied, deflecting the question as he led the way to the elevator. They got off on the first floor and headed outside onto a covered walkway. Davis felt a concoction of curiosity and fear as they marched towards a lone building she'd yet to ever visit.

A second security clearance check was required. As Davis swiped her ID, a downbeat chirp emitted from the reader.

"She's with me," bellowed the DDI to the security guard.

"Audrey, what you're about to see, you can't speak of to anyone." Ashcroft stopped at an unmarked door, swiped his badge one last time, and opened the door for them both. When they entered, Davis's mouth fell open.

"Where are we?" The puzzled look on her face remained as she stared about the room covered with TV screens and military and civilian personnel on desktop computers. On the screens were various live feeds, satellite maps and a digital countdown clock of some kind.

"How close are they?" Ashcroft asked a uniformed officer.

"Ten minutes out, sir."

"O'Neil reported over the radio they've no indications of any other aircraft about." This time it was Shelby, who got up from a swivel chair holding a Coke can. Davis noted Clark, Skylar, and Koufax sitting together while staring at the overhead feeds.

"Sir?" The spy turned analyst had only heard whispers of this place before. It had been above her clearance and no more than a passing thought. Until now.

"Audrey, as we speak, fifteen special ops members are en route over Libya on their way to Camp 47. Justice is about to be served."

The pilots at Okba Ben Nafi Air Base saluted their commanding officer one final time before heading to their fighters. They were thankful for the overcast skies this evening. It would make things easier on them as they went out on their mission.

Ten Soviet-made MiG-23s took off from the runway and headed out to sea. The young pilots felt a swell of excitement at their first opportunity to encounter the Americans. The older, more experienced ones, still remembering past dogfights, were much more subdued.

Alongside the MiGs flew a lone TU-22 Backfire. The three-man crew of the strategic bomber had been conspicuously kept apart from the other pilots during the briefing.

The orders had been clear: demonstrate strength and authority over the contested waters in the Gulf of Sidra and be ready to ward off any American planes that refused to acknowledge Libyan superiority. Even if they were well outside the disputed boundary. Rumors of a bounty on shot-down aircraft had circulated, but none knew if such a prize still stood.

"This is SG-29," said the lead pilot flying out front of the squadron as he scanned his plane's Saphir-23 pulse Doppler radar. "Detecting three bogeys fifty kilometers out. Requesting orders."

"Move back in closer formation," radioed the squadron commander. "We will hold our ground and force the Americans back out of the sector. Over."

It was unknown if the bogeys were merely testing them or on patrol. Considering the respective speeds of the MiGs and the American planes, contact would be made in five minutes.

"Satellites should be in range in T-minus thirty seconds," said Shelby in between sips of his soft drink. "Man, if only I had a bag of popcorn."

Clark, Ashcroft, and several others gave glaring looks of offense at the remark. Ashcroft was just about to utter a blistering rebuke when a young staffer sitting at one of the computers threw up his hand. The staffer's senior came over to see what it was.

"Director Ashcroft," the supervisor spoke up. "All three Blackhawks radios are offline."

Skylar's head cocked immediately towards the breaking news. "You sure it's not something on our end?" Ashcroft asked.

"I don't know. Communications down. That's all we know."

"Ten seconds."

"Do we abort the mission?" Skylar asked in an increasingly panicked voice.

Ashcroft shook his head. "It's too late for that."

Suddenly the main center screen showed a lone satellite image. Davis immediately recognized it for the camp. Through heat-seeking technology, they could see where people were. Most were lying asleep in what appeared to be two bunkrooms. Meanwhile, three red and yellow figures moved about the perimeter, no doubt on night watch duty.

"Here they come!" Shelby exclaimed as no more than fifty yards out, the first members of the op's team approached one of the perimeter guards. The American intelligence officials watched from a birds-eye view as the bright red figure appeared to slump to the ground, the team members now advancing. For whatever flippancy Shelby had shown in his earlier popcorn remark, the scene playing out before them on the TV was, to Davis, one of surreal suspense.

Another guard fell, and then finally, the last. The team members split into two groups: one went towards the supposed bunkhouse, the other headed for the garage.

The whole room was now completely still. With bated breath they watched, knowing what was next.

Then suddenly, a bright flash emitted over the bunkroom. The commando recruits perishing in their bunks with not even a second to react. Another bright flash came from the garage where several grenades had been launched inside, destroying any chance of driving off for help.

Davis's blood turned cold. Never before had she viewed anything like this in real-time.

All three choppers moved in over the camp. Two of the Libyans appeared to have made it outside. Whether by the gunfire from the Blackhawks or O'Neil's men on the ground, they were both quickly eliminated.

"When will we know if we got him?" Koufax asked in a low tone. No one answered.

"Sir, what do you…." Davis stopped speaking as she watched Ashcroft grit his teeth. His breathing was heavy and his eyes were bloodshot. She was about to call for help when he relaxed somewhat. "We'll know as soon as the radios are back up again."

Davis accepted the answer before returning her attention to the screen.

"This is Eagle 103. Fast approaching group of eleven bogeys continuing to move in a tight formation towards our present position." The E-2C Hawkeye Combat Information Center Officer who'd first spotted the Libyans as they took off 150 miles away while cruising at 27,000 feet, focused on his own radar, his concern rising. "Appears to be ten MiGs and a Backfire."

"Eagle 103, head fifteen degrees north along with your two Tomcat escorts. We're sending reinforcements now to join you."

The pilot of the Hawkeye, who was listening on the same frequency, turned the aircraft tasked with airborne early warning and headed to safer airspace. A routine racetrack pattern patrol flight had quickly taken a turn for the worse.

The whole of Task Force 60, including the USS *Nimitz*, was close by. Pilots from three squadrons rushed to the flight deck and hopped in their cockpits. All around their Tomcats, the deck crew hustled. The yellow-shirted flight deck director waving each jet forward to the catapult track. Red-shirted ordnancemen readied the Sparrow, Phoenix, and Sidewinder missiles underneath the planes. Proper cables attached, the first aircraft takes on tension and awaits as the seconds ticked by. Jet blast deflector raised, missiles armed, final check. The signal is given and the afterburners are ignited. One more moment they wait, while taking hold of the catapult grip to maintain the throttle position. Then, the moment arrives: the shooter gives the signal and the catapult fires. The

Tomcat shoots off toward the bow as the pilot feels the full effects of three g's. Off the runway and into the darkness of night, they prepare to meet whatever challenge the opposing MiGs might bring.

Commander Billingsley was out front leading Knight Squadron. As the Tomcats neared the rendezvous point, where the Hawkeye had been on patrol well within international waters, the Libyans were already pinging on their radar.

"Prepare to intercept bogeys. No one gets past us tonight, much less anywhere near the fleet. Especially the Backfire. Understood?"

"Roger that, Birddog. Taking defensive counter-air positions now."

The order given, Billingsley pulled the control stick back, causing the Tomcat to climb fast at a speed close to Mach 2. While flying Phantoms over Vietnam, the Commander had learned the powerful advantage of thrust and the ability to climb fast. With this advanced fighter, he could make the jump and be able to make a diving attack.

In the darkness of night, he relied on Ned Landry to keep him abreast of the radar situation. Without the light of the moon over the sea below, little could be seen outside the canopy.

"Lead bogey coming in at four miles, Birddog. Elevation, twenty-thousand. We've got the high ground. Get ready."

Within seconds, Billingsley could see the lights of the approaching lead MiG. *Wait for it...wait for it...*

"In position!"

Both pilot and RIO were immediately hit with heavy g-forces as the Tomcat dove hard in pursuit of their bogey. The lead MiG banked hard to the right as it attempted to evade. All around, Tomcats from the other squadrons were lining up to intercept the rest of the opposing aircraft.

Billingsley kept his eyes locked on the lights of the MiG. He was going to show this Libyan just how pointless it was to try and outfly an F-14 Tomcat and its veteran crew.

Within two minutes, it was over. The MiG had given up trying to shake him and returned to a normal cruising speed. It was time for this one to return back to Tripoli.

"Birddog, this is Greaser. Two of the MiGs are staying close to the Backfire. They're breaking off from the rest of the group but aren't directly heading for *Nimitz*."

"Roger that. Anyone not assisting with an interception will pursue the Backfire and its escorts. I'll join you as soon as this guy turns back."

What game are you guys playing? Another mock attack? If so, why fly the Backfire, your carrier killer, away from Nimitz?

Billingsley's concerns became heightened as the rest of the MiGs, even though intercepted and held off from reaching Task Force 60, had yet to return to their base. *It's like you're trying to distract us. But why?*

Finally, the lead MiG Billingsley had tangled with carefully turned and headed back to the coast. Seven other MiG aircraft did likewise, allowing the leader of Knight Squadron to race toward the mysterious Backfire and its accompanying escorts.

"Birddog, we've intercepted the escort bogeys, but they won't let us get near the Backfire.

"Size up the target. Prepare your phoenix missiles just in case there's...."

"Woah!" Landry exclaimed as he looked up from his radar. "You see that?"

"Birddog, the Backfire appears to be stalling. It's going down!"

The tension was building throughout the command center. The ops team continued moving through the camp buildings. *But what for?* Davis felt it. *Something had gone wrong. But what?*

Behind her, Ashcroft was pacing the room. He tried to pop a pill discretely, but Skylar noticed. "Boss, why don't you sit down? You can't do anything now. It's out of all our hands."

The DDI ignored him, though, and kept on as he was.

"Come on, guys, it's time to wrap this up," Clark barked out loud.

"O'Neil to ops command. Come in," the voice coming through the static over the sound system in the room. It was Clark, steamed at being the head of Operations yet mysteriously left in the dark on this mission and needing to save face, who took the lead.

"O'Neil, this is ops. What's the situation?"

"All opposition eliminated. However, the target has not been found. I repeat, the target has not been found."

"Sir!"

Davis ran to a white-faced Ashcroft, now on the floor, both hands gripping his chest. "Somebody get a paramedic in here now!"

They flew through the rising smoke while scanning the sea below as best they could.

"Did anyone get out?"

"Not sure. There's a ship less than a mile out from here. A cargo ship, we likely cataloged it earlier. If anyone did survive, I imagine they'll try to flag them down. That plane's wing, though. It exploded out of nowhere. Are we sure none of us is responsible for downing it?"

"No indication it was one of ours."

The two Tomcat fighters did a low flyby of the area twice to no avail before heading back. The two escort MiG's did the same.

Only under the cover of darkness did they miss the figures clutching to the edge of a flotation device. The three survivors watched as the approaching cargo ship came closer, waiting until it was close enough to signal with a waterproof flashlight they carried.

The crewmembers of the *Phaedra* saw the signal and alerted the wheelhouse. The ship carefully edged near them. A lifeboat was then hastily lowered and sent out to rescue the crash survivors. Once aboard, almost all the crew looked on in amazement at the men of the Backfire, which only minutes before thundered above at twenty thousand feet.

They were soon brought to the bridge. "I'm Major Faruk Osman of the Defense Ministry," the shortest of the three said wrapped in a blanket. "I've come to inspect your cargo. Where is General Zhukov?"

"I'm right here," the General answered as he approached them. "I see you brought a friend of mine. How was the flight?"

Konstantin Boytsov stepped forward from behind Major Osman and the pilot of the Backfire. "It has been a long time since I've been required to use a parachute, my friend. Much less be ejected from a plane along with my seat."

"All part of the act. Did they take it?"

"It's too early to tell for sure," Boytsov answered, "but I believe they did. The Americans will have a hard time believing the Libyans would purposely crash a bomber into the sea. Now, shall we let Major Osman begin the inspection?"

"Yes. The sooner the inspection, the sooner we can complete this deal."

Billingsley's F-14 hit the third hook on its landing aboard the *Nimitz*. As Squadron Commander, he made a bee-line to the Bridge where the Admiral was waiting for a full report.

"Well, Commander, what exactly happened out there?" Rear Admiral Truett spoke as he turned from a table covered with charts. "Did you see if the crew of the Backfire ejected or not?"

"No, sir. In the dark, I couldn't tell one way or the other. We flew near the crash site for several minutes but didn't even spot a flare. There was, however, a ship in the area."

"*Phaedra*. Yes, the same one we spotted earlier this week. I know we can't keep tabs on them all, but just in case...."

"Yes sir, I'll see that we position a recon plane on it."

"There weren't any signs the Backfire was having problems before it went down?"

"Not that we could see. We can review the fighter cameras, though."

The Rear Admiral nodded and dismissed the Squadron Commander. He took about thirty seconds to think out what he'd report back to the Theatre Commander. Even if none of his men had taken a shot at the Libyan planes, there still could be diplomatic issues. *And just why are we keeping tabs on all these cargo ships anyhow?* If he'd known the reason, he would've found something more to sweat about than diplomatic niceties.

CHAPTER 36

Ashcroft was pronounced dead shortly after the paramedics arrived. A lifetime of carrying the weight of the Agency's intelligence division on his shoulders had finally caught up with him. The following morning, the seventh floor was hushed in a quiet reverence. For Davis, it was but another loss compounded by the failure to get Boytsov.

Word had traveled quickly: Skylar was to be named acting DDI for the time being. A few supposed the promotion would likely become permanent.

The lingering questions seemed only to multiply and intensify. *Where'd Boytsov gone to? Did Benny pass me bad intel? Who really is the mole? Had Ashcroft uncovered anything else? Would her family ever be safe without federal protection? What was next?*

Davis sat at her desk lost in thought just as a knock came at the door.

"Thought I'd come by to chat," Skylar said as he entered and shut the door behind. "It's awful, just awful what happened. You doing okay?"

"Feels like a punch to the gut, Jack." Davis stared despondently down at her desk. "I learned a lot from him. When it came to working here, the man left it all on the court."

"He meant the world to all of us, Audrey. No doubt about it," Skylar remarked in a chipper manner that grated on Davis. "Unfortunately, we have to move on." *Easy for you to say 'Acting DDI'.* "Which is why I wanted to speak with you. A couple options. Both I think would be great for you. Both I think you'll like. One, you could get out of this windowless space and get back to field training at The Farm. Get some fresh air and stop with the analysis work, if you like."

"And the other option?" she asked, looking up.

"Be the Assistant Deputy Director of Intelligence. I can make it happen once I get this job on a permanent basis."

"But Camp 47…"

"What about it? So Boytsov wasn't there. We still bagged some bad guys who would've caused trouble one day or another." Davis knew that opinion wasn't widely shared within their intelligence community. Those who knew Ashcroft leaned on her analysis for targeting the camp seemed to universally share the opinion she lacked the brains for intelligence and needed to be moved.

"Why Jack? Why me? I'm not oblivious to what they're saying. Plus, I'd figure you'd have a chip on your shoulder after the secretary incident not long ago.

"Water under the bridge," he said with a wave of his hand. "I don't hold grudges and I can laugh that off. Because I think there's something special about you, Audrey. You know how to think sharp. You've been in the field. Ashcroft saw something in you, and so do I."

It was the way he was looking at her, the same way he looked at her late last year, which made Davis doubt his words. Whatever was going on in that head of Jack Skylar's, she had no idea.

"Let me think about it, Jack. Give me a few days and I'll give you my answer."

"Unscrew the forward panel, please." Major Osman was now on his third hour of inspections. No detail missed his eyes. He asked few questions and made many a comment. The condition of the Oka's propulsion system, wiring, the warheads themselves, etc. Any possible defect which could allow his country to haggle on the price. The Russian renegades grumbled as they did what the Libyan officer asked. Zhukov, meanwhile, said nothing, instead standing at ease waiting alongside Boytsov for the man's final evaluation.

"From what I can tell, General, it would appear that you've successfully avoided any rust from the salt water. Everything appears to be in order. Where might I use a radio?"

"I will escort you to it. I take it we will have a deal?"

"That will be ultimately up to Colonel Gaddafi himself. As for my recommendation, it will be to proceed with the deal and pursue delivery," Osman answered.

"The same for me as well," answered Boytsov.

It was all Zhukov could do to keep from smiling. *This close to a new life, a new future. This close Yakov. All those years, wasting away in that cold mountainous region guarding those weapons of destruction. Serving a failed ideology. It wouldn't be all in vain. If we can just complete the transaction.*

"Come with me then, Major," the General said as he escorted the Libyan to the communications room. "Lieutenant Tamarkin, see that everything is secure on the three Okas."

"It will be done, General," the young officer said with a salute. He turned and began directing the men back toward the missiles. Walking around each of the launchers and inspecting them thoroughly, he began to wonder about the future. He'd receive his own share, a sizeable one at that. It would be enough to start anew. More likely, though, he would continue in service of the man he felt he owed so much. *It would be a much easier life than that of a Soviet Army officer. Still… But no, now is not the time to think of ethics. Besides, Zhukov has done so much for you. How could you refuse him?* Tamarkin's fate was sealed as far as he was concerned, for better or worse.

CHAPTER 37

Bab al-Azizia Compound – Tripoli, Libya

The Defense Minister felt a knot in his stomach as he listened to the orders. He knew the grave risks that were about to be embarked on. It was not within his power, however, to stop it. All he could do was utter the words: "It will be done as you say, Colonel Gaddafi".

Closing the large cedar wood door behind him as he left Gaddafi's presence, the ramifications of the order he'd been given were not lightly felt.

"So you have spoken to him. What did the Colonel say?"

The Defense Minister turned to his top Air Force General. "He's ordered that we finalize the deal and prepare to secure the cargo with our forces."

The General could sense the hesitation and concern in the Minister's voice. "You don't approve?"

"I do as Gaddafi commands. I don't question orders."

The two had now stepped out into an open courtyard on their way back to an armored SUV. Security and Intelligence Director Raza ensured long ago that no listening devices were placed here in the courtyard.

"You were saying?"

The Minister sighed. "A united Arab nation, I support. Standing up to the west and those who tormented us for so many years, I agree with. Obtaining weapons of this magnitude, much less the cost, is one not to be taken lightly."

"So you have concerns but no outright disagreement with them, Defense Minister?" The words sent chills up their spines as they turned to see Director Raza, still beaming from his newfound status as Gaddafi's favored one. The heist's success had not only inflated his stock in the eyes of the Libyan leader but also his own ego and self-esteem. "Don't you see, with even one of them, we finally take our place among the ruling nations? Fear begets respect. That's what the Colonel sees in this. Only with these, purchased with money from our oil, can we begin to craft new trade agreements, receive less pushback from the US, and found a unified Arab state."

"Fear can beget respect, my friend," replied the Defense Minister. "It can also bring forth dangerous actions on both sides. If this deal does go through, what measures can be taken to prevent international panic? Or reckless use of these weapons of mass destruction?"

"Regarding international concern, I leave that to the foreign minister," said Raza before lowering his voice. "Reckless use, well, should these warheads fall under our watchful eyes, I trust we'll be able to act as needed if an issue arises. Mind you now, that stays between us."

"That gives me some relief," the Defense Minister nodded. The Air Force General did likewise. "Thank you, Director Raza."

"I do hear your more underlying concern. It's up to you and me to balance the power of these weapons aboard the *Phaedra* with the inclinations of the Colonel," Raza said as he saw his ride pull up through the main gate behind the Defense Minister's car, not far from where they stood. "Think of the possibilities when we control such devices."

The Minister nodded his head in solemn concession. "Well put. It's good to know that steady hands such as yours are leading our military."

"And steady hands dealing with the Colonel. Do not worry. Despite the American carrier patrolling off the coast and the issues of handling these weapons, we'll be fine."

The three men entered their chauffeured vehicles and headed on their way. Sky-high confidence resting in the heart of one, and a strong dose of caution weighing heavily on the latter two. All, however, believed their goal would soon be achieved: the completion of the heist and the Okas brought onto Libyan soil.

Yet even the most well-thought-out plans created by sound military or intelligence tacticians is destined to encounter the unseen. The same held true in this case. No one had taken into account the Mossad spy, concealed in their midst behind a large marble pillar on the outer edges of the courtyard.

CHAPTER 38

Bar Dayan's first concern was whether anyone had seen her. After realizing she was safe for the moment, her next thought turned to how she could get this information out of the country. *If only there was time to reach Daniel Meir.*

With her movements heavily monitored and ability to leave the compound limited, it would be at least a week before she could make contact with or leave a dead drop for her Mossad handler. Time was ticking. There was now only a matter of days before a sworn enemy of Zionism became a nuclear power. Still standing in the shadows of the courtyard, her mind sifted through a number of ideas. All were risky. Few offered any real chance.

Then, it hit her. *Maybe one in a hundred chances. It just might work, though.*

She hurried from the courtyard, heading toward a lone, grey, rectangular structure just off the rally site. She had access to its door with a set of keys entrusted to her for guard duty. Inside the darkened room were supplies, from bleachers to flood lights to oil drums. Dayan shut the door behind her and pulled out a small flashlight to illuminate the windowless room. Getting down on her knees, the Mossad spy searched the tiled floor carefully before her hand found the latch. Months of exploring Bab al-Azizia Compound and its hidden layers were about to pay off. *Hopefully.*

Lifting up the latch to the dusty trap door, Dayan made her way down a flight of stairs and into a dark tunnel. *Two miles until the roundabout. First turn on the right, and then you'll be there.*

How she hoped no one else was down here tonight. *They had to be at some time or another,* she thought to herself while trying to avoid stepping on the rats scurrying about. She knew the military used some of the tunnels. Others such as this one, however, had become abandoned and forgotten. Dayan could see the remains of running wires connected to bulbs above from the glow of her flashlight. Graffiti in Arabic lined the walls.

Suddenly she tripped, falling on several large rodents. A tail hit her in the face as she felt small but sharp teeth sink into her left hand. It was all she could do not to scream. Getting up, she leaned down to pick up her flashlight when she heard something.

Not now. Please, not now. Holding her breath, she waited and listened. Then she heard it once more. *Just the cars driving up above, Bar. Relax.* Dayan continued onward. But as much as she tried to stay calm, she remained on edge and fearful of what lay ahead.

Davis paced through the open area of cubicles where the junior analysts worked. Only a few remained by their desks at this late hour. "You still here?" Tyler Baskins, the duty officer for the evening, asked as he noticed her passing by.

"Couple items I need to look over. How's the family?" she asked.

"Doing fine. My oldest is shopping with her mom this weekend for prom dresses, and the youngest is killing it with the finger paintings in pre-school."

"And the other five?"

Baskins chuckled. "That's where having the grandparents only twenty minutes away pays off."

"Never a dull moment in your house, I imagine. Well, I better get back to it. Clark and Skylar are both gone by now, but if you need anything, just holler."

"Will do."

Davis headed on to the breakroom to grab a cup of coffee. Her mind alternated between Skylar's offer earlier in the day and the lingering questions regarding the mole. She decided to spend the night continuing the search, looking over a set of microfilm of the FIELDGOAL operation, the same file loaned to her by Ashcroft hours before his fatal heart attack. Maybe somewhere there was a trinket of information that pointed to Clark, Koufax, or perhaps even Shelby. She still hadn't ruled out Skylar but a deeper dive would have to wait another night. *Long, quiet and uneventful evening. Let's get right to it, Audrey.*

Four times. That was the answer to the trivia question of just how many sorties Bar Dayan had made in a MiG-29. As part of her Amazonian Guard training, she'd been instructed in flying the Soviet-made jet, among other aircraft. Now, looking out to where one sat parked on the edge of a barren runway, the Israeli was prepared to fly the MiG-29 a fifth time.

Dayan emerged from the tunnel in the early hours of morning, just before sunrise through a discrete bunker near a hangar. Covered in soot and grime, she blended into the night, evading the sightline of the patrol guarding the hangar, not far from where half a dozen MiG-29's always sat parked on alert status. If only she could get past a much larger patrol guard blocking her path.

This is madness! The Israeli kept telling herself over and over again. The odds seemed to be ever-shrinking for her to get across the tarmac, into the plane, take off, and still be in the air once she reached the sea. The element of surprise, however, is a funny thing.

Dayan watched for several minutes before getting down the guards' pattern near the aircraft. Every fifty-two seconds, there was but a brief moment when the guard turned from his path losing sight of the runway behind him. Two large cargo pallets, about eight feet high, and standing twenty feet apart marked the distance between her and the nearest MiG she'd commandeer. *Be with me, Adonai.*

Forty-nine. Fifty. Fifty-one. Right on cue, the guard began to turn. *Now.* Quickly, the spy ran towards the first pallet, careful not to kick up anything or shuffle her feet along the pavement. She pressed her back against the first pallet as her heart beat fast. Dayan peered out to see no one had detected her. Waiting once more, she ran again to the second pallet. *One more time.* At exactly fifty-two seconds, she bolted a final time. Reaching a yellow steel ladder, the spy climbed aboard. Her whole body shuddered from a rush of adrenaline as she looked over the controls and attempted to recall all that she'd once learned. With the engine already running, she pulled down the polycarbonate canopy and began to drive the aircraft down the runway.

At first, the guard looked on in disbelief, unsure if perhaps a Libyan pilot had received emergency orders to get to the sky at once. When he saw her dark hair pulled in a bun, he ran to the nearest hangar, yelling for help

Dayan switched on the thrusters and prepared to take off. The aircraft picked up speed, racing down the runway. Soon, she was off the ground as the airfield faded behind her. Looking down, lights twinkled on the grown below before water appeared. *Take a deep breath.* That, of course, reminded her to keep the plane below 10,000 feet lest she suffer hypoxia with no air mask. It seemed almost surreal to be flying after so long away from behind the controls. Dayan did her best to contain her nervous and excited energy. There was nothing quite like flying solo at more than 600 kilometers an hour. The speed, tranquility of the skies and solitude would always have a strong appeal to her. Now, she was combining that love of flying with the very real need to escape the enemy nation at once and find the American aircraft carrier somewhere out at sea.

You don't even know where this aircraft carrier is. Only that it's somewhere out in the Gulf. Flying east from Tripoli and locating the Americans wouldn't be an easy task. The NO19 radar installed in the MiG detected only so far as 50 kilometers. It would be at least seven minutes before the plane reached the Gulf and had a shot at finding them. Everything also depended on five incoming aircraft, no doubt part of the group of MiG-29's on stand-by alert. She figured on having roughly an eight-minute lead on them. Just barely out of range of their air-to-air missile capabilities, for now.

Nearing the edge of the Gulf, Dayan decided to go with a hunch. She knew the Americans viewed the international boundary to be twelve nautical miles and knew from intel debriefings for Gaddafi that they were in the area now. In her mind, they'd likely be somewhere between the international boundary and the sixty-two-mile mark Libya argued was its sovereign territory. With that knowledge, she headed to the sweet spot of thirty seven miles or so off the coast and hope to catch the carrier on her radar.

CHAPTER 39

Time was of the essence. Reaching the Gulf, Dayan noted the position of the five MiGs. *They're getting closer.* She took stock once more of the situation. Her aircraft was still far enough out of the reach of any incoming Libyan jet's air-to-air missiles. But at the current rate they were gaining on her, that certainty wouldn't last long. *Head in a straight line between the international boundary and Gaddafi's declared one. Radar has to pick it up.*

It paid off. Soon, her radar found Task Force 60. With it came several Tomcats heading her way.

Now's a good a time as any to let them know. She switched on the radio and tuned it to a general frequency that someone among the American planes and ships would be bound to hear. "This is an Israeli intelligence officer seeking permission to land aboard your aircraft carrier. I'm being pursued by at least five Libyan fighters. Repeat, seeking permission to land."

"Intelligence officer," came a quick reply. "Turn back at once, or we'll be forced to open fire."

"Look, this isn't some sort of a ruse. I'm a Mossad agent, on the run from Colonel Gaddafi with intelligence of great value. I…"

"Oh, really? If you're Israeli, what are you doing in that plane?"

"The case officer I report to is unable to be reached soon enough," Dayan replied, doing her best not to get flustered. "I'm serious. I have vital intelligence for both your country and mine, but there are several Libyans on my tail."

Just as she finished speaking, two F-14 Tomcats did a hard and fast flyby, roaring above her cockpit. Dayan did her best to keep her agitation in check, hoping someone would take her seriously.

"They say they're what?" Rear Admiral Truett scratched his balding head in confusion. "I'm going to need more than that. For all we know, it could be a trick ambush with those other incoming MiGs bringing the firepower. Someone get me EUCOM. Ask this pilot just what sort of 'vital intelligence' she has."

It took two minutes to track down the Commander-in-Chief of the US European Command at Patch Barracks in Stuttgart-Vaihingen, Germany. Just as perplexed at the situation as the Rear Admiral, he ordered his subordinate to patch in the Central Intelligence Agency, in case they could verify anything in the mystery flyer's story.

"Alright, what intel do you have that's so vital?" the pilot asked as his F-14 kept close on top of Dayan's MiG.

"Are you crazy? I'm not going to relay this over an unsecure frequency! I need to land this instant."

"You try, and you'll be shot down instantly."

Dayan swore under her breath. The Libyan fighters were now within firing range. Any second they could launch a homing missile on her plane. *Give them something they can verify.*

216

"Audrey! Pick up Line 5. Call from EUCOM."

Davis looked at the out-of-breath duty officer. "What?" she asked with a confused expression.

"Something important. Look, everyone's gone home. From where I'm standing, you're next in line at the moment. Besides, Skylar gave orders to go to you if anything comes up while you're still here."

Jack must be serious about that offer. She picked up the phone instantly. "This is Audrey Davis."

"Ms. Davis, this is General Gavin, Commander-in-Chief of EUCOM. Our carrier in the Gulf of Sidra, USS *Nimitz*, has intercepted a Libyan MiG-29. The pilot is claiming to be an Israeli with vital intel for our country and their own. You're patched into a call now with the commanding officer of Task Force 60, Rear Admiral Truett."

"General Gavin," Truett spoke up. "The MiG pilot won't say what the intel is. They've expressed concern about an approaching group of five other MiGs. For all we know, it could be a trap. I don't like it one bit."

Both Gavin and Truett recalled the previous years of Libya challenging their right to the Gulf within international waters, as well as the aftermath of Operation El Dorado not even two years prior. Combine that with the recent test of Task Force 60's aerial defense by ten MiGs, and there was enough real concern for a surprise attack.

"Hold on. General Gavin, the pilot just said: 'Caleb'. That's it, just one word."

Instantly, the recall of the long-ago code word struck Davis. *The code word for Cooper's agents within Gaddafi's security detail. But how? What if the Libyans got that out of Omar years ago and this is all a trick? Or...this could be the Mossad asset who tipped us about the camp. Same camp that led to the failed mission to catch Boytsov. But they still pinpointed a site where terrorists and commandos were being trained. That's something too valuable for the Libyans feed to us by way of a double agent. No, Mossad must've instructed this woman about the history of the mission and told her the code word. Trust your instinct, Audrey.* "General Gavin, I can't explain, but somehow, you've got to bring this person in."

"Truett, give the plane permission to land aboard *Nimitz,* but if it makes one false move, eliminate it. That's an order."

"Yes, sir."

"Davis, once we get the pilot out, we'll be keeping them in the brig for further questioning."

CHAPTER 40

"It's all here. Jack, it's surreal. This woman, Bar Dayan, plays the part of one of the Colonel's select female bodyguards and gets her intel straight from the source."

Skylar kept his gaze focused on another memo. "She's also the one who told us it was Camp 47."

Davis was caught off-guard by the remark. "I thought you said we still bagged some bad guys who would've caused trouble?

"I did. However, while the Israeli most likely believed she was passing on good intel, the fact remains that it wasn't. Why? I don't know. What I do know is I'm not going to stick my neck out less than a week into this gig for the word of an agent that's already been off."

"But if you read what she's said in the transcript. Look, Boytsov moved. According to the post-op report, the site was a commando/terror training camp. He just wasn't there at that exact moment. Now she's got the scoop on what both us and the Soviets have been on the edge of our seats looking for. She's given us the name of the ship, and the Navy has even verified it's in the area. Why wouldn't we push this news up to the top?"

"Like I said, the agent has already been off considerably." Skylar could sense he needed to shift tactics. "Audrey, did you ever think we'd make it this far? Out of anyone in this building, after all those years spent in Moscow doing what you did, you deserve this. You're a top-notch analyst. One day, you and I will have enough capital to take a few risks. Maybe, for now, we have the Navy do a few flyovers over this cargo ship to check it out."

"A few flyovers?" she asked.

"Yes. Just the right amount of due diligence needed for this situation."

"So you're not going to report this to Director Webster then?"

"No, Audrey, I'm not. Besides, he's in South Korea till the end of the week. Enough of this. Look, let's hit reset and get lunch. I know a good spot...."

Davis's blood was boiling. She didn't know what to think of Skylar or whether he ever really trusted her analysis and critical thinking to begin with. This bombshell intel was too big to ignore. Someone needed to be told and she knew exactly who.

"That's fine, Jack. I can meet you there. Got an errand I need to run first, though."

Within three minutes, Davis was outside the CIA building as her FBI agent driver swung the car around and pulled up to the curb. "Glenn," she said as she hopped into the shotgun seat. "I need you to start driving to DC. We're going to go see someone."

"Who?"

"The National Security Advisor."

CHAPTER 41

Washington DC.

Davis's palms were sweating profusely as the car turned off Pennsylvania Avenue and pulled up to the gate of the White House. It was only the second time she'd been here. Never had she imagined her next visit would have so much at stake.

"Assistant to Acting Deputy Director of Intelligence, Audrey Davis," she answered as she handed the guard her driver's license and ID badge. *Well, that seems to be the title for the moment.* "Here to see the National Security Advisor."

"Do you have an appointment with him?"

"No, but it's important he see me."

The guard gave no expression of what he thought of the surprise visitor, instead pointing out where to park. Coming through the east entrance, she went through the security and metal detectors before she was given further directions. Throughout her decade spent in Moscow among the elite and driving forces of the Kremlin, she'd always maintained a coolness that transcended her cover. Now, she was in awe of the halls marking her nation's history as she walked toward the most significant section of the building: the West Wing.

Seeing the name she was looking for engraved on a small gold-plated sign, she entered through an open door to a waiting area. A secretary sat behind a small desk.

"What can I do for you today?"

"I'm here to see General Powell."

"And you are?" the middle-aged woman asked, curious as to who thought they were important enough to interrupt the schedule of a three-star general and the President's own Senate-appointed advisor.

"I'm the assistant to the Acting Deputy Director of Intelligence. I need five minutes of the General's time."

"I'm afraid he's busy this morning. Maybe if you schedule an appointment, you could come back...."

"It's a national security matter! Ma'am, please. I wouldn't be showing up like this unless it was of vital importance."

"Look, you can't just...."

A door swung open causing both to shift their gaze. Standing six-foot-two, it was hard to miss him, even without the uniform. "Margaret," spoke General Colin Powell, National Security Advisor. "What does my schedule look like after this meeting?"

"Conference call with the joints chiefs of..."

"General, I'm CIA and I need to speak with you now." The less-than-graceful words fell out of Davis's mouth before she could think.

"Okay," Powell replied as he adjusted his large gold-rimmed glasses. "Who are you again?"

"Audrey Davis. I worked with Trent Ashcroft. I'm now assisting the Acting Deputy Director of Intelligence."

"Walk with me." Powell continued on towards the hallway as Davis hurried alongside.

"General, we've just gained intel on the whereabouts of Zhukov and the missing Okas. The Mossad spy that Task Force 60 picked up worked undercover as a bodyguard for Gaddafi. The Libyans are the buyers, sir, and the weapons are aboard a Cypriot cargo ship called the *Phaedra*."

"If true, we might be able to do something about it," the National Security Advisor replied. The two moved past the main lobby and now were just outside the Director of Communications' office. Staffers of various levels of importance moved alongside them to and fro. "But your source, is it the same one who gave us the earlier information?"

Not again. Davis was dreading where this might go, or rather, end. "Yes, General, it is."

"Tell me, why are you the one briefing me on this? Why not the Director or your boss?"

"The Director is out of the country and, frankly, the Acting Deputy Director of Intelligence doesn't think the source is reliable."

"What you're doing is insubordination. Cut and dry. There'd better be a good reason, Ms. Davis."

"General, I know I'm out of my depth and don't know everything. But I know this: I took an oath fourteen years ago to protect my country. I trust the source and believe dismissing and burying the intel would be a grave mistake. Because of that, I'm here to present *all* the information, leaving it to you to make the call you see fit."

"Even if the decision is not to take action on this? Even if I recommend you be fired for what you're doing now?

"Sir, absolutely," she answered without missing a beat.

They reached the outside of the Cabinet Room and made a right turn at the corner. Standing outside a door opposite the Roosevelt Room, Powell stopped and pulled Davis aside. "Assistants to acting deputies don't normally come to the White House uninvited and leapfrog their direct reports. Then again, your background isn't normal."

"General?"

"I've read your file. A bit of a renegade. Whenever you've put it all on the line, though, you've been proven right and ended up saving the day." Powell continued walking several feet to another open door, leaving Davis standing alone with a confused look. He turned back. "You coming?"

"Where to?"

Powell gave no answer. He wasn't going to ask twice. Davis followed. Entering another room, they passed a receptionist's desk and stood before a door guarded by a young, tough-looking Marine in full-dress uniform.

"He's ready to see you now," spoke a middle-aged woman from behind the desk.

Watching the Marine reach to open the door, the realization suddenly struck Davis. She looked up to Powell, expecting to get some sort of advice. There was none.

"Let's go," was all he said as the two entered the Oval Office.

CHAPTER 42

"Mom? What are you doing here?" Sergei stood at the door of his mother's bedroom with a look of confusion. Just home from school, he didn't expect to see her of all people at this early of an hour. Setting down the football he was carrying, he plopped down on the bed and peered into the small carry-on suitcase that lay open.

"Work, Sergei. I'm flying out tonight. Hand me that sweater, please."

"But where to?" he asked again as he handed her the black turtleneck. "Can't I come?"

Davis shook her head. "I'm sorry, honey. You know how we've talked about what I do every day, how I work to protect the country and keep it safe but have to keep some things secret. This is one of those times. I'll be back soon. Just a few days and I'll be home next week. Mary is returning to duty later this afternoon and will be here."

"You're leaving?" It was now Nikita at the doorway. She could tell from his expression and shaky tone that he was already upset. "But Mom, we need you! Please don't go. Please."

"I have to, son." *This isn't how I wanted to leave.* "It's part of my job," she answered while continuing to pack, lest she became emotional.

"Will you be safe? You won't... won't..." the younger son's voice cracked as his head shifted downward.

"Hey now, come here, Sergei," Davis said as she set down her toiletry bag and wrapped an arm around him. "I'm coming back. I mean it."

"You have to!" Tears began to stream down his face. "Promise us."

"Please, Mom," Nikita spoke up. Promise us, or don't go. *Papa* went off to work and never came back." He began to choke up. "Not you too. Not you. I don't want to lose you. Can't you find another job? We'll still be happy, even if you make less. We're fine if we don't have a big home."

It's come full circle. Dad twenty years ago. Now my own children. I can't let them go through what I did.

"Both of you, listen to me. I love you. So much. More than you'll ever know. I give you both my word: I will return home safe. I promise."

All three came in for a family hug, and she kissed them both. Nothing on earth could break the bond she had with each of her sons. For all the pain, difficulty, and grief that she'd endured during her career of espionage and analysis, these two had been the shining bright spot. It was for them that she'd complete the mission and return home once more.

Darkness had begun to fall as the C-130 Navy plane warmed up on the runway at Andrews Air Force Base. Their flight time would be nearly fifteen hours. Non-stop. As Davis got out of her vehicle, her plainclothes attire stood in stark contrast to the regulation olive-green flight suits of the crew, her adrenaline was pumping. The sort of energy that always seems to appear at the start of a mission. It gives no such indication how everything will turn out, only a strong aroma of the significance of what is about to take place.

Climbing aboard the aircraft, Davis was greeted by a crew member before taking a seat. Once settled, she reached into her bag and removed a brown folder marked Operation Silent Cyclone. *Thirty-six hours from when I reach the carrier. Barely enough time to make this work. I can only imagine what it's like right now at Virginia Beach. Those guys must be moving fast.*

It impressed Davis just how quickly this had come together. The President and the National Security Advisor could be thanked for that one. It was now her job to see that the capture of the Okas and the rogue Russian General succeeded, a responsibility that weighed upon her heavily. Whatever had gone wrong during the strike against Camp 47, this was a chance to redeem herself as a valued member of the CIA.

Davis began to review the operation file when a name caught her eye. *Commander Kyle Billingsley, squadron commander of the Knights with Task Force 60. Billingsley? The Navy guy from the White House party last December. What are the odds?*

CHAPTER 43

The *Phaedra*

Tamarkin watched and listened to Boytsov with complete awe. There alone on the top deck, looking out towards the east while clutching the railing, the former *Spetsnaz* commando sang the ballad. His deep baritone voice intoned each verse with a mournful cry. The man was a mystery to the Lieutenant. Oh, Zhukov had explained to him that the stranger was a Russian responsible for brokering the deal that allowed them to sell their stolen missiles to Libya. The rest, however, remained unknown. Silent, Tamarkin stood some feet away as he listened to the words sung with passion.

When he'd finished, Boytsov turned around. "You've been there quite a while."

Tamarkin wasn't sure, but in the moonlit evening, he thought he saw more than one tear that had streamed down the hardened man's face. "That song. I've never heard it before."

"Every young Russian should be taught that song. *On The Nameless Height*. It tells the true story of a soldier during the Great Patriotic War.

Eighteen men, brothers in arms, left to defend a hill with no meaningful name near a town with no meaningful name as well. All but three die. For what? The *Rodina*? Yes, those were the wretched Nazis they were fighting. But let me tell you, Lieutenant, the men pulling the levers in the Kremlin could care less if we die for a piece of land or cause with no real significance. We're mere pawns to them. But you understand this. You saw the light yourself, I take it, when you helped steal those three warheads below deck."

Tamarkin nodded. "Those men showed such bravery. Perhaps their sacrifice saved others?"

"Was their position even strategically important?" replied Boytsov. "More lives may have been lost than if they had pulled back and fought another day. All to appease bureaucrats with little empathy for the sacrifice of the proletariat.

"It is better to do as we are now, than to follow fools blindly and die on a nameless height."

"Care for some?" Tamarkin held out a flask. He liked this strange comrade. The interaction had allowed him to break formality. Boytsov gladly accepted and took a swig.

"Where did you come by such a fine label of vodka? Where I've been the last few years has kept me from tasting the drink of my people."

Tamarkin gave a shrug. "The General would get it back in Sochi. I stored a bottle of the stuff in my gear when we left our home base." Boytsov handed back the flask and the young officer took a sip. "Did you fight in Afghanistan?"

"*Nyet.* But I did see action."

"Where?"

Boytsov looked at the young man before him. Memories, subsided momentarily by drink, returned like the roaring tide. The images of his comrades, his brothers in arms, would never leave him. No amount of revenge exacted would erase the painful recall, nor rectify tainted orders given and so blindly followed. Turning inward, he knew he was but an empty man without an answer to his hurt.

"Moscow," he replied. "On a snowy street in Moscow."

CHAPTER 44

U.S.S. Nimitz

The C-130 touched down on the deck of the *Nimitz* at mid-afternoon. As Davis exited the plane, she stopped for a moment taking in the sight of crewmen hustling around and Tomcats, Intruders, Vikings and Hawkeyes moving about. Just off deck, she could see several cruisers and destroyers on the both port and starboard sides of the ship.

"First time aboard a carrier?" a khaki-attired officer asked.

"It is," she nodded. "Pretty impressive."

"Most definitely so. Come on, the Rear Admiral's been expecting you."

Davis grabbed her bag and followed behind as they headed below to the gallery deck. Entering the stateroom, Rear Admiral Truett stood up from his leather swivel chair and welcomed her.

"Good to meet you, Ms. Davis," he said, shaking her hand. "We owe you a big thanks for confirming just who was really flying that MiG. That situation would likely have turned tragic had it not been for you."

"Thank you, Admiral," Davis replied. "Where is she now?"

"In the infirmary. It was a bit of a bumpy landing, her first time on a carrier. We gave her instruction over the radio and had the barricade raised. All things considered, she did well. Suffered only minor injuries. The doctor says she'll be fine but wanted to keep her there for observation. I've got an armed guard standing outside. You're welcome to see her as soon as you'd like."

"I'll do that as soon as we finish up here."

"Excellent." Truett then shifted gears. "We've got a Hawkeye keeping radar tabs from a safe distance on the *Phaedra*. The SEAL Team responsible for the boarding already has their plans drawn up. My Air Commander and I have our own orders. As I understand, you'll be joining the SEALs?"

"That's correct."

Truett looked at the woman before him, the wheels in his head turning. Finally, he shook his head.

"Part of me wants to say a woman like you shouldn't be putting herself in harm's way. Then again, I sense you've been in spots like this before. Maybe a little different, but still. Just be safe."

Davis simply nodded. *If only you knew all I've been through.* "I understand from the Operations file that you and your Air Command have been given latitude in crafting the airborne strategy. What should we expect?"

"Task Force 60 will disable the ship by air attack and set up a perimeter. If the Libyans make a move to reach the ship, we have orders to engage. Under no circumstances is the ship to reach harbor or communicate with the Libyan Air Force. If you get aboard and discover they've radioed them, we need you to alert the Squadron Commander and us at once."

"Captain Billingsley?"

"I see you've read through the file. Well, we can talk more later once the SEALs arrive. Welcome aboard, Ms. Davis. Please let me know if there's anything I can do."

CHAPTER 45

After getting lost twice down numerous corridors and wells, Davis finally located the infirmary on the third deck. Showing her credentials to the posted guard, she entered and was directed by a corpsman to an isolated cot cordoned off by curtains. There lay resting asleep was Bar Dayan. Davis stood at the edge of the cot for a moment, pondering just how consequential this mystery woman had been the last few weeks for her country.

Dayan's eyes began to open just then, sensing the presence of someone standing close by. "Mossad says hello," Davis began.

"Who…who are you?" the Israeli asked as she attempted to shake off the grogginess.

"A friend from Langley." Davis took a step closer to the side of the bed. "And let me tell you we have—or at least I have—been hanging on every bit of intel you've been passing along."

"I didn't know my reports were being sent to you Americans. Well, I'm glad someone was listening. If not, your Tomcats would've splattered me across the sky."

"That makes two of us. As soon as this is over, we'll notify Tel Aviv that you're safe and get you back home. Right now, though, we're preparing an operation against a certain cargo ship. Communications are blacked out and no one's allowed to leave. For now, is there anything we can get you?"

"Chocolate rugelach from Marzipan Bakery would be nice," Dayan cracked with a smile.

"I'll see what sweets I can find in the galley then."

Dayan began to stir in bed. Davis could see she was deciding whether or not to say something.

"I know you've got questions to ask. I imagine you're going to say as a citizen of a friendly nation, I'm not necessarily forced to answer them."

"Something like that, yes," Davis replied.

Dayan attempted to sit up, drawing closer to Davis. Davis could see the look of concern on the Mossad spy's face.

"If it relates to the upcoming operation your military has planned, I'll answer what I can. There is, however, another matter not related to missiles or rogue generals. You saved my life by intervening yesterday. Now I feel led to return the favor."

The sun was just beginning to rise early the next morning as Davis looked from the main hangar deck toward the south. Cup of coffee in one hand, she zipped up her bomber jacket with the other as the winds blew mercilessly. *Less than twenty-four hours to go.*

Just when did America first get pulled into this corner of the world? It stretched back farther in time than Gaddafi or the Cold War. It went back to the days of Thomas Jefferson and the Barbary Wars. Men such as the fearless Decatur and O'Bannon inspired the opening stanza of the Marine Corps Hymn, "From the Halls of Montezuma to the Shores of

Tripoli". It was they who made history here on both the high seas and coasts of Libya. Now, it was about to be made here again. *Only it wouldn't. The world will never know. If it's a successful operation, at least.*

"I always like to look out from here at daybreak too." Davis turned to her right and saw Commander Kyle Billingsley staring out onto the vast sea.

"Commander Billingsley, it's good to see you again. Been a while since that dance at the White House dinner party."

"It has at that," he replied. "Though I wish we were meeting again under better conditions." Out in the open hangar, Billingsley decided it best not to linger on the subject for now and shifted gears. "How are you getting along so far aboard the *Nimitz*?"

"When I'm not lost and asking for directions, I'm in my stateroom reading and analyzing."

"Still making a point of 'knowing a little bit about everything', I see," he said with a chuckle. "Well, have you had breakfast yet? If not, come join me in the Dirty Shirt."

"The what?"

"Oh, sorry. It's the galley and wardroom area for the air wing. We call it that because the menus are a bit informal and flight suits and deck work gear are allowed. It's as good a breakfast as you'll ever find aboard this floating city."

"Sure. I'm game, Commander."

The two headed up to the gallery deck and went through the buffet line. After grabbing a plate of hash browns, two scrambled eggs and a biscuit with honey, Davis followed Billingsley over to the Knight's squadron table.

Two pilots who'd already been there a while got up, leaving the spy and the squadron commander free to talk amongst themselves. Davis began by asking Billingsley just how he'd decided on a flying career, which led to his life story. A kid growing up near Cape Canaveral watching rockets soar, he dreamed of soaring to the heavens as well. He graduated from ROTC at Florida State, became a naval officer, learned to fly and was sent to Vietnam. The rest of course was history for the respected Navy aviator. When the conversation shifted to Billingsley's classmate at Annapolis, she began to dread the question she knew he would ask.

"How's Jack doing, by the way? You two still seeing each other?"

"Your old friend decided to have, well, shall we say a second date there that night. No, we're just colleagues now."

"Really?" Billingsley instantly perked up.

"Do your jets always get revved that fast, Commander?"

Billingsley gave a mischievous grin while trying to decide whether it'd be appropriate to respond with what he was thinking. "There are ways of finding out. But on another note, I thought I told you to call me Kyle the first time we met."

"Okay, Kyle. Well, Jack's moved up the ladder recently, there was a sudden death and he's now Acting DDI."

"Does he know you're here?"

Davis nodded. "I haven't spoken to him, but I imagine he does by now. Let me ask you a question: you spent four years with the guy at Annapolis, so what do you think he's thinking right now?"

"Oh gosh, pretty ticked-off most likely. The man always wants to be in the know. Don't get me wrong. I like Jack. He was a good midshipman, but he doesn't like being left on the outside. He thrives on being part of the action. The only reason I believe he left the Navy was because he thought there was even more excitement and thrills in this path he chose. But then again, maybe that holds true to most of you spy types."

The conversation continued a bit longer. Davis liked the squadron commander of the Knights. Her impression of him was a straight-talking aviator with just the right amount of bravado and charm. She appreciated how he didn't attempt to pry for the details of Silent Cyclone not privy to him. He'd likely only been told that a ship needed to be disabled and boarded before reaching Libyan waters, with nothing said about its cargo or the notoriety of the men aboard. The man was a true professional. When the time came the following day, she knew without a doubt their air support would be top-notch.

"I'd best be going," Billingsley said as he noticed a clock nearby. "I'll see you later in the briefing room?"

"Yes sir. Be there at 1600," she answered, getting up from the table.

The Commander got up as well but then stopped. His eyes expressed serious concern. "Audrey, one more thing."

"Yeah?"

"No matter what happens, I mean it, just radio us, and we'll have your back."

CHAPTER 46

The ticking sound of the wristwatch reverberated loudly throughout the lonely cabin. Zhukov checked to see the time as he sat atop his cot. Less than eight hours.

Sleep had been impossible to come by. Nearly all of his military career had been spent maintaining missiles and awaiting orders to unleash the wrath of some of the most destructive weapons on earth. For the first time, he was about to let them go.

Regrets? You've done your job, Yakov. Watched as others higher up than you, the bureaucrats and nomenklatura, profit off of others' misery. It's your turn now to have a better life. Regrets? Only about waiting this long.

A knock came at the door. "Come in," Zhukov answered.

"General Zhukov, my country's navy will have an escort to meet us soon at the rendezvous point," said Major Osman. "We'll have two platoons come aboard to secure the ship and then bring you into the harbor."

"That was not part of the plan. No one comes aboard without my consent. The transfer will happen only right offshore. You'll have three men, unarmed, come on ship to drive the Okas off. All of which will happen only after the funds have been transferred in full. Is that understood, Major Osman?"

"I cannot...."

"No Major, you can, or I shall speak to my comrade, Boytsov. Or dare I remind you of what I have aboard this ship?"

"I will let my superiors know. Is there anything else, General Zhukov?"

The General nodded to the door. "That will be all."

Davis finally fell asleep. Before turning out the light in her private quarters, she sat on the edge of the bed. For the second time in only a brief period, her intel analysis would result in men being put in harm's way. Already once, it had ended in failure to capture the target. *Dare it happen again? With so much at stake?*

Then it hit her. *Fear doesn't get a seat at this table.* She would not be moved. Even after the raid on Camp 47. A small but growing faith had been taking root. Now, she leaned into it with everything she had. It was not a faith that all would go as planned in the morning but rather that she would be given the strength to face what lay before her.

Reaching for the switch, Davis turned off the light and lay down. Her eyes soon shut as she tranquilly drifted off, resting until the bedside alarm clock went off at 0300.

CHAPTER 47

"There's something approaching off the starboard side," hollered one of the shipmen looking through a pair of binoculars. "A helicopter?"

Zhukov stood on the bridge, looking out onto the sea. It was not yet dawn There was no sign of their buyers. Then again, they were a bit early.

The sailor at the wheel seemed to be almost trembling as he kept the ship on course. All hands, both on the bridge and in the gangways, appeared uneasy. Those who spoke to one other did so in hushed whispers. The Captain, only hours before in a euphoric trance at the wealth awaiting him in his offshore account, was now on edge.

"Radar on," the Captain ordered. "What's out there?"

The words had barely left his mouth when the roar of F-14's passed over the Cypriot flag cargo ship.

"Evasive maneuvers! Major Osman, get ahold of your military at once!"

"You men," ordered the first mate to several deckhands who appeared barely old enough to drive a car, "Uncover and man the working guns on deck!"

"General, we need to get your men in position to return fire should they board. General?"

During those first seconds of chaos, the mastermind did not flinch. A certain level of coolness seemed to permeate from him. "Lieutenant Tamarkin," he said as he pulled out his silver cigarette case. "A light, please."

Tamarkin himself seemed to be caught off-guard by the man's demeanor. His right hand shook as he held up the lighter.

"Breathe, soldier," he replied before turning towards the Captain. "If they come aboard, then so be it. Let them."

The Captain was flabbergasted. "But General Zhukov…"

"Captain, don't tell me you didn't foresee either the Americans or my former Soviet Red Army interfering with this transaction? You have to have a contingency plan."

"How dare you lecture me at a time like this," the Captain snarled. "Do you even have a plan?"

Boytsov, standing to the side in quiet observation, straightened up as he began to realize what his old comrade had in mind. *A dangerous gamble…*

"Lieutenant, once the American forces board the ship, have the men open the bow doors and deck hatch as planned."

"You don't actually think you can escape in those amphibious launchers?" The Captain shook his head. "They'll cut you down before you even reach the Libyan navy."

Zhukov ignored the remark. There was no point in explaining it to this simple-minded sailor. When the time came, he'd be ready to meet the Americans face-to-face and win.

"Zulu Thirty-One Tango," Billingsley's Radar-Intercept Officer, Ned Landry, called into the microphone attached to his helmet. "There appears to be two 40 mm cannon placements. One on the bow and another on the stern. No other visible signs of resistance on the top deck. Preparing to unleash the M61 guns on the next flyby."

"Roger that, Stetson," radioed Lieutenant Commander Scott Spieth of the SEAL Team aboard the lead chopper. "Appreciate the heads up. Once you take them out, we'll begin boarding."

Billingsley pulled the choke to the right and turned the Tomcat around. As he lined up to attack, he could see that each high-caliber machine gun was now manned. *Still haven't turned out the lights aboard.* Closing in, it was now or never. He squeezed and held the trigger. Just as he did, he saw a bright flash of fire come from one of the gunners.

One of the sailors was securing a hatch atop deck when he watched a rain of 20 mm bullets strike the front of the deck, destroying the attached machine gun and ripping down the ship to the other end. A small fire erupted, caused by a bullet hitting a two-gallon oil can used for deck equipment. He rushed to where the sailor manning the front deck gun once stood, only to realize halfway there that no one could have survived such a hailstorm.

"Captain, I've given the distress signal. They are not far away," Major Osman said, hoping to bring some semblance of calm and order to those on the bridge.

"They better get here quickly," the Captain answered with impatience in his voice. "I've ordered my men to open up our armory and prepare to fight. What? What are you laughing at, General?"

"My apologies, Captain, but—no, I don't apologize. Your men won't stand three minutes up against the trained special forces of the United States military." Zhukov continued to chuckle. "Did you not see what just became of your gunners?"

The Captain's face turned red with anger as he strode towards Zhukov and came within an inch of his face. "Idiot! It's you and your cargo that's brought ruin upon my ship. My men are the only line of defense we have until your buyers arrive! We'll be lucky to survive."

It seemed as if the man of the sea was daring the warrior to laugh once more, daring the man to push him but a little more until he attempted to kill him with his bare hands. Their eyes bored into each other's, neither blinking, neither throwing down the baton just yet. It was Osman who finally broke up the standoff.

"Stop it! Both of you! There is no time for this. We must organize some sort of resistance. Several squadrons of Floggers are on their way as we speak now. If we can just hold on for a little while longer."

"Very well, Major," answered Zhukov before turning to leave the bridge with Boytsov following behind. "You'll find my men and I below deck. When the time comes, you'll hear from me."

"Coward," the word escaping under the breath of the Captain, who then turned to the Libyan officer. "You say Floggers? What else?"

Major Osman nodded. "MiG-23 Floggers. They'll arrive first, followed by three frigates and a half a dozen patrol boats." They could both see from the bridge that the American choppers now getting closer. "Hold until relieved. That's all we can do now."

"Ship is all yours, boys," said Billingsley as he checked his rearview and was satisfied with his work on the *Phaedra*. "We'll begin setting up our no-fly zone as planned."

The pilot of the chopper took note. "Prepare to board," he announced to the SEALs waiting anxiously, as well as one Audrey Davis.

It was moments like these that the U.S. Navy SEALs of SBT-20 trained for. Skilled in Visit, Board, Search, and Seizure operations, or VBSS for short, they trained daily as part of Naval Special Warfare Group Four in Little Creek, Virginia.

An officer named Tannehill sat next to her clutching an M4A1 carbine and noted the intense look on her face. "Don't worry. You'll have two SEAL team platoons in front of you the entire time." You're the one with the Agency, aren't you?"

Davis nodded. "Yeah."

"You know how to use that thing?" the officer asked, pointing to her sidearm.

"Let's just say I've had an occasion or two to practice with it."

The officer nodded before looking out as they hovered over the cargo ship. A gunner had the side door open, scanning for any electronic or heat wave signals indicating the use of a SAM rocket launcher. Once satisfied everything was clear, the pilot quickly made way for the ship's helipad and began circling downard.

"Let's go! Go! Go! Go!"

The special operations team, some of America's most physically fit and well-trained men, jumped out and onto the pad. Each held their gun in ready position, moving with speed away from the chopper. Davis was the second to last to get out. Once all were aboard and their ride took off, another chopper carrying a second platoon was already preparing to land.

"This is Birddog, incoming bogies. Repeat, incoming bogies. We'll hold them back. Please use caution."

Davis felt a knot in her stomach as she heard those words. For a brief moment, she thought about Nikita and Sergei. However, there was no time to lose as the American forces rushed forth to secure the *Phaedra* and capture its deadly cargo.

The entire Knights squadron was in the air, along with two full squadrons of F/A-18 Hornets, as the numerous bogies lit up every Radar Intercept Officer's screen. If this was the real deal, it would be the third time in less than seven years that Task Force 60 would face off against Libyan forces.

"Birddog, I've got at least thirty bogies coming up from the south, range fifteen miles at nine thousand," Stetson noted.

"If I knew for sure what they were up to, we'd launch all our Phoenix missiles now," Billingsley growled. "When they get within two miles, if you see a single Atoll launch from those MiG's, we attack."

"Might need to keep some of our powder dry. Appears they've got a flotilla of patrol boats behind them. Probably a corvette or two thrown in."

"Just be ready for anything, Stetson." The squadron commander then radioed the rest of his men. "This is Birddog. Maintain defensive perimeter in a racetrack pattern. Do not engage with bogies unless fired upon. Repeat, do not engage unless fired upon. Under no circumstances can they reach the *Phaedra*. Get below Angels Five," Billingsley noted, referring to five thousand feet of altitude. "We're going to stay in their blind spot."

"Just keep staying behind me," Tannehill turned and spoke to Davis as they prepared to enter a hatchway. Beads of sweat trickled down her forehead. The SEAL team platoon she'd come with, consisting of sixteen operators, had now broken off into two eight-man squads to fan out and secure both ends of the vessel. The squad she was with now treaded slowly down the passageway, ready for anything, including the sudden loss of light throughout the ship.

"Get ready," muttered the veteran SEAL under his breath.

A bright burst of light immediately erupted from up ahead. Davis, still adjusting to the dark, was momentarily blinded. The SEALs, using the latest cutting-edge night-vision technology, were better prepared. They returned the gunfire with a hailstorm of their own.

"This is squad one. Gunfire inside the ship. We've encountered resistance."

When her eyes had finally adjusted, Davis looked down and saw two crew members lying on the floor. Their AK-47 rifles, smoke still coming from the barrels, rested beside them. The squad continued on. Moments later, radio chatter announced a firefight at the other end of the ship. One of the SEALs with the second platoon had taken a bullet to the shoulder. He'd live. The crewmember that fired at him didn't. The rest of the *Phaedra* crew now could see the writing on the wall. Slowly, they appeared—hands over heads and weapons on the ground.

"Where is your captain?" barked the platoon leader, a Lieutenant (O-3) named Gaines, at one of the sailors.

The man began speaking rapidly in Greek, waving his arms down at the other end of the ship.

Gaines turned to one of the SEALs specially selected for the operation, the son of first-generation immigrants from Athens. The operator with Greek heritage stepped forward to translate the sailor's words.

"He says the captain hasn't been seen since last giving orders while on the bridge to put up a fight. A Libyan officer, however, is currently in the communications room."

"Let's get this Libyan and keep moving towards the hull."

Davis held back with the rest as three SEALs were sent to the communications room not far away. Immediately it was apparent Major Oman had locked the door and barricaded himself in. Orders were shouted to open up and surrender. No reply came.

"You know what to do, Mark," one of the SEALs said to his teammate, who began to pull out a detonation charge and apply it to the hatch door. Moments later, the three men moved around a corner as a loud blast echoed throughout the metal-lined hallway.

The communications room was thick with smoke and debris as they rushed in guns blazing. Major Oman, thrown against the opposite wall from the blast and with a bloody gash to his right forehead, now rested on the floor in a daze trying to reach for his sidearm.

"Leave it," yelled one of the SEALs whose index finger was already against the trigger and ready to squeeze. Oman failed to obey in time and took a bullet to the shoulder. Immediately, he was dragged from the room and taken back to where the platoon had congregated for the moment.

"So this is how it's going to go," the platoon leader declared to Oman. "If you want medical attention fast, you tell me everything I want to know," he said staring down at the Major. "Where is the captain and General Zhukov?"

"You will not win. Our forces are fast approaching and will crush you," Oman weakly but defiantly replied. "We could've destroyed your meager F-14s several nights ago if we wanted to."

The platoon leader's face reddened with anger as he slammed and then pinned Oman against the wall. His left arm pressed into the wound in the Major's shoulder, causing the man to howl in pain.

"It's over. You can either answer my question or share their fate. I think you know well what that is."

"Gone to the hold with the missiles," Omar gasped with a grimaced expression.

Letting loose of him, the platoon leader turned towards his men. "We'll join back up with the rest of our platoon and Commander Spieth before entering the hull. Ms. Davis, your expertise is about to be required."

CHAPTER 48

It was too quiet. Their footsteps were the only audible sound. The lights, save for the red emergency lamps overhead, were still out. Davis's heart pounded fast inside her chest. Her head suddenly jerked hard to the right as she heard something down a side passageway. Several other SEALs did the same. One jerked his rifle in that direction before seeing a mouse scurry about.

"This is it," SEAL Team Commander Spieth turned and spoke in a hushed tone as they neared a white-painted steel hatch with the word *ampári* emblazoned in blue.

Two men moved forward and carefully approached. It was their job to inspect for any potentially dangerous trip wiring and blast it open as needed. All members of the platoon as well as Davis collectively held their breath as they anxiously watched.

"What the..."

"Jackson, what's the matter?" the Commander asked with concern.

"Sir, it appears to already be unlocked."

The Commander squinted his eyes and shifted his head to the right. "You sure?"

"Yes sir."

Davis reached down to feel for her sidearm. *I have a bad feeling about this.*

Preparing for the operation, the SEAL Team Commander had studied the layout of various types of cargo ships as well as those converted from WWII-era L.S.T.'s to craft an idea of what to expect. He could only make an educated guess, however, as to what could be waiting for them behind this hatch. Now it was time to see if his leadership would pass the test.

"You boys remember what we said. There's likely a stairway leading down to the right of the hold. Garcia and Jones will go first toward the protective cover near the stairs while the rest of us provide cover fire. After that, we move in and make our way down. Understood? Let's roll!"

The hatch was yanked open, resulting in a brash clanging noise of the steel door hitting the metal wall. The first two men found the stairs to the right just as guessed and rushed towards a large piece of freight nearby. M16A1 rifles poked out of the doorway, ready to for anything.

"Huh," Davis heard one of the men up front say. "Where are they?"

"Their radars should have trouble picking us up from down here," said Billingsley. "Well, hopefully…"

Stetson's eyes meanwhile were zeroed in on the radar. "Bogies are two miles out. I've got three descending."

"Birddog here. Outrigger, Razor, and Blue Heeler follow behind as we intercept approaching bogies. Again, do not fire unless fired upon."

"Say your Angels?" said Blue Heeler.

"Heading up to Angels Seven," Billingsley replied.

Stetson's voice suddenly interjected, "Incoming Atoll, Birddog! Repeat, incoming Atoll!"

It's on.

"Welcome aboard the *Phaedra* gentleman," came a loud but calm, accented voice. "Nice to have you join us on our Mediterranean cruise. Please, please, do come on in."

"What do we do, Spieth?" one of the men ask the SEAL Team commander.

"I'll go," the Commander replied. Stepping out to take the lead, he was surprised to hear the ocean as clearly as he did before noticing the open overhead deck hatch. Directly beneath it lay the three green-painted Oka missile systems parked alongside each other. Taking up defensive positions on front of the launchers were the group of renegade Russians. Cargo and various bulk supplies acted as a makeshift barrier for them.

The rest of the SEAL platoon followed behind their leader, before spreading out as they reached the bottom of the hold. Davis immediately noticed that one Russian remained out in the open, standing atop the center Oka.

"Allow me to introduce myself. My name is General Yakov Zhukov, formerly of the Soviet Red Army. Don't be shy. Come closer."

"We're fine right where we are," the SEAL Team Commander quickly replied, unamused.

"And your name?"

"Lieutenant Commander Scott Spieth, United States Navy. You know why we're here. It's time to surrender."

"Pleasure to meet you, Commander Spieth. I believe, however, you're mistaken.

"General, this isn't a game. I'm giving you...."

"No, I'm the one who tells you how this will go. You and your men will leave the ship and your carrier group will sail away. If you do not, I will have no choice but to fire directly at the U.S.S. *Nimitz*."

"Are you mad? At that close range, the blast will kill us all!"

"Perhaps," Zhukov answered coolly. "You see, if I cannot complete my business venture, then I'm left with little choice. I think we can both imagine the consequences not just for me," he said before pausing to survey his armed guard and give added effect. "But for my men as well."

Davis could make out a man seated inside the cabin of the far left launcher vehicle. *It takes fifteen minutes to prepare the Okas for launch and only twenty seconds for the missile to rise, facing upward before launching. If they started turning everything on right when we got on board, then a launch could take place at any moment. But if they haven't...*

The loud sound of a gunshot, from where nobody was quite sure, stopped Davis in her thoughts. Both the Russian line and the SEALs were firing now. Davis ducked behind a shipping container with Tannehill opposite her, across an open area behind another container.

Screams of pain reverberated off the steel hull as men began to fall on both sides. Quickly, Davis removed the M9 from her holster and moved to the edge of her cover. *There's got to be a way to reach that launcher.* She peered out for a moment, just long enough to see where things stood.

The SEAL platoon had already taken three casualties. One appeared to be dead already. At the end of the hull, the Soviet casualties were higher. At least four of the original ten, not including Boytsov, were down. Zhukov was nowhere to be seen. That same could be said, Davis noted, of the figure she first saw inside the Oka cabin.

It happened in half a second. For Billingsley, however, it all seemed to take place in slow motion. With the lead descending MiG already locked on, he instantly fired a Sparrow missile. Stetson, as Radar Intercept Officer, fired an A.I.M. Phoenix almost immediately before then launching countermeasures. Chaff, flare, and decoy dispensers were released, and the Tomcat raced upwards in the sky, turbofan engines lit. G-forces throttled both men into their cockpit seats.

"Atoll went for the decoy, Birddog."

He barely had time to comprehend the welcome news as he piloted their rapid ascent. There in the early hours just before sunrise, Billingsley was about to apply the nighttime dogfight training he'd acquired at TOPGUN.

Using the 'Egg' maneuver, the powerful aircraft rocketed to the heavens, passing above and leaving far behind the MiG before finally making an inverted loop. Stetson looked below the best he could, all the while upside-down, to game the situation.

"Phoenix is locked on to bogey and closing in. Blue Heeler is entering into attack with the second, and the third is dealing with Razor."

The nose of the Tomcat began pointing back toward the sea below as they began to dive. With precision, Billingsley navigated the jet into a flight pattern that gave him a shot at coming in right behind the tail of the enemy Blue Heeler was dogfighting. Never did he let his eyes leave his target. *Lose sight, lose flight.*

"Now!"

Firing off another Sparrow as he came from behind, Billingsley watched the missile streak toward the target. Two bright flashes, one forward and another starboard, soon illuminated the dark skies.

"That's what I'm talking about, Birddog! Whoop!"

Billingsley could hardly believe it. Stetson was ecstatic.

"Two birds at once. Way to go!" radioed Air Wing Commander Chamberlain.

With the Sparrow hitting the Libyan plane tangling with Blue Heeler and the A.I.M. Phoenix taking out the lead descending MiG, a rare feat had been achieved by both pilot and R.I.O.

"Alright, Stetson," Billingsley finally said, his adrenaline rushing. "Let's send the rest of them back to Tripoli or the bottom of the sea."

Davis had figured out a way. A spot in between tightly situated freight and fifty-five-gallon drums where one might fit into. The Russian eyes and firepower were focused away from it. She could see how it led up within just a foot of the makeshift barricade.

Next chance, go to the right, she mouthed, point out the spot to Tannehill, who was still across from her. The SEAL nodded, then silently prayed this would work.

"Now!" Davis exclaimed as the shooting momentarily let up. Tannehill went first as the CIA instructor covered for him before making a dash. In less than a second, the shooting restarted in their direction. A second later, and they were protected again, now hidden behind a metal crate.

The shooting around them continued as the two slowly moved on, keeping low to the ground. The space between cargo was at times no more than a foot wide. With each shuffle, Davis did her best to steady herself without touching anything, lest she cause an object to fall and crash against the floor. Each moment seemed like an hour in the race against time. *Men are dying. More still if you don't get up there fast.*

The SEAL raised his hand suddenly to stop her. "This is it," he whispered to her.

"How many of them can you see?" Davis asked.

"Five."

"Zhukov?"

"Nope."

"How about in any of the Okas?"

"Still no. I can outflank those behind the barricade. You watch my six if anyone appears from behind the launchers." That proposal was fine by Davis, considering the simple semi-auto handgun she carried.

"Sounds good. You lead the way."

The Russian closest to where they jumped around the edges of the barricade was in complete shock as he turned to see the SEAL on his side aiming to fire. He tried to get a shot off at the American but it was in vain.

"*Chto*?" yelled one of the men nearby aloud in Russian. "*Kak oni popali …*" unable to finish before his sentence before taking a bullet to the chest.

Davis, meanwhile, kept her eyes focused on the launchers, scanning for any signs of a hidden shooter. Then something caught her gaze. Someone moved up in the cabin of the middle launcher.

"Duck!" The words escaped her lips just as she fired her pistol. The barrel of the sniper rifle jerked from the incoming shots just as it took aim at Tannehill. A bullet grazed the SEAL, causing him to drop down for a moment before gripping his shoulder and moving out of the line of fire.

Davis quickly moved behind the closest Oka. Her eyes scanning all around, searching for the gunman in the shadows. None could be seen, only the few remaining Russians at the far end of the hold.

You'll have to continue outflanking them. She looked up at the overhead deck hatch, now displaying the early rays of approaching sunrise and echoing the noise of the naval aircraft, presently engaged in an aerial battle. Beside her, opposite of the Oka, was the hinged door of the bow slightly open, though with the ramp drawn up. A powerful spray of sea salt suddenly came through it, hitting her square in the face. It all seemed hard to fathom. She was here now, trying to stop a madman from not just selling multiple nuclear warheads but maybe even launching them. Just three days ago, she sat at a desk in Langley, Virginia, wondering what lay next in her turbulent career.

She treaded carefully along the end of the enormous launcher. It was not the first time Davis had seen a weapons system capable of blasting off a nuclear warhead. It was, however, the first time she'd been faced with the possibility of having to stop one from firing mid-launch sequence.

Taking cover at the end of the launcher where the tip of the warhead would conceivably rise and point out towards the open hatch door, Davis peered out and saw him. She knew right away. The man who killed Cooper and tried to take out her family. There with a sniper rifle, Konstantin Boytsov scanned the narrow walkaways between the Okas.

Dayan never mentioned anything about him being aboard! How often had she thought about this moment? Confronting the man responsible for the terror inflicted on her family? More than she cared to admit. Sometimes, if Davis were honest, a part of her wanted revenge. She wanted him to pay. But then character, instilled in her by mentors with integrity and faith, would overcome the raw emotion. *You know what to do, Audrey.*

She raised her pistol, taking aim at Boytsov's shoulder, to disable rather than kill. Just as she prepared to fire, the Russian's eyes made contact with hers.

Two rounds streaked toward her as she took cover and attempted to return fire

"I know who you are," Davis spoke in Russian. "Drop your weapon and come out. There's no escape back to Libya or wherever else you thought you'd go from here."

The sound of bullets clanking within a wisp of her head was his reply.

"This is it. You're out of options. Surrender and you'll be treated fairly. You have my word."

Boytsov lowered his weapon and looked out across the chaos in the hold. "I've been out of options for a long time," his voice betraying a desperate mix of fear and anger. "All because of you and that old man!"

"Last chance. Please."

Davis could see the butt of the sniper rifle returning to his shoulder as Boytsov raised it back and aimed at her. *Now.*

Three rounds left her M9. Traveling at thirteen hundred feet per second, two struck the former Spetsnaz just above his protective vest, straight into his neck, causing his body to immediately drop to the floor.

In his final seconds, a bloodied and choking Boytsov looked up through the upper hold hatch and into the morning skies. *I return to you, comrades. Back to that nameless height.* Then, it was over.

Davis stood nearby, clutching her firearm and staring at the lifeless figure. *Breathe. Just breathe.* She worked to calm herself. *You did what you had to do. It's done.*

Reloading another magazine, Davis carefully moved past the body lying just outside a metal ladder leading atop the Oka launcher's cabin.

"I suggest you stop, Miss, or I'm afraid you'll end up like him." Davis looked up to see a Makarov pistol pointed at her by General Yakov Zhukov, smugly grinning as he poked up through the Oka's roof hatch.

"You're just in time to witness Soviet arms technology at its finest. Do come in. Oh, but please leave your weapon outside." Zhukov gestured for her to climb up the ladder and enter the Oka's cabin. As Davis dropped her weapon and climbed aboard, the barrel of Lieutenant Tamarkin's AK-47 peered out of the cabin shotgun window. Zhukov returned to entering the correct computer commands for the impending launch.

Her eyes fixed on the young man. Desperately she wished she could read his thoughts. Once inside the cabin through the hatch, she could see the firing key, no longer hidden beneath the General's military uniform, resting around his neck. *It all comes down to this.* The intelligence gathering, special ops mission, shootout with rogue Red Army soldiers, all of it down to this moment in the waters of the Gulf of Sidra.

"Just a few more moments and the missile will be ready to rise into place, firing directly through the open upper hatch. Unless, of course, you'd care to call off this incursion on a business transaction between two parties that doesn't concern you," Zhukov said pointedly as he took a seat in front of the control panel and set his Makarov beside him.

A nauseous feeling instantly hit Davis at the General's words. She'd come all this way only to become a prisoner and be forced to witness a nuclear disaster firsthand. The analyst & instructor did her best to keep her composure steady. Then suddenly, a recall from the past came to Davis.

"Does it ever get tiring? The going along to get along. Play it safe and never rock the boat once, so to speak?" she spoke, still in Russian, as her eyes bore into Tamarkin's.

"Excuse me?" the Lieutenant asked perplexedly

"You heard me. All your life, Grigory, you've been quiet. Oh, you had things to say, but you kept them to yourself, even when other's actions went against your own convictions."

The junior officer's facial expression appeared both at ease and twisted in confusion all at once. Davis continued. "You're a good man, Grigory

Tamarkin, like your father before you. A loyal one as well. Too loyal, maybe. Is this really how you wanted it to end for you?"

"You really think that's going to work, guilt-tripping my most trusted officer?" Zhukov interrupted. "Useless, that's what it is. He and all the rest think as I do. They are soldiers—trusting and obeying to the maximum degree." The General grinned as he continued inputting the final commands. As he did, the mechanized steel sound of the missile rising outside signaled less than twenty seconds until it could be fired.

Davis looked into the young soldier's eyes. It seemed in vain, but she searched for any sign she was getting through to him. The gray-colored eyes, however, appeared only focused on shooting her if she made the slightest move.

The General took the key from around his neck. As he reached towards the launch lock with it, a powerful force struck from behind. It caught him by surprise, knocking him out of the chair and causing him to drop the key. The Makarov pistol, meanwhile, flew off the seat beside Zhukov and traveled across the cabin. A blow with the butt of Tamarkin's rifle barely missed the General's head, instead connecting with his shoulder, knocking the wind out of him.

A scuffle ensued. An emboldened Tamarkin wrestled for the key while Zhukov desperately fought to take the AK-47 away. Davis rushed toward where the Makarov lay on the cabin and quickly picked it up. Desperately she attempted to aim at the General. Her efforts, however, were in vain with no way to get a clear shot.

The upper hand was abruptly gained when Zhukov finally ripped the rifle away. In an instant, he fired several rounds into the man who had trusted him since the day he arrived at the base. Tamarkin's body slumped over.

Davis wasted no time. Immediately she discharged every last round in the Makarov pistol at the General. Each bullet hitting its target, tearing through the Soviet uniform he still wore and piercing his chest. Zhukov violently fell backward into the controls. Hand gripping the key, he gasped for air before breathing his last.

It took several seconds before Davis shook out of fight or flight mode and lowered her gun to survey the aftermath. Reaching down, she confiscated the key and looked at the two bodies before her.

When asked later, Davis could not recall any suggestion as to what the rogue Russian General, once entrusted with weapons capable of changing the world forever, was thinking as he took his last breaths. Regret? Frustration? There was no way to tell.

It was the look, however, on Lieutenant Tamarkin's face that she never forgot. His eyes shut, pulse gone, yet she could see the countenance of a man who'd finally taken a stand, found courage and followed his own conscience. There would be no hero's funeral back in the *Rodina* for him; his crimes against the state deemed unforgivable. But to Davis, this young man had become a hero in his final moments.

"Ms. Davis, you alright?" She turned to see a lone SEAL peering into the bloodied Oka cabin as he clutched his M16A1 rifle. Just outside, the sound of the battle between SEALs and Russian renegades had gone silent.

"It's over," she said softly, staring at the launch key she clutched in her hand. "It's finally over."

The sight of smoke plumes on the horizon immediately caught Davis's attention when she returned to deck. It was now 0900. *Phaedra* was secure with a destroyer class and a smaller frigate sailing on each side of the ship. She rubbed her tired eyes, reflecting on how close they'd all come to a potentially devastating alternate outcome. Every fiber of her being was exhausted: physically, mentally and emotionally. *To sleep for ten hours.* For all real practicality, it was a pipe dream at the moment. Now was the time for giving reports and answering the questions from the top brass. Heading towards the ship's helipad, Davis held a hand up over her eyes as a chopper slowly hovered downward, ready to unload a group assigned to operate the captured vessel and investigate the Okas below.

Aboard the chopper, Davis found herself dozing off for a few minutes before they landed on the deck of *Nimitz*. She quickly noted the celebratory atmosphere. All around, sailors, SEALs and returning pilots and crew were high-fiving one another.

"Good to see you're alive," Billingsley said as he shook her hand in congratulations. There was a look of genuine concern and just a bit of excitement to see her. "I heard it got a bit rough where you were this morning."

"We lost two men. It was rough, but we got the job done and completed the mission. That's all I can really say."

"All that you need to."

"I saw the smoke as I was leaving the ship. What happened?"

"A dogfight for the history books—if they'll ever let it be known, that is," Billingsley replied as he led her off to the side away from passing sailors and officers in the passageway. He then lowered his voice to a hushed tone. "The official word from Navy brass to Task Force 60 is that Libya got too cute with war games and overstepped the line firing on us, to which we retaliated. Just like back in '81. Any word beyond that— at least to those not already directly involved in Operation Silent Cyclone, such as you—is strictly forbidden. Everyone within Task Force 60 will be required to sign nondisclosures. No press are aboard at present, which should be a plus."

Davis recalled the rest of what she'd been briefed before leaving D.C. If successful, the U.S. would, via backchannels, put the squeeze on Gaddafi to remain silent about the whole thing, lest the extent of the attempted nuclear weapons purchase be known to the world and he face the fallout. The INF Treaty would no longer be in jeopardy due to mistrust or misunderstanding between two world powers, nor would an enemy that sponsored terrorism come into possession of three nuclear missiles. In the end, what happened today would be but a rumor of another firefight in the Gulf of Sidra and no more. *Just as it should be.*

"So what's next for you?" Billingsley asked. The two began moving again through the passageway.

"Well, I've got to speak to the Rear Admiral and give my report."

"I mean when you get home. Hopefully take some time off and relax."

"No, not really," she replied without stopping her stride.

"What then?"

"Unfinished business."

The two stopped walking, alone now in the passageway. "Then I wish you the best." Billingsley paused before speaking again. "They're saying after this I may be sent stateside soon. Back to Miramar to work as an instructor. If you're ever in San Diego…."

"A drink? You name the time and place, Birddog," Davis said, finishing his sentence and leaning in just a bit. "Likewise, if you're ever in Washington…"

"Tell me where and I'm there in Mach 2."

CHAPTER 49

Bakri Assad appeared to have it all. Leaving the small two-bedroom apartment in Benghazi and coming to the U.S. with his family when he was only seven, Assad was immediately instilled with the belief that anything was possible in this country. His parents reinforced this idea by pushing him in his studies. The boy was bright and brought his parents, owners of a local dry cleaner, much pride when he graduated valedictorian from high school and was accepted to Harvard University. It was there that his journey began. During a political science class, his professor extolled the promise of socialism and advancement Muammar Gaddafi was bringing to his country, as well as his goal of one united Arab state. The young student hung on every word of the lecture, requesting extra reading materials from the professor after class on his homeland and the revolutionary leader. Before freshman year was over, he became the type most students try to avoid on their way into libraries and student unions—a loud, red-in-the-face activist.

How he eventually became an agent of the Libyan intelligence service was unknown. Upon reviewing the intel provided by Dayan aboard *Nimitz*, Davis guessed that he either made a trip to his former country or was approached on campus. One thing was sure, though. Before graduation, Assad had done a complete one-eighty.

He went on to get an M.D. and marry a girl from a prominent family outside of Boston. For a time, he was an associate professor at the university. During that period, he'd kept an eye out for potential recruits. Finally, Tripoli ordered him to move to D.C. The in-laws were upset at losing their daughter and two grandchildren, but Assad explained it was a major career opportunity that couldn't be missed.

For three weeks, Davis stalked his every move. When he left home for the hospital every morning, she was only a few cars away in the traffic. When he went to lunch, she was disguised at a nearby table. And when he made a detour before returning home from work to his family, she was there as well.

It was neither difficult nor time-consuming to get what was needed. In twenty minutes of observation, she'd listened in, snapped photos of the exchange, and got the license tag of the congressional aide who'd just sold information from a closed-door intelligence committee meeting. Now she only needed to introduce herself.

Waiting outside the hospital, she watched as the young and polished heart surgeon left work for the day. Davis got out of her car and walked in his direction, carrying a yellow envelope.

"Call the number in five minutes," she said as she shoved the envelope in his chest and kept walking. Flabbergasted, he looked back at the woman before picking up the pace toward his car. He quickly shut the side door, looked around, and opened the envelope. His whole body began to tremble as he saw the evidence before him. Finding the number written down on an index card, the Libyan spy ran out of his car in search of a pay phone.

"How can we fix this, Doctor? Or do you prefer Bakri?" he heard the female voice saying over the line.

"What do you want?"

"Let's back that up, shall we. What do you want? That's the real question."

"I don't want to go to jail!"

"Traitors always to go to jail. But what if I said I could make it easier on you, providing a path to see your family after today?"

"How so?"

"I need to know about your CIA contact."

Now, Davis was ready. Getting the key from Assad before turning him over to the FBI, she sat upright in a recliner, waiting patiently from the darkened room of a safe house a block away from Georgetown. It was here the Libyan spy would meet with his CIA source. The one-bedroom unit was small but quaint. The curtains had been drawn (the understood okay signal), blocking out the pale moonlight. A recovered Agent Mary Holden, the one person she could trust to help her, stood hiding in the bedroom, awaiting the moment she could come into the room and arrest the man responsible for her near-death experience.

Davis's hands were clenched into each of the respective armrests. At first, she'd tried a breathing exercise, to no effect. Her mind was in overdrive wondering how this would play out. Her eyes trained on the front door.

The proper signal had been given for a meeting. A call made to an area code in Frederick, Maryland and a message left on an answering machine asking "if Cliff was down for getting drinks after work this Friday."

Suddenly, she could hear it. With each footstep climbing the stairs outside in the hall, she her breath. *Could it be? Have they really taken the bait? Soviet Select, or just a lost pizza deliveryman?*

Finally, they reached the top of the stairs. Their pace continued, closer and closer to the safe house door. A lone bead of sweat began to form at the top of Davis's brow. She could see the lone glint of light coming from the peephole eclipsed by a figure just on the other side. The sound of keys clinking as they were wrestled from the figure's pocket. A key into the lock. The deadbolt slowly sliding back. The ominous doorknob twisting to the right.

As the figure entered, Davis could make out the dark silhouette of a man. By now, her fingernails had nearly dug a hole through the cheap upholstery of the armrests. *Stay calm, Audrey. Whatever you do, just stay calm.*

He shut the door behind him, his face scanning the darkened room in vain. Whether he assumed he was the first to arrive or sensed trouble, he stood in the entryway for several seconds. Then the light came on.

"Hello, Audrey."

For weeks following the arrest, Agent Holden found herself wondering which of the two was the most shocked by the presence of the other. As she stood in the kitchen peering through a cracked door, she waited with bated breath for Audrey to reply.

"Why, Koufax? Why?"

The Soviet division director shrugged his shoulders and sighed. "Like I told you a while back," he said passively. "It pays to keep up a facade."

"You were born in this country, Toby Koufax. Graduate of Yale. You swore an oath to protect the nation when you join the CIA. The same oath I swore."

Koufax shook his head before scratching his beard in a fidgeting manner. "Oaths are made to be broken. Especially when convenient."

"Was it money? Were the East Germans not able to fully meet your financial needs, POTOMAC?" her tone frigid as she said his former code name. "I doubt Gaddafi ever could."

"You're welcome to psychoanalyze me all you'd like," he replied, this time with a tinge of defiance. He sat down on a couch. "Visualize me as some sort of Kim Philby. I don't really care. I've no need for any flag-waving ideologies and it's never been entirely about the money. Though that doesn't hurt."

"Then what?"

For once, looking uncomfortable as he shifted in his seat and fidgeted with his wedding ring, Koufax contemplated just how to answer that. "You do this job for thirty years. Blend in. Keep your head down. You do that and after a while people come up with their own subjective take on you. 'Koufax, he's the quiet type. Steady cloak and dagger work, now desk work on the Soviet division. Goes home to his wife every night. Stays out of trouble. A loyal Company man. Meanwhile, you gain a new perspective, see the flaws and see the openings. You ask yourself if you do it. This time, independent and up against them all. To be a player again in the game and always one step ahead of everyone else. There's a thrill to it. An exhilaration unlike anything else." He chuckled as he appeared to be reflecting on it all.

"Did your wife even know?"

"Unlike myself, Val really was a quiet bore. All she ever wanted to do was paint landscapes of the Chesapeake Bay and fawn all over her three cats." Koufax began to chuckle to himself

"So it was all an act at the hospital that day about knowing what it's like to lose someone? The nerve of you to show up that day after the part you played." Davis's blood began to boil. You're sick, Koufax. My kids, my friends, my life, the target of a hit squad because of your need for a thrill." She got up from her seat now as he continued to snicker. Holden was quickly becoming concerned.

"Tell me this. Who was with Stephen Banks, the Archives Director, on the night he died? I know you couldn't have jumped out of the car during that short of a blind spot. You're too out of shape and been out of the field too long."

Koufax ceased laughing and looked up at her. "That would be Shelby. I convinced him long ago to go to lean on Banks for whatever files I needed, including yours and Carson Cooper's. Shelby believed he was acting on Clark's orders passed through me, that it was top secret and that it should be discussed with no one but myself. If he did anything I didn't like, I threatened to leak the dirty details on a certain escapade of his that went south. By the way, in case you're wondering, a junior field officer was arranged to move Shelby's car parked outside of Bank's before the FBI arrived."

"Which leads us to Pat Clark. Were you trying to frame him?

"It's not hard to frame that egotistical blowhard. I long expected someone would eventually look into his trip for that operation FIELDGOAL. You see, I coordinated my first meeting with the East German Stasi when Clark was there. If anything went wrong, his itinerary would lead counter-intelligence to assume he was POTOMAC."

"I've heard enough. You're going to pay for this, Koufax," she answered, standing directly in front of him with clenched fists. "For Carson Cooper's life, the hell you put my family through, and the wake of destruction you've left."

"Maybe. Then again, maybe not." A Cheshire cat smile formed on his lips. "I know too much about the other side. Names, contacts, insight into the Stasi, Libyans and a couple other players you still don't know about. Maybe I go to jail but I think not. I imagine the Feds and I will come to some sort of an agreement. Besides, it's just your word against mine." He pointed his stubby right index finger at Davis, grinning even more. "You've lost."

Holden could see it in Davis's eyes. The desire for revenge is a strong force. A force that Davis had wrestled with for months. It was in that moment that she began to give in.

"Audrey, no!" Holden bolted into the living room as Davis removed and cocked her Beretta M9 before aiming it at Koufax, whose eyes widened at the sight before sickly grinning one more.

Davis waved off Holden with her other hand. Pressing the barrel firmly into the side of Koufax's skull, she held it there for what seemed like an eternity.

"You almost won," she said finally.

"What?" asked the mole.

"You want me to pull the trigger, Koufax. Your mind's warped. Warped to the core. This would be too easy an out for you. It'd only destroy me, which is exactly what you want." She drew the gun back, still keeping it pointed at him. "I'm not giving you that satisfaction."

Koufax was left dumbfounded as Holden quickly moved in to handcuff him and formally make the arrest. Backup from the Bureau arrived shortly thereafter to take the traitor away. For the first time, a wave of peace was felt by Audrey Davis.

"What were you thinking before you lowered your gun?" Holden asked later that night as they completed necessary papers and statement forms at the J. Edgar Hoover Building. "I thought you were going to do it."

Tired but not downtrodden, Davis answered. "I wasn't thinking. I was praying. Praying just to let go… and take hold of something better."

EPILOGUE

April 1988

Owings Mills, Maryland

Davis still wasn't entirely sure she wanted to do this. As she pulled off the main highway into Owings Mills, she continued trying to come up with reasons to turn the car around. For four months, she'd put this off. An unspoken fear had held her back all that time. *No more. It's time to face this. You're ready, Audrey.*

The sun had not quite yet risen in the early morning hours as she pulled into a front parking spot at the First Owings Mills Bank. Shutting the engine off, Davis got out of the car and headed inside. The bank manager, who'd received a call from Don Wainwright the night before, was here early to assist her. He offered her a cup of coffee, which she declined, before leading her to a vault door towards the back. Turning the dials, he led her inside.

"2631. Here it is. You have the key with you, Ms. Davis?"

Reaching inside her purse, she pulled out the envelope given to her on Christmas Day and removed the key.

"Go right ahead then," he motioned towards the safety deposit box. Slowly, Davis stepped forward. An almost nauseous feeling in her stomach tried to ward her off, yet she continued. Inserting the key and turning it to the right, she slid out the twelve-by-six-by-four-inch metal container.

"I'll leave you alone here. If you need anything or whenever you're finished, just hit the buzzer. Shouldn't be anyone here for at least a couple more hours."

She gave a nod as he turned to leave, closing and locking the door behind him.

This is it then.

A steel table with two chairs stood in the center of the vault. Taking the deposit box, Davis sat down and took a deep breath.

Opening the top lid, she found a letter inside, sitting on top of several large envelopes. She shuddered as she began to read the first few words before stopping.

Lord, help me do this. Davis folded her hands over her nose and mouth and collected herself. It was time. Starting once more, she read the last words from her mentor and friend.

Audrey,

If you're reading this, I've finally made it Home. Where I am now, there's no more pain or suffering. I'm in a better place here with my Savior. Please don't cry over me.

I cannot fully express what your friendship has meant to me. The same can be said for Nikita and Sergei. From our time in Moscow to the get-togethers on the tree farm, I treasure each memory. I've watched you and the boys find your footing here back in the states these past few years with strength and perseverance. There will be more trials ahead as there are for all of us. I've no doubt you'll overcome those too.

There are some things I wish I could've told you. Things I so badly wanted to say to you since the day we met at the safe house in Moscow but couldn't. It's been a burden to keep these from you. Now in death, it's time you heard.

I was stationed in South Vietnam in late 1964, doing what I did best. It was just on the eve of the Gulf of Tonkin incident. While there, I got to know a gentleman by the name of Rick Davis, your father.

Rick's specialty was paramilitary operations. We worked in conjunction off the intel I was able to pick up from sources along the border region and areas where the Viet Cong had infiltrated. Over time we became friends, playing poker and talking all things Orioles baseball after hours. He talked about you, Audrey. Spoke often of his twelve-year-old daughter, who liked to ride horses out on the family farm, could shoot with the best, and had an adventurous outdoor spirit just like him.

One evening, after gaining information from an agent of mine about an enemy general on the move, Rick was needed to help launch an ambush along with several South Vietnamese soldiers and take the general prisoner for questioning. He and four others never returned.

At the time, due to the fact our country had yet to officially enter the War, the work we were doing over there was highly classified. It remains so to this day. I've wanted to tell you about the man I knew, his drive, focus, kindness and continual love for his family even while thousands of miles away. I wanted to tell you the real story of what happened to him that night. Shortly before the mission, your father gave me a letter addressed to you. Due to the sensitive nature of our work and red tape surrounding it, however, we were soon forbidden to send anything to the families of the CIA officers who died that evening.

Until now.

In death, I finally have the freedom from repercussion to share this with you. In this deposit box, you'll find his letter, sealed just as it was more than twenty years ago.

The road has finally reached an end for me. Yours is far from over. Sometimes I've seen an unspoken hurt in your eyes. On one occasion, you shared a small bit about your Dad and how you wished you could've said goodbye. I hope what's contained in the box can bring some small sense of healing and closure.

Your friend forever,

Carson

Doing her best to keep her composure, Davis looked down at the second envelope that had lain underneath Carson's letter. She opened it up slowly. The handwriting was one she hadn't seen for many years. As she read, her throat tightened. First, a single tear streamed down her right cheek, followed by sobbing. The last words from her father, the ones she'd longed to hear one more time, brought forth a flood of emotions. Pain, sadness, grief, but most of all, joy. Tears of joy. *I love you, Audrey,* were the last words. At the end of the letter, she noted the date: a month after she'd last spoken to him and five days before he was killed. *I love you too, Dad.*

Fifteen minutes later, she was back in her car on her way to work. The sun was now peaking above the eastern horizon. In its light, the world was awakening. Spring had arrived. *A new beginning.*

After work that day, Davis planned to take the boys along to check out houses near the farm she once called home. It was time to get out of the city, out of the suburbs and let her kids live in wide-open spaces. She'd seen them enjoy the woods of western Maryland and knew as the FBI protection finally ended that it was where all three of them needed to be.

Getting on the highway, she tried to mentally prepare herself for her first day as the head of a new task force, known as the Tallmadge Order, to take the place of the Soviet Select. The Director had personally chosen her for the position rather than Skylar or Clark. She'd report to the Director alone and be responsible for an organization within CIA charged with both analysis and taking precise action as needed against rising international threats to the nation. It was a big step for the woman who'd started at the Agency only fifteen years before in an NCO

274

position. *What were the odds, Audrey? Dad, Cooper, Ashcroft—if they hadn't pointed me in the right direction and been there to offer words of wisdom, what then?*

She arrived at the gate just before the start of work. Davis took the elevator up to that sacred seventh floor. Her office, next door to the Director's, looked out onto the wooded area that hid Langley from much of the world's peripheral view. A stack of folders upon folders awaited her on the desk. After pouring her first cup of coffee for the work day, the head of the Tallmadge Order walked toward the floor-to-ceiling window, looking out past the trees toward the Potomac River. There, in close proximity to a complex constantly responding to the threats of a turbulent world, the tranquil waters of the river stood in stark contrast.

Davis walked back to her desk and skimmed through the folders. *Glasnost and warhead dismantlement in the Soviet Union. Underground democratic movements on university campuses in China. Noriega in Panama. Unrest in the Middle East.* She shook her head and sighed. *More rivers to cross. But Lord willing, as Cooper would say, we'll conquer these too. Lord willing.*

The phone rang. It was the Director wanting to discuss the latest reports in two hours. "Yes, sir. I'll be in your office then," she answered. Taking a seat in the leather swivel chair, she opened up the top folder and got to work.

CHIEF

OF

STATION

J.D. Narramore

SAMPLE READING OF SELECT CHAPTERS

1

The First Day- March 9th, 1983

Yuri Ustinov had always been and would always be, a particular and timely man. Believing in absolute orderliness and attention to detail, he kept everyone he supervised at the Ministry of Railways on their toes. A subordinate arriving but a second late to a meeting with him would suffer a severe verbal lashing. The opposite held true, however, for Ustinov's superiors. Waiting to meet with the Minister himself, his stubby fingers tapped loudly against the wooden armrest of his chair. The secretary seated at her desk across the room was becoming increasingly annoyed with him. At ten minutes past nine, he finally arose somewhat exasperated and approached her. Just when should he expect to see the Minister of Railways, Viktor Molotov? The brusque secretary reluctantly pressed a button on her desk. Immediately a voice came from the intercom.

"Yes, Katya?"

"Minister Molotov, Yuri Ustinov is here to see you for your 9 o'clock appointment."

"Tell him unexpected business requires me to postpone our appointment. Please reschedule with him."

The Minister of Railways released his finger off the intercom button, returning his attention back to the conversation with his old friend: Major Pyotr Ivanovich of the KGB.

The Major sat lost in thought as he looked out the near frosted-over windows and onto the heavy snow blanketing Red Square. From the warm comfort of the Minister's office, he could see the Kremlin guards doing their best to cope with the frigid temperatures and icy air blowing hard from the east. If the weather reports were correct, they would find little solace for some time. The same of which, he considered, could be said for the state of their own country.

"Sorry about that, Pyotr."

"Oh, you're fine," he replied as he turned back to look across the desk at his old comrade. "Please continue."

"As I was saying, the Central Committee's next meeting is not that far away. The snow will soon melt, spring shall arrive in the *Rodina*, and we'll be faced with the undercurrents of so-called reform. Do not misunderstand me. I'm in full support of our General Secretary. However, I can't help but suspect that some manipulate him now in his advanced years."

"Might it be that those whom you are anxious about are just younger than you and I, Viktor?"

"Young, yes, but also ignorant of what reckless reform can lead to. It was reckless reform that led to Khrushchev's downfall nearly twenty years ago. The younger generation is susceptible to materialistic ideas from the West, as well as such selfish pursuits that would destroy the common good and pave the way for us to be under the boot of the Americans."

Major Ivanovich nodded in agreement. "So we must set an example for them and lead in the way that Brezhnev did."

"That we shall, but it won't be enough. See now, Brezhnev is gone and Andropov is in the autumn of his years. It's within the realm of possibility that we shall soon be faced again with choosing a new leader. What is stopping a younger, charismatic, reform-minded man from winning over the Committee?"

"Chernenko would be the most logical next in line."

Molotov leaned back in his chair and pondered his friend's remark. "That I'm not so sure. He failed to gain enough support when Brezhnev died. He could very well fail again next time around."

"You suppose maybe that young man that used to oversee Stavropol?"

"And now has a seat on the Politburo? Yes, Pytor, I most definitely suspect Mikhail Gorbachev could be our next leader," replied Molotov disgustedly. "Andropov shows favor to him. At times he even allows him to chair meetings! As shrewd as that old KGB headmaster is, he's making a mistake. Gorbachev would make irreversible changes that would harm our power and system of rule."

The Major nodded his head in agreement. "Maybe if he had fought in the Great Patriotic War, he would have greater respect for this communist system of ours. It's remarkable that one with such ideas could work their way up The Party ladder as he has."

Molotov's eyes suddenly turned cold and calculated. "Comrade, that is why something must be done. That is why something will be done. And that is why I have asked you to come here today."

"Go on."

"What I am about to say to you is said in the strictest confidence."

"Understood, Viktor."

"There is a group of staunch Soviet patriots, like you and I, who wish to prevent this fool from ever taking power. Men on the Central Committee, the upper hierarchy of your own KGB, and even the Politburo. We have formed a pact to work together in seeing that he goes away."

"How so?"

With a stone-faced expression fitting of an executioner, Molotov spoke but a single word. "Permanently."

A deafening silence filled the room. Finally, Ivanovich spoke.

"How can I be of help?"

A smile slowly formed on the old Soviet oligarch's face. "Only with the most important part, comrade. Only the most important part."

***

It was at the end of a long day at the Lubyanka that Ivanovich returned to his apartment shortly after six. Slowly pulling up to the curb of the building where the privileged and ruling class resided, the driver got out and opened Ivanovich's passenger door. The Major nodded his head in quick acknowledgment before making his way inside to where the elevator doors were just then opening. The operator, a small balding man who had four sons currently fighting in Afghanistan, greeted him. "Good evening Major Ivanovich."

"Good evening to you, comrade Somov. How is your family?" Ivanovich asked as the doors shut and the elevator made its way to the 6th floor.

"Doing fine, Major. My wife and I received a letter from our youngest today. He's been promoted to sergeant."

Ivanovich recalled a memory but chose to shut it out immediately, lest his emotions show. "Treasure your children, comrade. They are the ones who go before us and leave a legacy when we're gone."

"Very true, comrade."

The doors opened and Ivanovich proceeded down the hall to his door. Before opening, he attempted to put aside the pressing issue still swirling in his mind. Taking a deep breath, the Major entered to the joy of his family.

"Oh, Pyotr! You're home. Come, I've made dinner and am just setting it out onto the table," his wife spoke from another room.

The Major took off his overcoat and went to look for his wife. Thirty-six years they had been married. Of those thirty-six years, this was his favorite part of each day. He entered the kitchen to find her picking up two bowls of soup to take into the dining room. "How was your day?" she asked with a welcoming smile.

He gave her a quick kiss. "The usual. More paperwork. How is Fyodor?"

"In his room studying," she said as she went into the dining room to set down the bowls of beet and cabbage red soup known as *Borscht*, looking everything over before deciding dinner was ready. "Fyodor, dinner is ready and your father is home."

Pyotr's teenage son soon entered the room. With his blue jeans and affinity for anything Western, he was a picture of the new generation of Russians. The old guard was losing a war to turn back the tide on its young people's passions as the father could easily see.

As they ate their dinner, the Major sat in silence while his son excitedly explained all he was learning for his upcoming engineering exam. He loved his son whole-heartedly, however, it was all he could do to feign a smile and pretend to show interest. The meeting with Molotov engulfed his thoughts. *How can they ask me, a veteran KGB officer, to become a co-conspirator in a plot to eliminate a member of the Politburo and possibly any hope of saving this country from itself?*

He could see the writing on the wall. The system was built on a foundation of lies that infected nearly every system of the government. Everything from the news of the goings-on in the West to economic reports of the *Rodina* itself—nothing could be trusted. If it really were a 'worker's paradise,' why were there constant food shortages and long lines for the working class? Change was needed. Change led by one who wouldn't give in to the greybeards and the corrupt.

Lying in bed later that evening while his wife slept beside him, his pressing thoughts remained. Ivanovich turned and reached over for his alarm clock: half-past three. *It's pointless trying to get sleep tonight. I know what needs to be done.*

Rising carefully so as not to wake up his wife, he made his way to the kitchen to find a bottle of *Stolichnaya*. He poured himself a shot of the Soviet-brand vodka and downed it fast. The tense feeling throughout his body eased somewhat as the warmth from the liquid went down. Ivanovich cleared his throat and sighed. He couldn't let this good man get killed. There was but one way to stop it from happening.

Pouring himself several more shots into a glass, the KGB Major walked into the living area and opened a cabinet. Inside were several photograph albums. Reaching for a dusty green one with gold trim on its cover, he carried it over to his favorite chair. His body plopped down into the seat like that of a much older man who had long carried a heavy load. Indeed, he had been carrying a heavy burden now for nearly fifteen years. He opened the album and looked with fondness at the first two photos of a young boy, no more than five, spending the day at a resort by the Black Sea with his parents. Pyotr remembered that time from so long ago before he was in the commanding position he had now—when life seemed simpler and his allegiances more straightforward—when the most precious things to him were his wife and his first-born son, Misha.

He turned to the next page to see his son now ten years old and with the biggest smile on his face—a photo of him on a camping trip out in the woods. Like all Russian parents, Pyotr adored his children. He recalled proudly how outgoing and adventurous Misha was from an early age. The father knew early on that his son would never choose a career behind a desk if he could help it. The son longed to be a hero like those he'd heard about from the war. His mother often caught him in their bedroom, peering inside their dresser drawer at his father's "Order of the Red Star" medal, awarded for bravery at the Battle of Stalingrad.

Ivanovich continued looking fondly at the pictures of his son until coming to one of him in uniform with his newly sewn-on shoulder marks befitting a commissioned officer. A mixture of anger and pain took hold of him.

Misha had been in the army for no more than a year when, in August of '68, he was sent to take part in Operation Danube. In an effort to thwart a Warsaw Pact member nation's reforms and movement towards democracy, the Soviets invaded Czechoslovakia with little warning. In Prague, the young officer received orders to take his tank and provide the support needed for soldiers to storm a radio station that was encouraging resistance. However, Czech citizens barricaded the station with transit buses. As his tank pushed through the barricade, it caught fire and was forced to stop. Several young men rushed towards their armored vehicle and tried to climb on top. One succeeded, and to his luck, the crew had failed to lock the top hatch of the T-62. Misha and his comrades suddenly looked up to see the light from outside and two petrol bombs hurled down. The glass bottles smashed against the floor as flames rushed forth, blanketing all of the men. They frantically attempted to push open the hatch but to no avail. The Czech outside, along with another compatriot, had succeeded in jamming it shut. By the time help arrived, the human faces were burned beyond recognition, with only Misha still alive.

Pyotr recalled that very last time he ever saw his son. In the hospital room here in Moscow, it was all that he could do to hold back tears in front of Misha. His skin completely burned off; every moment the young man had left was spent in agony. When it was over, the Major's views about everything changed. The lingering questions and concerns he once held were pushed aside. Now, an intense hatred fermented for the strong men pulling the levers in the Kremlin—the very ones he worked alongside for decades and to an extent was one of. For too long, he'd ignored what was plain to him until this loss forced him to open his eyes. Misha had no business being in Czechoslovakia. If the people there chose a different path, let them. Maybe it was time for his own country to try democracy and reform for a change. The system needed to be torn down. He was sure of it. From then on, Pyotr would do whatever possible to make that a reality.

Several months later, he made the fateful decision that had changed everything: he became a spy for the United States.

Was he a traitor to his country? Ivanovich didn't think so. Just as his son saw him for his service in the war, he saw himself as a patriot, trying to save his country from men who had consolidated power for themselves atop a worker's paradise that never was and never would be.

When he next met with his handler, a young CIA officer in his early thirties, he would tell him all about this plot. Would the Americans do anything to foil this assassination attempt? That was a perplexing question. What he did know, however, was that it would be his best chance to do something without risking exposure. There was no way of knowing who all was involved. If he could make the Americans understand the potential of having a man like Gorbachev as both General Secretary and negotiating partner one day, they'd have to step in.

Ivanovich looked for a moment longer at the last photo taken of his son. "I do this for you, Misha," he said softly aloud. Taking the glass of *Stolichnaya*, he emptied it before closing his eyes and finally falling asleep in his chair.

A few hours later, he awoke to the ill effects of his late-night drinking. He knew just the cure. Getting dressed as his wife still slept, he called for his driver and headed downstairs. When he got into the car, the driver immediately noticed the bloodshot eyes and worn look on the Major's face.

Often he would drive Ivanovich like this early in the morning. Unlike so much of Soviet life, however, these trips were unpredictable. Several blocks away from the Kremlin, the car pulled up in front of the Tenishev Steam Baths. There, others like the Major arrived early to soothe the hangovers that plagued them. Ivanovich entered the building and made his way to the men's steam rooms. Once inside, he undressed in the changing room and took a towel and a handful of birch tree branches. Opening the door that led to the steam rooms, he immediately felt the warm air rush towards him. It was through this sweating out of the poisons that he felt both renewed and mentally refreshed.

There were already several other men inside the *banya* when he entered. Their heads hung low, breathing in deeply and slapping the birch branches against their backs. He recognized some of them, regulars, as he took a seat at the far end away from everyone. He was in no mood to visit.

What exactly would he say to his American handler? The next rendezvous was in four days. He pondered how best to present his intel in the short time they would have.

Soon it was time to go. The Major rose and headed to the showers where the ice-cold water did the final trick in preparing his body for the long day.

"Major, it is good to see you this morning," an overweight man with a round face bellowed as he slapped Ivanovich's bare back. He appeared to still be drunk from the night before, or perhaps he had already started the day with a few drinks. "What brings you here this morning? I believe this is the first time I've seen you here on a Tuesday!"

Ivanovich's mind raced to remember who this man was until the answer came to mind. "Ah, General Samovich. It is good to see you. I come here every so often. It's good for an aging body like mine."

"Very true, and for an officer of the 2nd Directorate like me, it is best to stay in top shape, lest a capitalist spy gets by me on the streets."

Pompous louse, Pyotr thought to himself. *It's well-known throughout the inner circle of The Party that you only received your position within the KGB because of your wife's uncle, and that you've never exerted yourself any more than when cheating on her with your secretary.*

"I'm afraid I must be going now, comrade. Can't be late to the office," he said in a deflective manner as he reached for a towel lying on a nearby cart, hoping to return to his thoughts and escape from this idiot.

General Samovich missed the visible social cue. The KGB officer leaned in towards the Major, revealing the liquor on his breath. "Comrade," he spoke in a slightly lower but still easy-to-hear voice. "I must congratulate you for taking a role in defending our *Rodina*."

"I do not understand..."

"You know! Our plan to put away that fool whose ideas are as bad as Khrushchev."

Ivanovich's heartbeat nearly stopped at the sound of this man's loose words. *He must be out of his mind drunk. What if someone should hear what he's saying? Someone loyal to The Party would implicate me to all of this in an instant!*

"Comrade, I don't think..."

"You are not the only brave Soviet who has taken a stand," he said as he raised a fist in the air. "There are others such as..."

Ivanovich's eyes began to dart around, looking for any sign of someone that could be watching. Part of him instinctively desired to run away lest he be seen with this drunken KGB General who was foolishly speaking out loud, not just of his own role in an assassination plot of a member of the Politburo, but the names of his fellow conspirators too. The Major's brain overrode these instincts by telling himself just how valuable this intel was.

"Now, comrade, please be careful who you tell," he said as if the effects of the booze had worn off momentarily. "We must exercise caution or our very lives could be at risk."

Ivanovich briskly nodded. With that, Samovich smiled and went on his way towards his own locker to change. The Major rushed to put on his clothes. His hands fumbled with the buttons on his crisp white shirt as he tried to wrap his mind around what he'd just heard. *It's much bigger than I first imagined. Molotov must've had no problem making a case for others to sign on. I have to tell the American as soon as possible...*

Putting on his jacket, he stepped out of the men's changing room and towards the lobby where his car was waiting outside to take him to work. He replayed the impromptu exchange in his mind during the drive. *No, there wasn't anyone around paying attention to that drunk. You're overthinking things, Pytor.*

Little had he noticed the lone figure discreetly hidden behind the towel cart.

3

The Third Day

O'Neil saw the signal. Taking his regular morning jog, he began at the diplomatic compound and ran down the same streets each and every weekday. It had become predictable to the point that the KGB's surveillance had grown lax, often times leaving it to the militia men posted along the route to report their sightings of him. It was halfway through his run that the Deputy Chief of Station looked across the street at a particular apartment, up to the eighth floor, third and fourth windows from the right.

Tonight? What's so important that he needs to move up the meeting?

The shades on the third window, belonging to Major Pyotr Ivanovich, were halfway drawn up and open while the fourth's shades were closed in reverse. *Guess we'll see how the new sheriff in town handles it.*

An hour later, O'Neil reported what he saw to his boss at Moscow Station. The Chief of Station had yet to even have his first cup of coffee on the job when he learned of the signal.

"You see anything else?" Carson asked once he was finished.

"No sir. Like I said before, security around me is light. If anyone gets near, I can spot them fast. It seems like the real deal."

289

Just then, James Shephard entered the Station to start the workday.

"Change of plans, James," said Cooper. "You're meeting in person with Torchlight tonight."

"What?"

"We just received word that he's signaled he wants to talk sooner than planned. He could have something important. He could also very well be compromised. You know the drill. Use your gut instinct on this one. If something doesn't seem right, abort the meeting and get out of there. Remember, you'll have Shroud with you as well. We don't need to put her at risk too."

"Understood."

"By the way, speaking of Torchlight, the care package for him arrived this morning."

Shephard looked to his right to see the Chief of Station get up from his desk.

"Did they get everything he asked for?" Shephard asked.

"Medicine for his wife. Pink Floyd, Led Zeppelin, and Whitesnake albums for his son. Poem collections by Joseph Brodsky, several of the latest issues of Time magazine. The only thing missing from the package is a cassette tape of Billy Joel."

"Any particular reason for it not being there?"

Cooper shrugged his shoulders. "They didn't give a reason. Just plain forgot it seems."

Shephard walked over to a wall with a large map of the city taped to it. Various pins marked dead drops and rendezvous points. *How could a high ranking Soviet Union official like Torchlight be a member of the upper echelon of Soviet society, yet still have basic needs and wants only met west of the Berlin Wall?* Yes, the CIA did pay their agent well via a secret bank account, should he ever need to be extracted. The packages meant so much to him though, and for good reason. His wife's chronic asthma had greatly improved since she had begun taking American medicine, rather than what had been prescribed by Soviet doctors. Meanwhile, Torchlight had made a breakthrough in his quest to connect with his teenage son who, despite being the son of a KGB officer, had a particular curiosity for rock music.

Shephard turned his attention to several photos pinned to the side of the map. He'd taken these three weeks ago while scouting out a new location. He and his agent never had any sort of contact at the same place more than once. This time they would meet by the Moskva River of off *Kalininsky Prospekt*.

"I've also got two new Tropel T-50's for you to give him," Cooper said. "I know we talked about it last night, but remind him to be mindful of the lighting when snapping photos of documents. Langley wasn't able to make out some of the papers from the last batch of film. Most of it was still good, but, of course, they're wanting to gain as much intelligence as they can from him."

Shephard nodded. "Most valuable asset—that's what he is to this country. I only wonder how much longer his run can last."

"Hard to tell. He's lasted longer than Oleg Penkovsky ever did."

"Now," Cooper spoke, a bit louder to get everyone's attention in the Station. "Let's go over the plan for tonight. Carpenter and Brock should be back soon, and then we can go over some new surveillance hotspots the Russians have put in place. Doug, how's... Doug, are you listening?"

Doug Brown, a liaison from the Office of Technical Services, was sitting at a table, face down at work with a pair of headphones on. Another case officer walked over and pulled them off, catching him by surprise.

Listening for a moment to the music coming from the headphones, she began to tap her foot. "Billy Joel. This a new album?" Lying on the table was a cassette of The Piano Man's new album, *An Innocent Man*, which she picked up and looked over.

"Does Torchlight have a Walkman?" she asked.

Shephard turned to Cooper with a smirk on his face. He then walked over and snatched Doug's Sony Walkman as well as the headphones.

"Hey! What gives?" protested Doug who had an irritated look on his face.

"He does now."

***

Boris Alexeev was clueless about his wife. He always thought it was his looks, class or maybe even his charm that had won the affection of the most beautiful woman to come from Kaliningrad. The hard facts, however, were that she neither married him for said attributes, nor did she come from Kaliningrad.

He awoke early that cold and snowy Monday morning to the familiar garish sound coming from the pipes within the walls. She was already up and showering. *Hopefully there will still be some warm water left.* He yawned and did his best to shake off the sleepy stupor. It wouldn't be too long until his car arrived to take him to the Kremlin.

Boris entered the steam-filled bathroom just as his wife was turning off the water. She stepped out from behind the shower curtain, dripping wet, and quickly grabbed a towel hanging nearby. Still enough time for Boris to take in an eyeful.

Tatiana's deep blue eyes met his, eliciting a somewhat dumbfounded expression on the young man's face. She gave a playful, flirtatious smile in return. "Good morning," she said while gripping the towel around

292

her. "Did you sleep well last night?"

"I did. Especially after..." he started to say just as she leaned in and interrupted with a long, slow kiss.

"Mmm, me too. You better start getting ready. I'll have breakfast waiting when you're finished."

And to think I almost didn't go to that party for Veselovsky. I would've never met her!

Twenty minutes later, he was seated at the table, dressed for the day in one of his newer suits with a dark red tie, along with a hammer and sickle pin on his lapel. He alternated between sips of coffee and bites of toasted black bread while reading *Pravda*.

"Anything interesting?" she asked while starting to clear some of the dishes.

"*CSKA Moscow* won four to zero last night and Viacheslav Fetisov scored two goals. I'd like to take Nikita to the game next week if work doesn't get in the way."

"His coach told me when I picked him up from practice Monday that he's become the best right wing on the team. Maybe he'll make the national team one day."

The proud father beamed at the statement. "Maybe. Whatever he does, he'll be a success at it. The boy is hard-working and sharp."

"You said if work doesn't get in the way. Anything important?"

"Meetings, speeches to be reviewed, tasks to be administered. All the sorts of stuff a regular Politburo member's staff must handle."

"Sounds boring."

"Tatiana, I love you, but you've never had a mind for politics or party business. It's okay. In every other regard, you're splendid." At this, he rose from the table and prepared to head out the door.

She walked over to him and wrapped her arms around his waist. "Good, because if you said anything different, you'd be on your own for dinner from now on."

He kissed her softly on the lips. "I'd best be going. Where are the kids?"

"Sergei, Nikita, come say goodbye to your father."

Their two sons, ages six and eight, ran from the living area where they were watching TV and hugged him. He kissed them both on the cheek. For all the hardships and struggles of Russian society, Boris was like many others who still loved and valued their kids.

"Both of you behave yourselves and do what your mother says. I'll be home tonight and maybe we can watch some hockey before bed."

"Yeah!"

Tatiana peered out the kitchen window. "The car just pulled in front of the lobby."

"Okay, I'm off now. *Do svidaniya!*"

Once outside, his driver opened the backseat door of a GAZ Volga for him to hop in. It was only a few minutes' commute from his apartment to the Kremlin. The roads were crowded this morning, but not for the Volga. The exclusive median lane was made available to him due to his status as a senior personal staffer to Mikhail Gorbachev, the youngest full member of the Politburo. Boris looked out on the vast sea of cars belonging to the proletariat stuck in traffic. He thought about Tatiana. Taking the kids to school, shopping, lunch with her friends at the Leningradskaya Hotel—she had her routine like all Soviets and rarely if ever deviated from it. Did she enjoy it like he did his own?

If Boris could have followed Tatiana Alexeev closely that day, he'd have realized just how wrong he was. It came at the Leningradskaya. There amongst her friends, mostly wives of *nomenklatura* such as Boris.

"I mean it, I'd rather shop at GUM no matter the lines than go back to that marketplace in Kyiv ever again," remarked one woman in between mouthfuls of caviar.

"The only place Sacha says is worthwhile to buy anything outside of Moscow is Budapest. Though I hear some of it is black market," another replied.

Just then their waiter, a rather short man, middle-aged with a receding hairline, returned to the table. He had worked here at the Leningradskaya's restaurant for more than twenty years, providing exceptional service that made the place well-known both with Muscovites and tourists alike.

"May I take your plate for you, madam?" he said to Tatiana.

"Thank you...actually, no. I think I may have room for one more bite."

The waiter set the plate, which he'd barely picked up, back onto the table, smiled and continued to serve the rest of the dining party. Not a single person had seen the brush pass. A sleight of hand that would make a magician proud. While everyone who was paying attention saw only the near-empty plate, the waiter had in fact dropped a single scrap of paper from the napkin cloth into her lap. Tatiana casually placed it in her pocket before he turned to serve the rest.

She waited until later back at the apartment that afternoon to read what it said. Alone, she regularly checked the place for listening devices and cameras, always careful to make note of them rather than remove them and raise suspicion. The bathroom with just one bug above the cabinet next to the sink, and no windows, was the safest room.

Once decoded, the message read:

"Torchlight meeting at 19:00 tomorrow night. Be at safe house III before
– Shepherd."

*Tomorrow evening? Barely a heads up. Guess I can make it work though.
Hopefully there'll be enough time before.* With that, the Russian
housewife tore the note to shreds, flushing the scraps down the toilet
before starting work on the family laundry.

ABOUT THE AUTHOR
J.D. NARRAMORE

Howdy! Thanks for purchasing a copy of *The Nameless Height*. I'm an author residing in the great state of Texas. I first became fascinated with the thriller genre after reading Tom Clancy's books in high school. My debut novel, *Chief of Station*, hearkens back to that same era of Reagan, the Soviets, and the Cold War. My hope with this and other future books is to paint a realistic picture of the world of espionage while conveying a message of hope.

Aside from spending lots of time with my awesome wife, I enjoy playing golf, eating good BBQ, studying history, and rooting for Texas A&M (Class of '15).

Lastly, I'm a Christian. My strongest desire is to live my life for Jesus and to tell others about the hope I have in Him

Instagram: @jdnarramore

Facebook: JD Narramore - Author

Twitter: @jd_narramore

Made in the USA
Middletown, DE
19 August 2023

36998455R00182